MAGGIE

broadview editions
series editor: L.W. Conolly

MAGGIE
A GIRL OF THE STREETS

Stephen Crane

edited by Adrian Hunter

broadview editions

Library and Archives Canada Cataloguing in Publication

Crane, Stephen, 1871–1900.

Maggie : a girl of the streets / Stephen Crane ; edited by Adrian Hunter.

(Broadview editions)
Includes bibliographical references.

ISBN 1-55111-597-2

I. Hunter, Adrian, 1971– II. Title. III. Series.

PS1449.C85M3 2006   813'.4   C2006-903346-3

Broadview Editions

The Broadview Editions series represents the ever-changing canon of literature by bringing together texts long regarded as classics with valuable lesser-known works.

Advisory editor for this volume: Marie Davis Zimmerman

Broadview Press is an independent, international publishing house, incorporated in 1985. Broadview believes in shared ownership, both with its employees and with the general public; since the year 2000 Broadview shares have traded publicly on the Toronto Venture Exchange under the symbol BDP.

We welcome comments and suggestions regarding any aspect of our publications–please feel free to contact us at the addresses below or at broadview@broadviewpress.com / www.broadviewpress.com

North America
PO Box 1243, Peterborough, Ontario, Canada K9J 7H5
Tel: (705) 743-8990; Fax: (705) 743-8353
email: customerservice@broadviewpress.com
PO Box 1015, 3576 California Road, Orchard Park, NY, USA 14127

UK, Ireland, and continental Europe
NBN International
Estover Road
Plymouth PL6 7PY UK
Tel: 44 (0) 1752 202 300
Fax: 44 (0) 1752 202 330
email: enquiries@nbninternational.com

Australia and New Zealand
UNIREPS, University of New South Wales
Sydney, NSW, 2052
Australia
Tel: 61 2 9664 0999; Fax: 61 2 9664 5420
email: info.press@unsw.edu.au

PRINTED IN CANADA

Contents

Acknowledgements

I am grateful to the Carnegie Trust for the Universities of Scotland for financial support during the preparation of this volume. Staff at the Lower East Side Tenement Museum in New York City gave an account of slum life that considerably altered my understanding of Crane's story. I was happy to act on advice given by Broadview's anonymous readers and editorial staff, particularly Julia Gaunce. Finally, I thank Jennifer Ellis for reading aloud in her best Ayrshire accent.

Introduction

"Ambiguity," William Empson once said, "is a phenomenon of compression." He was remarking, straightforwardly enough, upon an oddity of language, namely that the fewer words one deploys, the greater the range of possible meanings one produces. Less is more, if you like: not saying enough cuts uncertainty loose. It is a situation that prompts some to superabundant talkativeness, in the hope of making words behave themselves. Legal discourse, for example, with its fretful proliferation of clauses, qualifiers, and correctives, is only trying to tell it like it is, like it *really* is. But for the critic Empson, as for the writer Stephen Crane, the volatility of a stripped-down language made for all sorts of creative adventure. *Maggie* may be a short book, but as the vast critical industry it powers attests, it is long on meaning; Crane's words are few, but fit.

The shortness of *Maggie* has always disturbed its readers. An early respondent, Hamlin Garland, declared the book a "fragment" lacking in "rounded completeness," though he was broadly satisfied that it marked an auspicious debut (Appendix F1). Other reviewers complained that Crane told only half the story of the slum—the terrible half—and was thereby derelict in the novelist's duty to provide "an aspiration in the uplifting of humanity's heart" (Appendix F3). More sharply, the English critic H.D. Traill took *Maggie*'s brevity as evidence of a vapid authorial imagination and lack of expressive range. The abstemiousness of the language was for Traill symptomatic of Crane's general failure to give his story a fulsome moral shape and purpose. As a narrative, *Maggie* went nowhere: it merely followed its characters around, from one squalid intercourse to another, in a "series of loosely cohering incidents" (Appendix F4).

And yet, for all *Maggie*'s transitoriness as a reading experience, it has enjoyed a remarkable longevity within the canon of American literature. One might wonder, then, if its shortness, far from being a flaw, isn't truly the hiding place of its power. After all, it's the text's silences and ambiguities, the things Crane left out or left unresolved, that have kept readers wondering about *Maggie*, and scholars in the business of interpreting it. There is the matter of the ending, for example. Just how *does* Maggie meet her death? Is it by suicide, foul play, accident?

Moreover, what is going on in her mind as she suffers, in those final desperate chapters, cumulatively insult, rejection, and personal violation? Crane neglects—that is, he refuses—to tell us. Maggie gets literally nothing to say for herself as her life comes apart. Condemned by her mother and brother as a "fallen" woman, she neither defends herself nor registers guilt: faced with their accusations and abuse, we are told, she merely "turned and went" (77). It is still, even for the contemporary reader, disconcerting to encounter the central character of a novel at so impersonal a distance. Indeed, so little access to Maggie does Crane permit that in the final chapter in which she appears, chapter 17, she is not even referred to by name but becomes, rather, "A girl of the painted cohorts of the city"—one of a "legion" of prostitutes (81). As Crane presents her, Maggie is destitute of depth: she is an entirely performative figure. Her inner life becomes a determining absence in her story. For all her narrative centrality—the book itself bears her name, after all—we know next to nothing about what she feels or thinks about what she says and does.

The enigma of Maggie, as of *Maggie*, is largely an effect of Crane's punishing economy of expression. Not only does he frequently withhold crucial information from his narrative, thereby restricting our view of the main character, but the relentless compression of his language means that the words he does provide are exercised to breaking point. On occasion, indeed, one might feel that ambiguity—or more precisely the unsettling of the reader's interpretative confidence—is just what Crane intends. Take the exhilarating opening staves of chapter 4:

> The babe, Tommie, died. He went away in a white, insignificant coffin, his small waxen hand clutching a flower that the girl, Maggie, had stolen from an Italian.
> She and Jimmie lived.
> The inexperienced fibres of the boy's eyes were hardened at an early age. He became a young man of leather. He lived some red years without laboring. During that time his sneer became chronic. He studied human nature in the gutter, and found it no worse than he thought he had reason to believe it. He never conceived a respect for the world, because he had begun with no idols that it had smashed.

He clad his soul in armor by means of happening hilariously in at a mission church where a man composed his sermons of 'yous.' While they got warm at the stove, he told his hearers just where he calculated they stood with the Lord. Many of the sinners were impatient over the pictured depths of their degradation. They were waiting for soup-tickets.

A reader of words of wind-demons might have been able to see the portions of a dialogue pass to and fro between the exhorter and his hearers.

'You are damned,' said the preacher. And the reader of sounds might have seen the reply go forth from the ragged people: 'Where's our soup?' (37–38)

We travel an astonishing distance in this passage, over several years and not a few profound happenings. I say "profound," but it's not as though profundity—in the sense of things deep-seated or far-reaching—is overtly signalled in the language. One must look twice to find it. The life and death of Tommie pass by like the "insignificant coffin" that bears him; Maggie and Jimmie "live"—but how? And the young man's "red years without laboring": were those years without profitable work, or years in which violence was readily, even blithely borne? And yet this journey from inexperience, to toughness, and finally to sneering, is only a fraction of the life of Jimmie that Crane's prose seems to evoke. This language, for all its compactness, leaks adversative, contrary meanings from every pore: Jimmie's disrespect for the world as much condemns that world, and what it considers respectable, as it does the man who once looked out with a boy's unpresuming eyes. And the soup-beggars, for all their wordlessness, have throats that are full of wounded mockery. One often feels that Crane's writing contains much more than it is prepared to say. His reticence captures in kind the straightened lives that are his subject; but it renders, by layered implication, all the agony of what those lives have lost and are without. One must lean close to hear the words of wind-demons.

Writing of this order of brilliance lies everywhere in wait for the reader of *Maggie*, and I am conscious as I compose this introduction of wishing not to give too much away or dull the sense to Crane's uniquely awkward genius. But it is useful to know a little of how this remarkable book came about, in what mud puddle it blossomed, and how in its own day it was received. In what follows, I trace a number of bit-parts in the making of *Maggie*: New York City has one, of course; but so too do religion, social reform, journalism, and literary theory. Though it feels, still, presumptuous to do so, I wish also to convey something of Crane himself—only twenty-two when this book was published, a young author of preternatural sensitivity already conscious, as he set down the blighted being of Maggie Johnson, of the malady that would end his own life before the age of thirty. As I go along, I will continue to draw attention to what I consider the most arresting feature of *Maggie*, namely its brevity, its reticence, its bold willingness to *stop short*.

Slum Reform and Slum Fiction

Stephen Crane first went to New York City in the fall of 1892. Born and raised in New Jersey, he had begun as a newspaperman at the precocious age of seventeen, reporting for the New Jersey Coast News Bureau, an agency run by his brother. His move to a cheap apartment house in the heart of a New York ghetto was a perilous one, for he both lacked money and the prospect of making any. What he saw around him in the Lower East Side Bowery were the effects of unrelieved squalour and poverty. It was a district of high-density slum tenement dwellings, lodging-houses, seedy saloons, and opium dens. God, as police reporter turned social reformer Jacob A. Riis remarked in 1890, had long since lost the battle for the Bowery: the Devil was doing all the building, and beer-pits outnumbered places of worship by forty to one (Appendix B1).

By December 1892 Crane had absorbed sufficient of his new milieu to have completed a first draft of *Maggie*.[1] It is also clear that he had read what others had written about the Lower East Side, and found it wanting. The subtitle he eventually attached to *Maggie*, "A Story of New York," was slightly disingenuous, for he was writing what was really *the* story of New York's slums, one told over and over by lesser talents, in which a virtuous young woman is seduced and

---

[1] It seems certain that he had begun drafting the story before moving to the city, basing his writing on visits he had made as a teenager.

ruined by her environment and the male predators lurking within it. It was a story much rehearsed in fiction of the time, but it also figured, in slightly different ways, in religious and reform writing of the sort that Crane would have been familiar with. Charles Loring Brace, a missionary in New York and founder of the Children's Aid Society, had published as early as 1872 a study entitled *The Dangerous Classes of New York* in which he dealt with, among other things, the "strange and mysterious subject of sexual vice" rife among young women (Appendix B3). Brace's book made the then common distinction between the "sexual sins of the lad" and the much more egregious wrongdoings of the female: her instinct being "more toward the preservation of purity," her "fall" was therefore all the "deeper." And it truly was a "fall" in every aspect of her nature, for the "crime of lust" quickly bred, according to Brace, an "evil" and "polluted soul."

Brace's brand of missionary preaching was widely reproduced throughout the 1880s and 1890s, and it reveals much about how the middle-classes thought of the slum and their relationship to it. On the one hand, it was a den of iniquity to be abhorred in this life as it would be justly punished in the next. At the same time, however, it was an arena to which the Godly reformer was called to do good and save souls. The slum was an evil blight, no question, but it also gave bourgeois philanthropic religiosity its mission. Brace quite appalled his readers by the portrait of evil he drew, but he also showed them wrongs that they could right in God's holy name. It was a call to constructive action bolstered by terrifying visions of apocalypse, and soon church missions and reform houses were springing up all across lower Manhattan.

The terrors of the slum were even more vividly represented by Thomas De Witt Talmage, a Presbyterian minister in Brooklyn whose horribly graphic accounts of his own night time wanderings in the Lower East Side were familiar to many thousands of newspaper readers (see Appendix B2). Like Brace, Talmage mixed compassion for the suffering poor with righteous declarations of self-approval. He worked the devices of sentimental fiction in his portrayal of the unfortunate—"I wonder if that gashed and bloated forehead was ever kissed by a fond mother's lips"—while providing direct evidence of those returned to grace by the efforts of Christian missionaries like himself. Agape, however, was only the most public of Talmage's motives in calling for slum reform; just as important was fear. "I am here this morning," one of his published sermons warned, "to tell you that there are deathful and explosive influences under all our cities, ready to destroy us with a great moral convulsion." The poor of New York were, it seems, more than just a threat to themselves. Not now the classic lumpenproletariat too drunk or docile to mobilize against its own discontent, Manhattan's underclass presented a very real danger to the moral structure of the Christian United States.

Many of the attitudes and fears prevalent in reform writing are to be found, too, in the urban fiction of Crane's day. As I mentioned earlier, the basic plot of *Maggie* was a familiar one conventionally used to voice anxieties about poverty and female sexuality. The novel that *Maggie* most closely resembles in terms of action is Edgar Fawcett's *The Evil That Men Do* (1889), which tells of the fall into destitution, alcoholism, and prostitution of Cora Strang. Like Maggie, Cora works for a time in the garment industry, is rejected by her lover, and meets her death at the river's edge in the company of a lecherous drunk. But here the similarities end, because Fawcett's language and attitude in the story closely resemble those of the reformer-moralists of the day, whereas Crane, as I'll show in a moment, forged an entirely new idiom in which to convey a more complex and contradictory vision of the slum.

Fawcett's novel frequently delays its advancing narrative by passages of sermonizing social commentary reminiscent of Brace and Talmage, and its vocabulary is likewise loaded with moral condemnation of what it depicts. Bowery life, we are told at one point, "seethes as though it were some sort of bubbling broth in a cauldron—hell-broth" (Appendix C). Describing the dwelling place of Cora's friend, Em Cratchett, Fawcett quite loses control of himself:

> Sin rioted in the reeking house, whose very stairs had rotten creaks when you trod them, as though fatigued by the steps of sots and trulls. To enter some of the rooms was to smell infection and face beastliness. Fever lived in the sinks and closets along the halls, where festered refuse more rancid and stenchful than stale swill, and so vile that to name it would be to deal with words which are the dung of lexicons.

Those halls had nooks of gloom where miasma might have fled in fright before the human grossness that spawned there. (Appendix C)

In pressing home the horror of slum, the true nature of Fawcett's book comes out: it is a tendentious essay on moral corruption. Repeatedly the narrative looks to place Cora's decline in its full ethical context: "Most human souls are lax in their receptivity to sin proportionately as they have once been fierce in their resistance of it. Cora did not satisfy herself with half-measures" (Appendix C). She becomes hooked on love's "narcotic," giving herself before marriage to the man she thinks loves her, and slipping by slow degrees into a "bacchanal revolt" of the senses. No longer is she simply the victim of the slum: she is, rather, one of its predators. Her moral fortitude having collapsed, she is deadly goods, wantonly purveying to others the poison that has destroyed her: "You might almost have fancied that she exhaled some odor at once delicious and deadly, like a blossom whose gaudy grace is akin to baleful creatures beamed on by the same tropic sun" (Appendix C).

Stephen Crane and Jacob Riis

Stephen Crane saw matters very differently from most slum reformers and novelists of his day. What he presented in *Maggie* was a vision of the Bowery and its people quite at odds with the one that bourgeois society, for all its toil and outrage, found ultimately affirmative of its own values and ideology. Crane granted the slum its "otherness." That is to say, he represented its psychological and ethnographic reality, rather than using it as a site in which to play out a moral or religious drama. What was scandalous about *Maggie*, as the critic Keith Gandal has argued, was not so much that it implied that social conditions rather than Godlessness were the cause of vice and criminality, but that it absented itself entirely from the traditional ethical scheme of Protestant Christianity that governed writing about the poor. "Crane's work," Gandal says, "contains no concept of will, conscience, moral character, eternal soul, or reason as a higher faculty or supreme arbitrator" (*Virtues of the Vicious* 9). When I said earlier that the originality and brilliance of *Maggie* lay as much in what it left out as what it declared, I had in mind the kinds of features Gandal lists here. It is

Crane's refusal to elaborate his story and his characters in terms of "will," "conscience," "soul," or "reason" that makes *Maggie* so significant a moment in American fiction.

Just how and why it should have come about that Crane, then only in his early twenties, was able to make this crucial breakthrough is, and will remain, one of the mysteries of his genius. Still, one can make a few determinations from surrounding evidence about the kind of literature that may have been shaping the young man's view of the slum during his New York years. One such document is Jacob A. Riis's *How the Other Half Lives* (1890). Several critics have explored correspondences between Riis's book and *Maggie* (see especially Gullason 1959 and Gandal 1997), and it is known that Crane heard Riis lecture in 1892. Among many obvious similarities, one might note that both texts avoid making any explicit moral judgements about what they describe. Riis, for his part, portrays slum culture not as it falls short of some putative middle-class standard, but as it operates according to its own norms and values. And crucially, those norms and values are not necessarily any less, nor any worse, than those prevailing in the dominant culture; they are simply different.

Riis devotes each of the twenty-five chapters of his book to a specific aspect of slum life. Subjects covered include the lodging-house, the tenement, the beer-dive, pauperism, child labour, the garment industry, and street violence. In Appendix B1 I have given extracts from chapters on the saloon and the Bowery "tough" as these are particularly germane to the action of *Maggie*. Many of Riis's observations serve to expose political corruption in the government of New York City—he explicitly lays the blame for alcohol abuse at the door of the city's aldermen and politicians, for example—but he was a more astute social analyst than such polemic implies, for he also appreciated, and was ready to state openly, the profound attraction of alcohol to the slum citizenry. In a witty appropriation of the discourse of the reformers, he notes that the saloon is quite often "the one bright and cheery and humanly decent spot" to be found in the tenement districts, and that it lures the patron with the promise of "refuge" and "relief" (Appendix B1). It was a point not lost on Crane. In Maggie's world, by far the most powerful and (within the terms of that world) successful character is the bartender, Pete; and his place of work is easily the most splendid venue in the book:

The interior of the place was papered in olive and bronze tints of imitation leather. A shining bar of counterfeit massiveness extended down the side of the room. Behind it a great mahogany-appearing sideboard reached the ceiling. Upon its shelves rested pyramids of shimmering glasses that were never disturbed. Mirrors set in the face of the sideboard multiplied them. Lemons, oranges and paper napkins, arranged with mathematical precision, sat among the glasses. Many-hued decanters of liquor perched at regular intervals on the lower shelves. A nickel-plated cash register occupied a position in the exact centre of the general effect. The elementary senses of it all seemed to be opulence and geometrical accuracy. (60–61)

Pete's bar is a place of order and clear boundaries: it is a little moral economy all of its own, and Pete in his white coat, polishing the glasses, is its elected guardian. It is somewhere men can go to enjoy the fellowship (another reform concept) of other men. Throughout Crane's New York writing the saloon functions in this way. In *George's Mother*, a companion piece to *Maggie* (reprinted here as Appendix A1), the central character, Kelcey, finds in alcohol the deep comforts of conviviality and homosocial combination:

Each man explained, in his way, that he was totally out of place in the before-mentioned world. They were possessed of various virtues which were unappreciated by those with whom they were commonly obliged to mingle; they were fitted for a tree-shaded land, where everything was peace. Now that five of them had congregated it gave them happiness to speak their inmost thoughts without fear of being misunderstood.

As he drank more beer Kelcey felt his breast expand with manly feeling. He knew that he was capable of sublime things. He wished that some day one of his present companions would come to him for relief. His mind pictured a little scene. In it he was magnificent in his friendship.

He looked upon the beaming faces and knew that if at that instant there should come a time for a great sacrifice he would blissfully make it. He would pass tranquilly into the unknown, or into bankruptcy, amid the ejaculations of his companions upon his many virtues. (Appendix A1)

To the reforming missionary, liquour lay at the heart of the slum problem. Crane certainly agreed, and Kelcey, like Maggie's mother and the countless other drinkers who stagger through the pages of Crane's New York writing, finds his life coming apart under the influence of alcohol. But where Crane differed from the likes of Brace and Talmage was in his understanding of why poor people drank. They did so not simply out of moral turpitude, but for a complex of motives, some of which had to do with the attainment of self-esteem and belonging in a world seemingly predisposed to their personal belittlement and alienation.

Riis was similarly insightful about the Bowery "tough," a figure also vividly rendered in *Maggie*. The "tough" was a cowardly thug, a wolfish, pack-hunting opportunist with pockets full of petty street weaponry who would nevertheless "resent as an intolerable insult the imputation that he [was] 'no gentleman'" (Appendix B1). In *Maggie*, it is Pete (to a lesser extent Jimmie too) who plays the part of the "tough": seething with violence and heartless hypocrisy, he swaggers the streets in eye-catching dandy outfits, wooing the girls with half-understood, ill-said epithets of suavity and honour. Yet he is admired and envied by Maggie and by the other men in the story—and even, dare one say, by the reader. For Pete, for all his ludicrous contradictions and cack-handed brutality, is a standard of defiance and creative self-fashioning in this lowly place: he can, and *does*, survive the slum. Maggie is drawn to him for this reason: "To her the earth was composed of hardships and insults. She felt instant admiration for a man who openly defied it" (45). His indifferent shrug and "air of distinguished valor," combined with his "infinitely gracious" manner towards her, make Pete Maggie's best, her only, role model. No one else around her seems remotely capable of transcending the twin injustices of heredity and environment. Consequently, when his attention is taken by the prostitute Nell and his ardour for Maggie cools, our sense of outrage at Pete's callousness may be tempered by the recognition that he has made himself fit for the purpose of enduring the slum. From his "peculiar off-handedness and ease" (71) with Maggie, to his finally telling her to "go teh hell" (80), Pete is practising the ruthless self-containment necessary to his survival.

The complexity of the portrayal of alcohol and of the "tough" in *Maggie* is, once again, intensified by Crane's reticence. By not elaborating any moral from what he depicts or involving his characters in any system of judgement, he stops short of the kind of reductive ethical evaluation that other literature of the time typically made. Like Riis, he was interested in producing an accurate ethnography of the Bowery, and that meant refusing to falsify or disentangle the difficult reality of slum. The result was a morally ambivalent but enduringly authentic literary masterpiece.

Literary Realism and the "New Journalism"

By granting the slum so complex—even intractable—a reality, Crane scandalized popular opinion. He also won approval, however, from those writers and critics who believed that urban modernity was the great subject that must be taken up by the contemporary novelist. Among these was William Dean Howells, novelist, critic, editor, and leading proponent of literary realism. During the 1880s, in his "Editor's Study" column for *Harper's Monthly*, Howells had argued that literature had a vital role to play in the progress of American politics and society, and that writers should therefore address themselves to the material reality of modern life. This meant rejecting the fantastic or romantic tropes of earlier fiction and dealing with what really went on in the world, even in garboiled, despicable quarters like the Bowery. Crane was praised by Howells for bringing to bear a sense of "constant reality" that eluded lesser, habitually sentimentalizing talents like Edward Townsend (Appendix F2). After Crane's death, it was *Maggie* that Howells singled out as the masterpiece of American fiction's most "distinctive and vital talent" (Appendix F3). In writing the city, Howells argued, Crane made a permanent contribution to the literature.

Crane himself was happy to be called a "realist." Howells's pleasingly spacious definition of realism as "the truthful treatment of material," which Crane recorded in his review of a lecture Hamlin Garland gave on Howells in August 1891 (see Appendix D1), certainly rings true for *Maggie* when one considers how far Crane goes to avoid the distortions of sentimentalism and Christian moralism. But Crane's realism, like that of his contemporary Frank Norris, was of quite a different sort from Howells', not least in the kind of subject matter it dealt with, which was on the whole far more socially and morally contentious than that of the older generation, and less obviously recuperable within the Howellsian grand project of American democratic progress and the advancement of middle-class decency.

Looking for some way to mark the difference between Crane and the first-generation realists, many critics have lighted on the term "naturalism." Unfortunately, however, naturalism comes too heavily burdened with its own intricate and conflicted history to really work in Crane's case. For a start, it is a term widely used to denote a distinctly European fiction, mainly associated with the French novelist Émile Zola, in which the twin determinants of heredity and environment are explored in the form of detailed socio-psychological character studies. Frank Norris referred to his own work as naturalist, but then he did not subscribe to the kind of deterministic philosophy that underpinned Zola's thinking. In turn, Norris did not consider Crane a naturalist writer at all because of the ironic attitude his narratives frequently took towards their characters.

Crane never claimed to be a naturalist, though he did famously inscribe copies of *Maggie* with the declaration that "environment is a tremendous thing." In many ways, *Maggie* simply does not fit within the naturalist nomenclature. For a start, its central character is largely untouched by the forces of environment. As Donald Pizer pointed out some years ago, Crane's description of Maggie as having "blossomed in a mud puddle" is hardly the stuff of naturalism, since it implies that she bloomed, at least in girlhood, *in spite of* her situation, that she came through the slum unscathed. This suggests that Crane was far more concerned with the meaning of Maggie herself than with what circumstance made of her. What's more, Maggie's family, and especially her mother, far from being the diseased victims of a particular place and time, are represented with deep irony. Mrs Johnson's condemnation of her daughter, for example, is really a hypocritical moralising pose that she strikes for the benefit of her neighbours. Crane's ironic narration allows us to view the woman's twisted impression of her own Christian piety, and this, as Pizer notes, is contrary to the kind of social determinism that drives the naturalist text.

The naturalist designation, then, falls somewhat short of the complex actuality of *Maggie*. For this reason scholars now tend to talk about Crane as a realist, albeit of a different sort from Howells and the earlier generation. One might wonder why critics should bother at all with this sort of classification when the terms of reference seem so slippery. Yet there is something to be gained from aligning Crane with realism as a literary phenomenon, for it provides a way of thinking about the relationship of his work to the advanced capitalist culture in which it was produced and to which it was addressed. Recent studies of American realism by Amy Kaplan, Alan Trachtenberg, and others have explored the ways in which realist writing can be said to participate in the rapid processes of cultural commodification that took place in America towards the end of the nineteenth-century. On the face of it, texts such as *Maggie* appear to criticize, at least by implication, the deleterious effects of the capitalist economy, particularly as these are felt in the urban space. But one might also view the realist text as colluding with the processes of commodification insofar as it renders working-class experience as *spectacle*, something to be consumed by a middle-class reading public voyeuristically intrigued by the "other half" and how it lives. In a curious way, this again has to do with the *shortness* of *Maggie*, with what it does *not* say: by refusing to situate his characters and story within a larger moral framework, and by refusing to guide the reader towards a particular conclusion, Crane arguably made a spectacle of Maggie's life and death. The reader gets to point and gape, to consume, without being compelled to any broader social or ethical understanding.

Reading realist fiction in this way actually takes us closer to the conditions of authorship in Crane's day. For it would be wrong to think of Crane, for all his obvious superiority to the popular sentimental writers of his day, as part of any literary elite. On the contrary, Crane was very much a working author, making a living from his fiction and journalism. If the realist text commodified its subject, it was in turn itself very much a commodity, and Crane understood it as such. *Maggie*, in common with most of his New York writing, was intimately bound up with the work Crane did for newspapers and his career as a reporter. In the years surrounding the composition of *Maggie*, Crane wrote extensively, and usually anonymously, for the *New York Herald* and the *Newark Daily Advertiser*. That he did so is significant of profound changes that were taking place during the 1890s both in newspaper journalism and in the identity of American literary authorship. For this was the period that gave birth to what

Michael Robertson calls a "central myth of modern American literature: the role of the newspaper as training ground for novelists" (*Stephen Crane* 75).

For the older generation of American novelists—Howells's generation—the "man of letters" had been a very different animal from the "man of business," or the journalist. It was a distinction that Howells was still insisting upon as late as 1893. For Howells, there was "something profane, something impious" in taking money for a work of art: "Business," he argued, was "the opprobrium of Literature" (Appendix E1). In the "huckstering civilization" of the 1880s and 1890s, however, that distinction had begun to falter, most visibly in the literary periodical, which now tended to be composed of "material which, however excellent, [was] without literary quality" (Appendix E1). What had taken over was journalism. While Howells stopped short of saying that the author "who approaches literature through journalism is not as fine and high a literary man as the author who comes directly to it" (Appendix E1), he was still, as the very terms of that statement show, certain that literature and journalism were quite different things. In the last analysis, literary art as Howells understood it was an end in itself, to be produced only to the satisfaction of the artist; journalists worked for other ends, often with "more zeal than knowledge," and all along knowing that they "would have been literary men if they could" (E1).

In the case of Stephen Crane, the difference between newspaper and literary writing is much harder to discern. It would be a mistake to suppose that his journalistic work was in some way inferior, or even anterior, to his literary output: the relationship between the two was far more tangled and creative than that. Crane came to prominence in a decade during which the journalistic profession was being revolutionized by brilliant newspaper editors like Lincoln Steffens. As city editor of the *New York Commercial Advertiser*, Steffens adopted a policy of recruiting gifted graduates with creative writing ability from the Ivy League colleges instead of seasoned professional newspaper men (Appendix E3). Expressive flair and originality, rather than house-style doggedness, became the employable qualities editors sought. For a young aspirant like Crane this meant being able to break into what had hitherto been the professional closed shop of news journalism.

Newspaper writing was transformed by this workplace innovation, but so too was literary fiction, for it meant that novels and short stories were now being produced by young authors who had adapted to the specific demands, practical and stylistic, of writing news and feature copy. In Crane's case, as Michael Robertson has demonstrated, there are many continuities of theme and style between his journalism and his New York fiction, including *Maggie*. Robertson notes how Crane's *New York Tribune* dispatches, for instance, assiduously avoided making moral judgements in their reporting of such topics as "overly daring bathing suits or backroom gambling" (*Stephen Crane* 78). Moreover, they deployed their prose in short paragraphs and paratactic sentence structures, cultivating a subtle syntactic discontinuity. As Robertson points out, this "abrupt style was a journalistic convention of the era" and reflected the fact that reports "got their unity from setting rather than sustained narrative" (79). Far from being the "opprobrium" (as Howells envisaged it) of his literary writing, Crane's paid journalism acted in brilliant symbiosis with it.

The New York stories and sketches included as Appendix A in the present volume show the *art* of Crane's journalistic work. They challenge the assumption that his feature writing was merely a trial-run of material that might make it into more substantial, literary publications. In fact, the newspaper pieces are the distilled essence of Crane's genius and demonstrate all the virtues of his so-called literary prose. In particular, as Robertson suggests, they show how he learned to write about a wide range of material, even that which was considered salacious or provocative, with an impassive irony. See, for example, how he brings issues of poverty, homelessness, vandalism, cruelty, and violence to the fore without any evaluative narrational commentary. Masterpieces of expressive concision, they show too how deeply Crane understood the aesthetic of writing "short." If, like *Maggie*, they strike the reader as wilfully open-ended or equivocal, that is very much the effect the author was after. They do not, for all that, *mean* any less. For as Crane understood, and William Empson would later affirm, brevity is an art not of economy but of amplitude.

[handwritten annotations:]
→ COLLEGE DROPOUT
→ DIED YOUNG (28)
→ younger in sig ham
→ journalist, poet

magois:
- joined 1891
- publ privately 1893
- publ revised 1896

Stephen Crane: A Brief Chronology

1871 Born November 1 in Newark, New Jersey, the youngest of fourteen children.

1885 Writes his first story while enrolled at Pennington Seminary, Pennington, NJ.

1890 Publishes a sketch, "Henry M. Stanley," in school magazine. Enters Lafayette College as a mining engineering student.

1891 Attends Syracuse University and works as correspondent for the *New York Tribune*. Publishes a story and begins writing *Maggie: A Girl of the Streets*. Drops out of university.

1892 Publishes five *Sullivan County Sketches* and the New York sketch, "A Broken-Down Van," in the *New York Tribune*.

1893 Publishes privately *Maggie: A Girl of the Streets* under the pseudonym "Johnston Smith." Begins work on *The Red Badge of Courage*.

1894 Short stories and sketches appear in *Arena* and the *New York Press*. Sells an abridged version of *The Red Badge of Courage* to a syndicate and it appears in the *Philadelphia Press*.

1895 Tours the American West and Mexico. Publishes a volume of poetry, *The Black Riders and Other Lines*. D. Appleton and Co. publishes *The Red Badge of Courage* to great acclaim.

1896 Publishes *George's Mother* and a revised version of *Maggie*.

1897 Shipwrecked en route to Cuba, which experience he immortalizes in "The Open Boat." Reports for the *New York Journal* and the *Westminster Gazette* on the Greco-Turkish War and continues to publish stories and sketches.

1898 Reports the Spanish-American War for the *New York World* and *New York Journal*. Publishes *The Open Boat and Other Tales of Adventure*.

1899 Publishes *War is Kind*, *The Monster and Other Stories*, and a novel based on his time in Greece, *Active Service*. Begins *The O'Ruddy*.

1900 Dies from tuberculosis in a sanatorium in Badenweiler, Germany, June 5. Buried in Hillside, New Jersey. *Whilomville Stories* and *Wounds in the Rain*, Cuban war stories, published posthumously.

A Note on the Text

Maggie: A Girl of the Streets (A Story of New York) was first published privately in New York in 1893 under the authorial pseudonym "Johnston Smith." In 1896, following the great success of *The Red Badge of Courage*, Crane's publisher, D. Appleton and Company, brought out an extensively revised edition of *Maggie*. This expurgated text altered dialogue where it was considered coarse or profane, and largely obscured Maggie's career as a prostitute. The Appleton edition prevailed until 1966 when Joseph Katz reissued the 1893 text in facsimile.

This Broadview edition reproduces the original 1893 *Maggie*. Obvious typographical errors have been silently corrected, both in the text of the novel and in the texts of the appendices in this edition.

MAGGIE:

A GIRL OF THE STREETS

CHAPTER I

A very little boy stood upon a heap of gravel for the honor of Rum Alley. He was throwing stones at howling urchins from Devil's Row who were circling madly about the heap and pelting at him.

His infantile countenance was livid with fury. His small body was writhing in the delivery of great, crimson oaths.

"Run, Jimmie, run! Dey'll get yehs," screamed a retreating Rum Alley child.

"Naw," responded Jimmie with a valiant roar, "dese micks can't make me run."   *Irish*

Howls of renewed wrath went up from Devil's Row throats. Tattered gamins on the right made a furious assault on the gravel heap. On their small, convulsed faces there shone the grins of true assassins. As they charged, they threw stones and cursed in shrill chorus.

The little champion of Rum Alley stumbled precipitately down the other side. His coat had been torn to shreds in a scuffle, and his hat was gone. He had bruises on twenty parts of his body, and blood was dripping from a cut in his head. His wan features wore a look of a tiny, insane demon.

On the ground, children from Devil's Row closed in on their antagonist. He crooked his left arm defensively about his head and fought with cursing fury. The little boys ran to and fro, dodging, hurling stones and swearing in barbaric trebles.

From a window of an apartment house that upreared its form from amid squat, ignorant stables, there leaned a curious woman. Some laborers, unloading a scow at a dock at the river, paused for a moment and regarded the fight. The engineer of a passive tugboat hung lazily to a railing and watched. Over on the Island,[1] a worm of yellow convicts came from the shadow of a grey ominous building and crawled slowly along the river's bank.

A stone had smashed into Jimmie's mouth. Blood was bubbling over his chin and down upon his ragged shirt. Tears made furrows on his dirt-stained cheeks. His thin legs had begun to tremble and

---

[1] Then Blackwell's Island in the East River; now called Roosevelt Island. In Crane's day it was the site of a prison, a workhouse, and a lunatic asylum.

turn weak, causing his small body to reel. His roaring curses of the first part of the fight had changed to a blasphemous chatter.

In the yells of the whirling mob of Devil's Row children there were notes of joy like songs of triumphant savagery. The little boys seemed to leer gloatingly at the blood upon the other child's face.

Down the avenue came boastfully sauntering a lad of sixteen years, although the chronic sneer of an ideal manhood already sat upon his lips. His hat was tipped with an air of challenge over his eye. Between his teeth, a cigar stump was tilted at the angle of defiance. He walked with a certain swing of the shoulders which appalled the timid. He glanced over into the vacant lot in which the little raving boys from Devil's Row seethed about the shrieking and tearful child from Rum Alley.

"Gee!" he murmured with interest. "A scrap. Gee!"

He strode over to the cursing circle, swinging his shoulders in a manner which denoted that he held victory in his fists. He approached at the back of one of the most deeply engaged of the Devil's Row children.

"Ah, what deh hell," he said, and smote the deeply-engaged one on the back of the head. The little boy fell to the ground and gave a hoarse, tremendous howl. He scrambled to his feet, and perceiving, evidently, the size of his assailant, ran quickly off, shouting alarms. The entire Devil's Row party followed him. They came to a stand a short distance away and yelled taunting oaths at the boy with the chronic sneer. The latter, momentarily, paid no attention to them.

"What deh hell, Jimmie?" he asked of the small champion.

Jimmie wiped his blood-wet features with his sleeve.

"Well, it was dis way, Pete, see! I was goin' teh lick dat Riley kid and dey all pitched on me."

Some Rum Alley children now came forward. The party stood for a moment exchanging vainglorious remarks with Devil's Row. A few stones were thrown at long distances, and words of challenge passed between small warriors. Then the Rum Alley contingent turned slowly in the direction of their home street. They began to give, each to each, distorted versions of the fight. Causes of retreat in particular cases were magnified. Blows dealt in the fight were enlarged to catapultian power, and stones thrown were alleged to have hurtled with infinite accuracy. Valor grew strong again, and the little boys began to swear with great spirit.

"Ah, we blokies kin lick deh hull damn Row," said a child, swaggering.

Little Jimmie was striving to stanch the flow of blood from his cut lips. Scowling, he turned upon the speaker.

"Ah, where deh hell was yeh when I was doin' all deh fightin'?" he demanded. "Youse kids makes me tired."

"Ah, go ahn," replied the other argumentatively.

Jimmie replied with heavy contempt. "Ah, youse can't fight, Blue Billie! I kin lick yeh wid one han'."

"Ah, go ahn," replied Billie again.

"Ah," said Jimmie threateningly.

"Ah," said the other in the same tone.

They struck at each other, clinched, and rolled over on the cobble stones.

"Smash 'im, Jimmie, kick deh damn guts out of 'im," yelled Pete, the lad with the chronic sneer, in tones of delight.

The small combatants pounded and kicked, scratched and tore. They began to weep and their curses struggled in their throats with sobs. The other little boys clasped their hands and wriggled their legs in excitement. They formed a bobbing circle about the pair.

A tiny spectator was suddenly agitated.

"Cheese it, Jimmie, cheese it! Here comes yer fader," he yelled.

The circle of little boys instantly parted. They drew away and waited in ecstatic awe for that which was about to happen. The two little boys fighting in the modes of four thousand years ago, did not hear the warning.

Up the avenue there plodded slowly a man with sullen eyes. He was carrying a dinner pail and smoking an apple-wood pipe.

As he neared the spot where the little boys strove, he regarded them listlessly. But suddenly he roared an oath and advanced upon the rolling fighters.

"Here, you Jim, git up, now, while I belt yer life out, you damned disorderly brat."

He began to kick into the chaotic mass on the ground. The boy Billie felt a heavy boot strike his head. He made a furious effort and disentangled himself from Jimmie. He tottered away, damning.

Jimmie arose painfully from the ground and confronting his father, began to curse him. His parent kicked him. "Come home, now," he cried, "an' stop yer jawin', er I'll lam the everlasting head off yehs."

They departed. The man paced placidly along with the apple-wood emblem of serenity between his teeth. The boy followed a dozen feet in the rear. He swore luridly, for he felt that it was degradation for one who aimed to be some vague soldier, or a man of blood with a sort of sublime license, to be taken home by a father.

CHAPTER II

Eventually they entered into a dark region where, from a careening building, a dozen gruesome doorways gave up loads of babies to the street and the gutter. A wind of early autumn raised yellow dust from cobbles and swirled it against an hundred windows. Long streamers of garments fluttered from fire-escapes. In all unhandy places there were buckets, brooms, rags and bottles. In the street infants played or fought with other infants or sat stupidly in the way of vehicles. Formidable women, with uncombed hair and disordered dress, gossiped while leaning on railings, or screamed in frantic quarrels. Withered persons, in curious postures of submission to something, sat smoking pipes in obscure corners. A thousand odors of cooking food came forth to the street. The building quivered and creaked from the weight of humanity stamping about in its bowels.

A small ragged girl dragged a red, bawling infant along the crowded ways. He was hanging back, baby-like, bracing his wrinkled, bare legs.

The little girl cried out: "Ah, Tommie, come ahn. Dere's Jimmie and fader. Don't be a-pullin' me back."

She jerked the baby's arm impatiently. He fell on his face, roaring. With a second jerk she pulled him to his feet, and they went on. With the obstinacy of his order, he protested against being dragged in a chosen direction. He made heroic endeavors to keep on his legs, denounce his sister and consume a bit of orange peeling which he chewed between the times of his infantile orations.

As the sullen-eyed man, followed by the blood-covered boy, drew near, the little girl burst into reproachful cries. "Ah, Jimmie, youse bin fightin' agin."

The urchin swelled disdainfully.

"Ah, what deh hell, Mag. See?"

The little girl upbraided him. "Youse allus fightin', Jimmie, an' yeh knows it puts mudder out when yehs come home half dead, an' it's like we'll all get a poundin'."

She began to weep. The babe threw back his head and roared at his prospects.

"Ah, what deh hell!" cried Jimmie. "Shut up er I'll smack yer mout'. See?"

As his sister continued her lamentations, he suddenly swore and struck her. The little girl reeled and, recovering herself, burst into tears and quaveringly cursed him. As she slowly retreated her brother advanced dealing her cuffs. The father heard and turned about.

"Stop that, Jim, d'yeh hear? Leave yer sister alone on the street. It's like I can never beat any sense into yer damned wooden head."

The urchin raised his voice in defiance to his parent and continued his attacks. The babe bawled tremendously, protesting with great violence. During his sister's hasty manoeuvres, he was dragged by the arm.

Finally the procession plunged into one of the gruesome doorways. They crawled up dark stairways and along cold, gloomy halls. At last the father pushed open a door and they entered a lighted room in which a large woman was rampant.

She stopped in a career from a seething stove to a pan-covered table. As the father and children filed in she peered at them.

"Eh, what? Been fightin' agin, by Gawd!" She threw herself upon Jimmie. The urchin tried to dart behind the others and in the scuffle the babe, Tommie, was knocked down. He protested with his usual vehemence, because they had bruised his tender shins against a table leg.

The mother's massive shoulders heaved with anger. Grasping the urchin by the neck and shoulder she shook him until he rattled. She dragged him to an unholy sink, and, soaking a rag in water, began to scrub his lacerated face with it. Jimmie screamed in pain and tried to twist his shoulders out of the clasp of the huge arms.

The babe sat on the floor watching the scene, his face in contortions like that of a woman at a tragedy. The father, with a newly-ladened pipe in his mouth, crouched on a backless chair near the stove. Jimmie's cries annoyed him. He turned about and bellowed at his wife:

"Let the damned kid alone for a minute, will yeh, Mary? Yer allus poundin' 'im. When I come nights I can't git no rest 'cause yer allus poundin' a kid. Let up, d'yeh hear? Don't be allus poundin' a kid."

The woman's operations on the urchin instantly increased in violence. At last she tossed him to a corner where he limply lay cursing and weeping.

The wife put her immense hands on her hips and with a chieftain-like stride approached her husband.

"Ho," she said, with a great grunt of contempt. "An' what in the devil are you stickin' your nose for?"

The babe crawled under the table and, turning, peered out cautiously. The ragged girl retreated and the urchin in the corner drew his legs carefully beneath him.

The man puffed his pipe calmly and put his great mudded boots on the back part of the stove.

"Go teh hell," he murmured, tranquilly.

The woman screamed and shook her fists before her husband's eyes. The rough yellow of her face and neck flared suddenly crimson. She began to howl.

He puffed imperturbably at his pipe for a time, but finally arose and began to look out at the window into the darkening chaos of back yards.

"You've been drinkin', Mary," he said. "You'd better let up on the bot', ol' woman, or you'll git done."

"You're a liar. I ain't had a drop," she roared in reply.

They had a lurid altercation, in which they damned each other's souls with frequence.

The babe was staring out from under the table, his small face working in his excitement.

The ragged girl went stealthily over to the corner where the urchin lay.

"Are yehs hurted much, Jimmie?" she whispered timidly.

"Not a damn bit! See?" growled the little boy.

"Will I wash deh blood?"

"Naw!"

"Will I—"

"When I catch dat Riley kid I'll break 'is face! Dat's right! See?" He turned his face to the wall as if resolved to grimly bide his time.

In the quarrel between husband and wife, the woman was victor. The man grabbed his hat and rushed from the room, apparently determined upon a vengeful drunk. She followed to the door and thundered at him as he made his way down stairs.

She returned and stirred up the room until her children were bobbing about like bubbles.

"Git outa deh way," she persistently bawled, waving feet with their dishevelled shoes near the heads of her children. She shrouded herself, puffing and snorting, in a cloud of steam at the stove, and eventually extracted a fryingpan full of potatoes that hissed.

She flourished it. "Come teh yer suppers, now," she cried with sudden exasperation. "Hurry up, now, er I'll help yeh!"

The children scrambled hastily. With prodigious clatter they arranged themselves at table. The babe sat with his feet dangling high from a precarious infant chair and gorged his small stomach. Jimmie forced, with feverish rapidity, the grease-enveloped pieces between his wounded lips. Maggie, with side glances of fear of interruption, ate like a small pursued tigress.

The mother sat blinking at them. She delivered reproaches, swallowed potatoes and drank from a yellow-brown bottle. After a time her mood changed and she wept as she carried little Tommie into another room and laid him to sleep with his fists doubled in an old quilt of faded red and green grandeur. Then she came and moaned by the stove. She rocked to and fro upon a chair, shedding tears and crooning miserably to the two children about their "poor mother" and "yer fader, damn 'is soul."

The little girl plodded between the table and the chair with a dishpan on it. She tottered on her small legs beneath burdens of dishes.

Jimmie sat nursing his various wounds. He cast furtive glances at his mother. His practised eye perceived her gradually emerge from a muddled mist of sentiment until her brain burned in drunken heat. He sat breathless.

Maggie broke a plate.

The mother started to her feet as if propelled.

"Good Gawd," she howled. Her eyes glittered on her child with sudden hatred. The fervent red of her face turned almost to purple. The little boy ran to the halls, shrieking like a monk in an earthquake.

He floundered about in darkness until he found the stairs. He stumbled, panic-stricken, to the next floor. An old woman opened a door. A light behind her threw a flare on the urchin's quivering face.

"Eh, Gawd, child, what is it dis time? Is yer fader beatin' yer mudder, or yer mudder beatin' yer fader?"

CHAPTER III

Jimmie and the old woman listened long in the hall. Above the muffled roar of conversation, the dismal wailings of babies at night, the thumping of feet in unseen corridors and rooms, mingled with the sound of varied hoarse shoutings in the street and the rattling of wheels over cobbles, they heard the screams of the child and the roars of the mother die away to a feeble moaning and a subdued bass muttering.

The old woman was a gnarled and leathery personage who could don, at will, an expression of great virtue. She possessed a small music-box capable of one tune, and a collection of "God bless yehs" pitched in assorted keys of fervency. Each day she took a position upon the stones of Fifth Avenue,[1] where she crooked her legs under her and crouched immovable and hideous, like an idol. She received daily a small sum in pennies. It was contributed, for the most part, by persons who did not make their homes in that vicinity.

Once, when a lady had dropped her purse on the sidewalk, the gnarled woman had grabbed it and smuggled it with great dexterity beneath her cloak. When she was arrested she had cursed the lady into a partial swoon, and with her aged limbs, twisted from rheumatism, had almost kicked the stomach out of a huge policeman whose conduct upon that occasion she referred to when she said: "The police, damn 'em."

"Eh, Jimmie, it's cursed shame," she said. "Go, now, like a dear an' buy me a can,[2] an' if yer mudder raises 'ell all night yehs can sleep here."

---

[1] New York City's most fashionable street at that time.
[2] A can of beer.

Jimmie took a tendered tin-pail and seven pennies and departed. He passed into the side door of a saloon and went to the bar. Straining up on his toes he raised the pail and pennies as high as his arms would let him. He saw two hands thrust down and take them. Directly the same hands let down the filled pail and he left.

In front of the gruesome doorway he met a lurching figure. It was his father, swaying about on uncertain legs.

"Give me deh can. See?" said the man, threateningly.

"Ah, come off! I got dis can fer dat ol' woman an' it 'ud be dirt teh swipe it. See?" cried Jimmie.

The father wrenched the pail from the urchin. He grasped it in both hands and lifted it to his mouth. He glued his lips to the under edge and tilted his head. His hairy throat swelled until it seemed to grow near his chin. There was a tremendous gulping movement and the beer was gone.

The man caught his breath and laughed. He hit his son on the head with the empty pail. As it rolled clanging into the street, Jimmie began to scream and kicked repeatedly at his father's shins.

"Look at deh dirt what yeh done me," he yelled. "Deh ol' woman 'ill be raisin' hell."

He retreated to the middle of the street, but the man did not pursue. He staggered toward the door.

"I'll club hell outa yeh when I ketch yeh," he shouted, and disappeared.

During the evening he had been standing against a bar drinking whiskies and declaring to all comers, confidentially: "My home reg'lar livin' hell! Damndes' place! Reg'lar hell! Why do I come an' drin' whisk' here thish way? 'Cause home reg'lar livin' hell!"

Jimmie waited a long time in the street and then crept warily up through the building. He passed with great caution the door of the gnarled woman, and finally stopped outside his home and listened.

He could hear his mother moving heavily about among the furniture of the room. She was chanting in a mournful voice, occasionally interjecting bursts of volcanic wrath at the father, who, Jimmie judged, had sunk down on the floor or in a corner.

"Why deh blazes don' chere try tch keep Jim from fightin'? I'll break yer jaw," she suddenly bellowed.

The man mumbled with drunken indifference. "Ah, wha' deh hell. W'a's odds? Wha' makes kick?"

"Because he tears 'is clothes, yeh damn fool," cried the woman in supreme wrath.

The husband seemed to become aroused. "Go teh hell," he thundered fiercely in reply. There was a crash against the door and something broke into clattering fragments. Jimmie partially suppressed a howl and darted down the stairway. Below he paused and listened. He heard howls and curses, groans and shrieks, confusingly in chorus as if a battle were raging. With all was the crash of splintering furniture. The eyes of the urchin glared in fear that one of them would discover him.

Curious faces appeared in door-ways, and whispered comments passed to and fro. "Ol' Johnson's raisin' hell agin."

Jimmie stood until the noises ceased and the other inhabitants of the tenement had all yawned and shut their doors. Then he crawled upstairs with the caution of an invader of a panther den. Sounds of labored breathing came through the broken door-panels. He pushed the door open and entered, quaking.

A glow from the fire threw red hues over the bare floor, the cracked and soiled plastering, and the overturned and broken furniture.

In the middle of the floor lay his mother asleep. In one corner of the room his father's limp body hung across the seat of a chair.

The urchin stole forward. He began to shiver in dread of awakening his parents. His mother's great chest was heaving painfully. Jimmie paused and looked down at her. Her face was inflamed and swollen from drinking. Her yellow brows shaded eye-lids that had grown blue. Her tangled hair tossed in waves over her forehead. Her mouth was set in the same lines of vindictive hatred that it had, perhaps, borne during the fight. Her bare, red arms were thrown out above her head in positions of exhaustion, something, mayhap, like those of a sated villain.

The urchin bended over his mother. He was fearful lest she should open her eyes, and the dread within him was so strong, that he could not forbear to stare, but hung as if fascinated over the woman's grim face.

Suddenly her eyes opened. The urchin found himself looking straight into that expression, which, it would seem, had the power to change his blood to salt. He howled piercingly and fell backward.

The woman floundered for a moment, tossed her arms about her head as if in combat, and again began to snore.

Jimmie crawled back in the shadows and waited. A noise in the next room had followed his cry at the discovery that his mother was awake. He grovelled in the gloom, the eyes from out his drawn face riveted upon the intervening door.

He heard it creak, and then the sound of a small voice came to him. "Jimmie! Jimmie! Are yehs dere?" it whispered. The urchin started. The thin, white face of his sister looked at him from the door-way of the other room. She crept to him across the floor.

The father had not moved, but lay in the same death-like sleep. The mother writhed in uneasy slumber, her chest wheezing as if she were in the agonies of strangulation. Out at the window a florid moon was peering over dark roofs, and in the distance the waters of a river glimmered pallidly.

The small frame of the ragged girl was quivering. Her features were haggard from weeping, and her eyes gleamed from fear. She grasped the urchin's arm in her little trembling hands and they huddled in a corner. The eyes of both were drawn, by some force, to stare at the woman's face, for they thought she need only to awake and all fiends would come from below.

They crouched until the ghost-mists of dawn appeared at the window, drawing close to the panes, and looking in at the prostrate, heaving body of the mother.

CHAPTER IV

The babe, Tommie, died. He went away in a white, insignificant coffin, his small waxen hand clutching a flower that the girl, Maggie, had stolen from an Italian.

She and Jimmie lived.

The inexperienced fibres of the boy's eyes were hardened at an early age. He became a young man of leather. He lived some red years without laboring. During that time his sneer became chronic. He studied human nature in the gutter, and found it no worse than he thought he had reason to believe it. He never conceived a respect for the world, because he had begun with no idols that it had smashed.

He clad his soul in armor by means of happening hilariously in at a mission church where a man composed his sermons of "yous." While they got warm at the stove, he told his hearers just where he calculated they stood with the Lord. Many of the sinners were impatient over the pictured depths of their degradation. They were waiting for soup-tickets.

A reader of words of wind-demons might have been able to see the portions of a dialogue pass to and fro between the exhorter and his hearers.

"You are damned," said the preacher. And the reader of sounds might have seen the reply go forth from the ragged people: "Where's our soup?"

Jimmie and a companion sat in a rear seat and commented upon the things that didn't concern them, with all the freedom of English gentlemen. When they grew thirsty and went out their minds confused the speaker with Christ.

Momentarily, Jimmie was sullen with thoughts of a hopeless altitude where grew fruit. His companion said that if he should ever meet God he would ask for a million dollars and a bottle of beer.

Jimmie's occupation for a long time was to stand on street-corners and watch the world go by, dreaming blood-red dreams at the passing of pretty women. He menaced mankind at the intersections of streets.

On the corners he was in life and of life. The world was going on and he was there to perceive it.

He maintained a belligerent attitude toward all well-dressed men. To him fine raiment was allied to weakness, and all good coats covered faint hearts. He and his order were kings, to a certain extent, over the men of untarnished clothes, because these latter dreaded, perhaps, to be either killed or laughed at.

Above all things he despised obvious Christians and ciphers with the chrysanthemums of aristocracy in their button-holes. He considered himself above both of these classes. He was afraid of neither the devil nor the leader of society.

When he had a dollar in his pocket his satisfaction with existence was the greatest thing in the world. So, eventually, he felt obliged to work. His father died and his mother's years were divided up into periods of thirty days.

He became a truck driver. He was given the charge of a pains-taking pair of horses and a large rattling truck. He invaded the turmoil and tumble of the down-town streets and learned to breathe maledictory defiance at the police who occasionally used to climb up, drag him from his perch and beat him.

In the lower part of the city he daily involved himself in hideous tangles. If he and his team chanced to be in the rear he preserved a demeanor of serenity, crossing his legs and bursting forth into yells when foot-passengers took dangerous dives beneath the noses of his champing horses. He smoked his pipe calmly for he knew that his pay was marching on.

If in the front and the key-truck of chaos, he entered terrifically into the quarrel that was raging to and fro among the drivers on their high seats, and sometimes roared oaths and violently got himself arrested.

After a time his sneer grew so that it turned its glare upon all things. He became so sharp that he believed in nothing. To him the police were always actuated by malignant impulses and the rest of the world was composed, for the most part, of despicable creatures who were all trying to take advantage of him and with whom, in defense, he was obliged to quarrel on all possible occasions. He himself occupied a down-trodden position that had a private but distinct element of grandeur in its isolation.

The most complete cases of aggravated idiocy were, to his mind, rampant upon the front platforms of all of the street cars. At first his tongue strove with these beings, but he eventually was superior. He became immured like an African cow. In him grew a majestic contempt for those strings of street cars that followed him like intent bugs. *enclosed/confined*

He fell into the habit, when starting on a long journey, of fixing his eye on a high and distant object, commanding his horses to begin, and then going into a sort of a trance of observation. Multitudes of drivers might howl in his rear, and passengers might load him with opprobrium, he would not awaken until some blue policeman turned red and began to frenziedly tear bridles and beat the soft noses of the responsible horses. *criticism*

When he paused to contemplate the attitude of the police toward himself and his fellows, he believed that they were the only men in the city who had no rights. When driving about, he felt that he was held liable by the police for anything that might occur in the streets, and was the common prey of all energetic officials. In revenge, he resolved never to move out of the way of anything, until formidable circumstances, or a much larger man than himself forced him to it.

Foot-passengers were mere pestering flies with an insane disregard for their legs and his convenience. He could not conceive their maniacal desires to cross the streets. Their madness smote him with eternal amazement. He was continually storming at them from his throne. He sat aloft and denounced their frantic leaps, plunges, dives and straddles.

When they would thrust at, or parry, the noses of his champing horses, making them swing their heads and move their feet, disturbing a solid dreamy repose, he swore at the men as fools, for he himself could perceive that Providence had caused it clearly to be written, that he and his team had the unalienable right to stand in the proper path of the sun chariot, and if they so minded, obstruct its mission or take a wheel off.

And, perhaps, if the god-driver had an ungovernable desire to step down, put up his flame-colored fists and manfully dispute the right of way, he would have probably been immediately opposed by a scowling mortal with two sets of very hard knuckles.

It is possible, perhaps, that this young man would have derided, in an axle-wide alley, the approach of a flying ferry boat. Yet he achieved a respect for a fire engine. As one charged toward his truck, he would drive fearfully upon a side-walk, threatening untold people with annihilation. When an engine would strike a mass of blocked trucks, splitting it into fragments, as a blow annihilates a cake of ice, Jimmie's team could usually be observed high and safe, with whole wheels, on the side-walk. The fearful coming of the engine could break up the most intricate muddle of heavy vehicles at which the police had been swearing for the half of an hour.

A fire-engine was enshrined in his heart as an appalling thing that he loved with a distant dog-like devotion. They had been known to overturn street-cars. Those leaping horses, striking sparks from the cobbles in their forward lunge, were creatures to be ineffably admired. The clang of the gong pierced his breast like a noise of remembered war.

When Jimmie was a little boy, he began to be arrested. Before he reached a great age, he had a fair record.

He developed too great a tendency to climb down from his truck and fight with other drivers. He had been in quite a number of miscellaneous fights, and in some general barroom rows that had become known to the police. Once he had been arrested for assaulting a Chinaman. Two women in different parts of the city, and entirely unknown to each other, caused him considerable annoyance by breaking forth, simultaneously, at fateful intervals, into wailings about marriage and support and infants. *Are you kidding.*

Nevertheless, he had, on a certain star-lit evening, said wonderingly and quite reverently: "Deh moon looks like hell, don't it?"

↳ stream of romonicsm

CHAPTER V

she's pretty!

diamond in the rough npc bot

The girl, Maggie, blossomed in a mud puddle. She grew to be a most rare and wonderful production of a tenement district, a pretty girl.

None of the dirt of Rum Alley seemed to be in her veins. The philosophers up-stairs, down-stairs and on the same floor, puzzled over it.

When a child, playing and fighting with gamins in the street, dirt disguised her. Attired in tatters and grime, she went unseen.

There came a time, however, when the young men of the vicinity said: "Dat Johnson goil is a puty good looker." About this period her brother remarked to her: "Mag, I'll tell yeh dis! See? Yeh've edder got teh go teh hell or go teh work!" Whereupon she went to work, having the feminine aversion of going to hell.

By a chance, she got a position in an establishment where they made collars and cuffs. She received a stool and a machine in a room where sat twenty girls of various shades of yellow discontent. She perched on the stool and treadled at her machine all day, turning out collars, the name of whose brand could be noted for its irrelevancy to anything in connection with collars. At night she returned home to her mother.

Jimmie grew large enough to take the vague position of head of the family. As incumbent of that office, he stumbled up-stairs late at night, as his father had done before him. He reeled about the room, swearing at his relations, or went to sleep on the floor.

The mother had gradually arisen to that degree of fame that she could bandy words with her acquaintances among the police-justices. Court-officials called her by her first name. When she appeared they pursued a course which had been theirs for months. They invariably grinned and cried out: "Hello, Mary, you here again?" Her grey head wagged in many a court. She always besieged the bench with voluble excuses, explanations, apologies and prayers. Her flaming face and rolling eyes were a sort of familiar sight on the island. She measured time by means of sprees, and was eternally swollen and dishevelled.

One day the young man, Pete, who as a lad had smitten the Devil's Row urchin in the back of the head and put to flight the antagonists of his friend, Jimmie, strutted upon the scene. He met Jimmie one day on the street, promised to take him to a boxing match in Williamsburg,[1] and called for him in the evening.

Maggie observed Pete. So short

He sat on a table in the Johnson home and dangled his checked legs with an enticing nonchalance. His hair was curled down over his forehead in an oiled bang. His rather pugged nose seemed to revolt from contact with a bristling moustache of short, wire-like hairs. His blue double-breasted coat, edged with black braid, buttoned close to a red puff tie, and his patent-leather shoes looked like murder-fitted weapons. → P. 36 clothing quote

His mannerisms stamped him as a man who had a correct sense of his personal superiority. There was valor and contempt for circumstances in the glance of his eye. He waved his hands like a man of the world, who dismisses religion and philosophy, and says "Fudge." He had certainly seen everything and with each curl of his lip, he declared that it amounted to nothing. Maggie thought he must be a very elegant and graceful bar-tender.

He was telling tales to Jimmie.

Maggie watched him furtively, with half-closed eyes, lit with a vague interest.

"Hully gee! Dey makes me tired," he said. "Mos' e'ry day some farmer comes in an' tries teh run deh shop. See? But dey gits t'rowed

---

[1] Part of Brooklyn, on the eastern shore of the East River.

right out! I jolt dem right out in deh street before dey knows where dey is! See?"

"Sure," said Jimmie.

"Dere was a mug come in deh place deh odder day wid an idear he wus goin' teh own deh place! Hully gee, he wus goin' teh own deh place! I see he had a still on an' I didn' wanna giv 'im no stuff, so I says:'Git deh hell outa here an' don' make no trouble,' I says like dat! See? 'Git deh hell outa here an' don' make no trouble'; like dat. 'Git deh hell outa here,' I says. See?"

Jimmie nodded understandingly. Over his features played an eager desire to state the amount of his valor in a similar crisis, but the narrator proceeded. PEROUNING, BRJGGING

"Well, deh blokie he says:'T'hell wid it! I ain' lookin' for no scrap,' he says (See?) 'but,' he says, 'I'm 'spectable cit'zen an' I wanna drink an' purtydamnsoon, too.' See? 'Deh hell,' I says. Like dat! 'Deh hell,' I says. See? 'Don' make no trouble,' I says. Like dat. 'Don' make no trouble.' See? Den deh mug he squared off an' said he was fine as silk wid his dukes (See?) an' he wanned a drink damnquick. Dat's what he said. See?"

"Sure," repeated Jimmie.

Pete continued. "Say, I jes' jumped deh bar an' deh way I plunked dat blokie was great. See? Dat's right! In deh jaw! See? Hully gee, he t'rowed a spittoon true deh front windee. Say, I taut I'd drop dead. But deh boss, he comes in after an' he says, 'Pete, yehs done jes' right! Yeh've gota keep order an' it's all right.' See? 'It's all right,' he says. Dat's what he said."

The two held a technical discussion.

"Dat bloke was a dandy," said Pete, in conclusion, "but he hadn' oughta made no trouble. Dat's what I says teh dem: 'Don' come in here an' make no trouble,' I says, like dat. 'Don' make no trouble.' See?"

As Jimmie and his friend exchanged tales descriptive of their prowess, Maggie leaned back in the shadow. Her eyes dwelt wonderingly and rather wistfully upon Pete's face. The broken furniture, grimy walls, and general disorder and dirt of her home of a sudden appeared before her and began to take a potential aspect. Pete's aristocratic person looked as if it might soil. She looked keenly at him, occasionally, wondering if he was feeling contempt. But Pete seemed to be enveloped in reminiscence.

"Hully gee," said he, "dose mugs can't phase me. Dey knows I kin wipe up deh street wid any t'ree of dem."

When he said, "Ah, what deh hell," his voice was burdened with disdain for the inevitable and contempt for anything that fate might compel him to endure.

[Maggie perceived that here was the beau ideal of a man.]Her dim thoughts were often searching for far away lands where, as God says, the little hills sing together in the morning. Under the trees of her dream-gardens there had always walked a lover.

CHAPTER VI

Pete took note of Maggie.

"Say, Mag, I'm stuck on yer shape. It's outa sight," he said, parenthetically, with an affable grin.

As he became aware that she was listening closely, he grew still more eloquent in his descriptions of various happenings in his career. It appeared that he was invincible in fights.

"Why," he said, referring to a man with whom he had had a misunderstanding, "dat mug scrapped like a damn dago.[1] Dat's right. He was dead easy. See? He tau't he was a scrapper. But he foun' out diff'ent! Hully gee."

He walked to and fro in the small room, which seemed then to grow even smaller and unfit to hold his dignity, the attribute of a supreme warrior. That swing of the shoulders that had frozen the timid when he was but a lad had increased with his growth and education at the ratio of ten to one. It, combined with the sneer upon his mouth, told mankind that there was nothing in space which could appall him. Maggie marvelled at him and surrounded him with greatness. She vaguely tried to calculate the altitude of the pinnacle from which he must have looked down upon her.

"I met a chump deh odder day way up in deh city," he said. "I was goin' teh see a frien' of mine. When I was a-crossin' deh street deh chump runned plump inteh me, an' den he turns aroun' an' says, 'Yer insolen' ruffin,' he says, like dat. 'Oh, gee,' I says, 'oh, gee, go teh

---

[1] Possibly a corruption of the name *Diego*; a dago refers to a man of Spanish origin.

hell and git off deh eart',' I says, like dat. See? 'Go teh hell an' git off deh eart',' like dat. Den deh blokie he got wild. He says I was a contempt'ble scoun'el, er somet'ing like dat, an' he says I was doom' teh everlastin' pe'dition an' all like dat. 'Gee,' I says, 'gee! Deh hell I am,' I says. 'Deh hell I am,' like dat. An' den I slugged 'im. See?"

With Jimmie in his company, Pete departed in a sort of a blaze of glory from the Johnson home. Maggie, leaning from the window, watched him as he walked down the street.

Here was a formidable man who disdained the strength of a world full of fists. Here was one who had contempt for brass-clothed power; one whose knuckles could defiantly ring against the granite of law. He was a knight. *very romanticized*

The two men went from under the glimmering street-lamp and passed into shadows.

Turning, Maggie contemplated the dark, dust-stained walls, and the scant and crude furniture of her home. A clock, in a splintered and battered oblong box of varnished wood, she suddenly regarded as an abomination. She noted that it ticked raspingly. The almost vanished flowers in the carpet-pattern, she conceived to be newly hideous. Some faint attempts she had made with blue ribbon, to freshen the appearance of a dingy curtain, she now saw to be piteous.

She wondered what Pete dined on.

She reflected upon the collar and cuff factory. It began to appear to her mind as a dreary place of endless grinding. Pete's elegant occupation brought him, no doubt, into contact with people who had money and manners. It was probable that he had a large acquaintance of pretty girls. He must have great sums of money to spend.

To her the earth was composed of hardships and insults. She felt instant admiration for a man who openly defied it. She thought that if the grim angel of death should clutch his heart, Pete would shrug his shoulders and say: "Oh, ev'ryt'ing goes."

She anticipated that he would come again shortly. She spent some of her week's pay in the purchase of flowered cretonne for a lambre-quin.[1] She made it with infinite care and hung it to the slightly-careening mantel, over the stove, in the kitchen. She studied it with

---

[1] Cretonne is a heavy cotton fabric, usually with a floral pattern; a lambrequin is a short curtain draped from the top of a door, window, or mantelpiece.

painful anxiety from different points in the room. She wanted it to look well on Sunday night when, perhaps, Jimmie's friend would come. On Sunday night, however, Pete did not appear.

Afterward the girl looked at it with a sense of humiliation. She was now convinced that Pete was superior to admiration for lambrequins.

A few evenings later Pete entered with fascinating innovations in his apparel. As she had seen him twice and he had different suits on each time, Maggie had a dim impression that his wardrobe was prodigiously extensive.

"Say, Mag," he said, "put on yer bes' duds Friday night an' I'll take yehs teh deh show. See?"

He spent a few moments in flourishing his clothes and then vanished, without having glanced at the lambrequin.

Over the eternal collars and cuffs in the factory Maggie spent the most of three days in making imaginary sketches of Pete and his daily environment. She imagined some half dozen women in love with him and thought he must lean dangerously toward an indefinite one, whom she pictured with great charms of person, but with an altogether contemptible disposition.

She thought he must live in a blare of pleasure. He had friends, and people who were afraid of him.

She saw the golden glitter of the place where Pete was to take her. An entertainment of many hues and many melodies where she was afraid she might appear small and mouse-colored.

Her mother drank whiskey all Friday morning. With lurid face and tossing hair she cursed and destroyed furniture all Friday afternoon. When Maggie came home at half-past six her mother lay asleep amidst the wreck of chairs and a table. Fragments of various household utensils were scattered about the floor. She had vented some phase of drunken fury upon the lambrequin. It lay in a bedraggled heap in the corner.

"Hah," she snorted, sitting up suddenly, "where deh hell yeh been? Why deh hell don' yeh come home earlier? Been loafin' 'round deh streets. Yer gettin' teh be a reg'lar devil."

When Pete arrived Maggie, in a worn black dress, was waiting for him in the midst of a floor strewn with wreckage. The curtain at the window had been pulled by a heavy hand and hung by one tack, dangling to and fro in the draft through the cracks at the sash. The knots of blue ribbons appeared like violated flowers. The fire in the stove had gone out. The displaced lids and open doors showed heaps of sullen grey ashes. The remnants of a meal, ghastly, like dead flesh, lay in a corner. Maggie's red mother, stretched on the floor, blasphemed and gave her daughter a bad name.

RED = ANGER, DANGER, aggression

CHAPTER VII

An orchestra of yellow silk women and bald-headed men on an elevated stage near the centre of a great green-hued hall, played a popular waltz. The place was crowded with people grouped about little tables. A battalion of waiters slid among the throng, carrying trays of beer glasses and making change from the inexhaustible vaults of their trousers pockets. Little boys, in the costumes of French chefs, paraded up and down the irregular aisles vending fancy cakes. There was a low rumble of conversation and a subdued clinking of glasses. Clouds of tobacco smoke rolled and wavered high in air about the dull gilt of the chandeliers.

The vast crowd had an air throughout of having just quitted labor. Men with calloused hands and attired in garments that showed the wear of an endless trudge for a living, smoked their pipes contentedly and spent five, ten, or perhaps fifteen cents for beer. There was a mere sprinkling of kid-gloved men who smoked cigars purchased elsewhere. The great body of the crowd was composed of people who showed that all day they strove with their hands. Quiet Germans, with maybe their wives and two or three children, sat listening to the music, with the expressions of happy cows. An occasional party of sailors from a war-ship, their faces pictures of sturdy health, spent the earlier hours of the evening at the small round tables. Very infrequent tipsy men, swollen with the value of their opinions, engaged their companions in earnest and confidential conversation. In the balcony, and here and there below, shone the impassive faces of women. The nationalities of the Bowery[1] beamed upon the stage from all directions.

[1] Part of the Lower East Side and home to many saloons and entertainment halls.

Pete aggressively walked up a side aisle and took seats with Maggie at a table beneath the balcony.

"Two beehs!"

Leaning back he regarded with eyes of superiority the scene before them. This attitude affected Maggie strongly. A man who could regard such a sight with indifference must be accustomed to very great things.

It was obvious that Pete had been to this place many times before, and was very familiar with it. A knowledge of this fact made Maggie feel little and new.

He was extremely gracious and attentive. He displayed the consideration of a cultured gentleman who knew what was due.

"Say, what deh hell? Bring deh lady a big glass! What deh hell use is dat pony?"

"Don't be fresh, now," said the waiter, with some warmth, as he departed.

"Ah, git off deh eart'," said Pete, after the other's retreating form.

Maggie perceived that Pete brought forth all his elegance and all his knowledge of high-class customs for her benefit. Her heart warmed as she reflected upon his condescension.

The orchestra of yellow silk women and bald-headed men gave vent to a few bars of anticipatory music and a girl, in a pink dress with short skirts, galloped upon the stage. She smiled upon the throng as if in acknowledgment of a warm welcome, and began to walk to and fro, making profuse gesticulations and singing, in brazen soprano tones, a song, the words of which were inaudible. When she broke into the swift rattling measures of a chorus some half-tipsy men near the stage joined in the rollicking refrain and glasses were pounded rhythmically upon the tables. People leaned forward to watch her and to try to catch the words of the song. When she vanished there were long rollings of applause.

Obedient to more anticipatory bars, she reappeared amidst the half-suppressed cheering of the tipsy men. The orchestra plunged into dance music and the laces of the dancer fluttered and flew in the glare of gas jets. She divulged the fact that she was attired in some half dozen skirts. It was patent that any one of them would have proved adequate for the purpose for which skirts are intended. An occasional man bent forward, intent upon the pink stockings.

Maggie wondered at the splendor of the costume and lost herself in calculations of the cost of the silks and laces.

[The dancer's smile of stereotyped enthusiasm was turned for ten minutes upon the faces of her audience] In the finale she fell into some of those grotesque attitudes which were at the time popular among the dancers in the theatres up-town, giving to the Bowery public the phantasies of the aristocratic theatre-going public, at reduced rates.   ↳ *phantasies*

"Say, Pete," said Maggie, leaning forward, "dis it great."

"Sure," said Pete, with proper complacence.

A ventriloquist followed the dancer. He held two fantastic dolls on his knees. He made them sing mournful ditties and say funny things about geography and Ireland.

"Do dose little men talk?" asked Maggie.

"Naw," said Pete, "it's some damn fake. See?"

Two girls, on the bills as sisters, came forth and sang a duet that is heard occasionally at concerts given under church auspices. They supplemented it with a dance which of course can never be seen at concerts given under church auspices.   → *southern black roe-son*

After the duettists had retired, a woman of debatable age sang a negro melody. The chorus necessitated some grotesque waddlings supposed to be an imitation of a plantation darkey,[1] under the influence, probably, of music and the moon. The audience was just enthusiastic enough over it to have her return and sing a sorrowful lay, whose lines told of a mother's love and a sweetheart who waited and a young man who was lost at sea under the most harrowing circumstances. From the faces of a score or so in the crowd, the self-contained look faded. Many heads were bent forward with eagerness and sympathy. As the last distressing sentiment of the piece was brought forth, it was greeted by that kind of applause which rings as sincere.

As a final effort, the singer rendered some verses which described a vision of Britain being annihilated by America, and Ireland bursting her bonds. A carefully prepared crisis was reached in the last line of the last verse, where the singer threw out her arms and cried, "The star-spangled banner." Instantly a great cheer swelled from the throats of the assemblage of the masses. There was a heavy rumble

---

[1] This word for a southern US Black originates in the mid-nineteenth century.

of booted feet thumping the floor. Eyes gleamed with sudden fire, and calloused hands waved frantically in the air.

[After a few moments' rest, the orchestra played crashingly, and a small fat man burst out upon the stage. He began to roar a song and stamp back and forth before the foot-lights, wildly waving a glossy silk hat and throwing leers, or smiles, broadcast. He made his face into fantastic grimaces until he looked like a pictured devil on a Japanese kite. The crowd laughed gleefully. His short, fat legs were never still a moment. He shouted and roared and bobbed his shock of red wig until the audience broke out in excited applause.]

Pete did not pay much attention to the progress of events upon the stage. He was drinking beer and watching Maggie.

Her cheeks were blushing with excitement and her eyes were glistening. She drew deep breaths of pleasure. No thoughts of the atmosphere of the collar and cuff factory came to her.

When the orchestra crashed finally, they jostled their way to the sidewalk with the crowd. Pete took Maggie's arm and pushed a way for her, offering to fight with a man or two.

They reached Maggie's home at a late hour and stood for a moment in front of the gruesome doorway.

["Say, Mag," said Pete, "give us a kiss for takin' yeh teh deh show, will yer?"] Double standard.

Maggie laughed, as if startled, and drew away from him.

"Naw, Pete," she said, "dat wasn't in it."

"Ah, what deh hell?" urged Pete.

[The girl retreated nervously.

"Ah, what deh hell?" repeated he.

Maggie darted into the hall, and up the stairs. She turned and smiled at him, then disappeared.]

Pete walked slowly down the street. He had something of an astonished expression upon his features. He paused under a lamp-post and breathed a low breath of surprise.

"Gawd," he said, "I wonner if I've been played fer a duffer."

POOL

CHAPTER VIII

As thoughts of Pete came to Maggie's mind, she began to have an intense dislike for all of her dresses.

"What deh hell ails yeh? What makes yeh be allus fixin' and fussin'? Good Gawd," her mother would frequently roar at her.

[She began to note, with more interest, the well-dressed women she met on the avenues. She envied elegance and soft palms. She craved those adornments of person which she saw every day on the street, conceiving them to be allies of vast importance to women.]

Studying faces, she thought many of the women and girls she chanced to meet, smiled with serenity as though forever cherished and watched over by those they loved.

The air in the collar and cuff establishment strangled her. She knew she was gradually and surely shrivelling in the hot, stuffy room. The begrimed windows rattled incessantly from the passing of elevated trains. The place was filled with a whirl of noises and odors.

She wondered as she regarded some of the grizzled women in the room, mere mechanical contrivances sewing seams and grinding out, with heads bended over their work, tales of imagined or real girl-hood happiness, past drunks, the baby at home, and unpaid wages[She speculated how long her youth would endure. She began to see the bloom upon her cheeks as valuable.]

She imagined herself, in an exasperating future, as a scrawny woman with an eternal grievance[Too, she thought Pete to be a very fastidious person concerning the appearance of women.]

She felt she would love to see somebody entangle their fingers in the oily beard of the fat foreigner who owned the establishment. He was a detestable creature. He wore white socks with low shoes.

He sat all day delivering orations, in the depths of a cushioned chair. His pocket-book deprived them of the power of retort.

"What een hell do you sink I pie fife dolla a week for? Play? No, py damn!"

Maggie was anxious for a friend to whom she could talk about Pete. She would have liked to discuss his admirable mannerisms with a reliable mutual friend. At home, she found her mother often drunk and always raving.

[It seems that the world had treated this woman very badly, and she took a deep revenge upon such portions of it as came within her reach.]She broke furniture as if she were at last getting her rights. She swelled with virtuous indignation as she carried the lighter articles of household use, one by one under the shadows of the three gilt balls, where Hebrews chained them with chains of interest.[1]

Jimmie came when he was obligied to by circumstances over which he had no control. His well-trained legs brought him staggering home and put him to bed some nights when he would rather have gone elsewhere.

Swaggering Pete loomed like a golden sun to Maggie. He took her to a dime museum[2] where rows of meek freaks astonished her. She contemplated their deformities with awe and thought them a sort of chosen tribe.

Pete, raking his brains for amusement, discovered the Central Park Menagerie and the Museum of Arts. Sunday afternoons would sometimes find them at these places. Pete did not appear to be particularly interested in what he saw. He stood around looking heavy, while Maggie giggled in glee.

Once at the Menagerie he went into a trance of admiration before the spectacle of a very small monkey threatening to thrash a cageful because one of them had pulled his tail and he had not wheeled about quickly enough to discover who did it. Ever after Pete knew that monkey by sight and winked at him, trying to induce him to fight with other and larger monkeys.

At the Museum, Maggie said, "Dis is outa sight."

"Oh hell," said Pete, "wait till next summer an' I'll take yehs to a picnic."

While the girl wandered in the vaulted rooms, Pete occupied him self in returning stony stare for stony stare, the appalling scrutiny of the watch-dogs of the treasures. Occasionally he would remark in loud tones: "Dat jay has got glass eyes," and sentences of the sort.

When he tired of this amusement he would go to the mummies and moralize over them.

---

1 That is, she takes them to pawnshops.
2 An amusement centre featuring novelty entertainments, including live human deformities, unusual objects, mechanical contrivances, and menageries. Dime museums were popular in downtown areas of American cities.

[Usually he submitted with silent dignity to all which he had to go through, but, at times, he was goaded into comment.]

"What deh hell," he demanded once. "Look at all dese little jugs! Hundred jugs in a row! Ten rows in a case an' 'bout a t'ousand cases! What deh blazes use is dem?"

Evenings during the week he took her to see plays in which the [brain-clutching heroine was rescued from the palatial home of her guardian, who is cruelly after her bonds, by the hero with the beautiful sentiments.]The latter spent most of his time out at soak in pale-green snow storms, busy with a nickel-plated revolver, rescuing aged strangers from villains.

Maggie lost herself in sympathy with the wanderers swooning in snow storms beneath happy-hued church windows. And a choir within singing "Joy to the World." To Maggie and the rest of the audience this was transcendental realism[Joy always within, and they, like the actor, inevitably without]Viewing it, they hugged themselves in [ecstatic pity of their imagined or real condition.] → cruelty, unfeel-ing

The girl thought the arrogance and granite-heartedness of the magnate of the play was very accurately drawn. She echoed the maledictions that the occupants of the gallery showered on this individual when his lines compelled him to expose his extreme selfishness.

Shady persons in the audience revolted from the pictured villainy of the drama. With untiring zeal they hissed vice and applauded virtue. Unmistakably bad men evinced an apparently sincere admiration for virtue. ~ Projection

The loud gallery was overwhelmingly with the unfortunate and the oppressed. They encouraged the struggling hero with cries, and jeered the villain, hooting and calling attention to his whiskers. When anybody died in the pale-green snow storms, the gallery mourned. They sought out the painted misery and hugged it as akin.

[In the hero's erratic march from poverty in the first act, to wealth and triumph in the final one, in which he forgives all the enemies that he has left, he was assisted by the gallery, which applauded his generous and noble sentiments and confounded the speeches of his opponents by making irrelevant but very sharp remarks] Those actors who were cursed with villainy parts were confronted at every turn by the gallery. If one of them rendered lines containing the most subtle distinctions between right and wrong, the gallery was immediately aware if the actor meant wickedness, and denounced him accordingly.

The last act was a triumph for the hero, poor and of the masses, the representative of the audience, over the villain and the rich man, his pockets stuffed with bonds, his heart packed with tyrannical purposes, imperturbable amid suffering.

Maggie always departed with raised spirits from the showing places of the melodrama. She rejoiced at the way in which the poor and virtuous eventually surmounted the wealthy and wicked. The theater made her think. She wondered if the culture and refinement she had seen imitated, perhaps grotesquely, by the heroine on the stage, could be acquired by a girl who lived in a tenement house and worked in a shirt factory.

CHAPTER IX

A group of urchins were intent upon the side door of a saloon. Expectancy gleamed from their eyes. They were twisting their fingers in excitement.

"Here she comes," yelled one of them suddenly.

The group of urchins burst instantly asunder and its individual fragments were spread in a wide, respectable half-circle about the point of interest. The saloon door opened with a crash, and the figure of a woman appeared upon the threshold. Her grey hair fell in knotted masses about her shoulders. Her face was crimsoned and wet with perspiration. Her eyes had a rolling glare.

"Not a damn cent more of me money will yehs ever get, not a damn cent. I spent me money here fer t'ree years an' now yehs tells me yeh'll sell me no more stuff! T'hell wid yeh, Johnnie Murckre! 'Disturbance'? Disturbance be damned! T'hell wid yeh, Johnnie—"

The door received a kick of exasperation from within and the woman lurched heavily out on the sidewalk.

The gamins in the half-circle became violently agitated. They began to dance about and hoot and yell and jeer. Wide dirty grins spread over each face.

The woman made a furious dash at a particularly outrageous cluster of little boys. They laughed delightedly and scampered off a short distance, calling out over their shoulders to her. She stood tottering on the curb-stone and thundered at them.

"Yeh devil's kids," she howled, shaking red fists. The little boys whooped in glee. As she started up the street they fell in behind and marched uproariously. Occasionally she wheeled about and made charges on them. They ran nimbly out of reach and taunted her.

In the frame of a gruesome doorway she stood for a moment cursing them. Her hair straggled, giving her crimson features a look of insanity. Her great fists quivered as she shook them madly in the air.

The urchins made terrific noises until she turned and disappeared. Then they filed quietly in the way they had come.

The woman floundered about in the lower hall of the tenement house and finally stumbled up the stairs. On an upper hall a door was opened and a collection of heads peered curiously out, watching her. With a wrathful snort the woman confronted the door, but it was slammed hastily in her face and the key was turned.

She stood for a few minutes, delivering a frenzied challenge at the panels.

"Come out in deh hall, Mary Murphy, damn yeh, if yehs want a row. Come ahn, yeh overgrown terrier, come ahn."

She began to kick the door with her great feet. She shrilly defied the universe to appear and do battle. Her cursing trebles brought heads from all doors save the one she threatened. Her eyes glared in every direction. The air was full of her tossing fists.

"Come ahn, deh hull damn gang of yehs, come ahn," she roared at the spectators. An oath or two, cat-calls, jeers and bits of facetious advice were given in reply. Missiles clattered about her feet.

"What deh hell's deh matter wid yeh?" said a voice in the gathered gloom, and Jimmie came forward. He carried a tin dinner-pail in his hand and under his arm a brown truckman's apron done in a bundle. "What deh hell's wrong?" he demanded.

"Come out, all of yehs, come out," his mother was howling. "Come ahn an' I'll stamp yer damn brains under me feet."

"Shet yer face, an' come home, yeh damned old fool," roared Jimmie at her. She strided up to him and twirled her fingers in his face. Her eyes were darting flames of unreasoning rage and her frame trembled with eagerness for a fight.

"T'hell wid yehs! An' who deh hell are yehs? I ain't givin' a snap of me fingers fer yehs," she bawled at him. She turned her huge back in tremendous disdain and climbed the stairs to the next floor.

Jimmie followed, cursing blackly. At the top of the flight he seized his mother's arm and started to drag her toward the door of their room.

"Come home, damn yeh," he gritted between his teeth.

"Take yer hands off me! Take yer hands off me," shrieked his mother.

She raised her arm and whirled her great fist at her son's face. Jimmie dodged his head and the blow struck him in the back of the neck. "Damn yeh," gritted he again. He threw out his left hand and writhed his fingers about her middle arm. The mother and the son began to sway and struggle like gladiators.

"Whoop!" said the Rum Alley tenement house. The hall filled with interested spectators.

"Hi, ol' lady, dat was a dandy!"

"T'ree to one on deh red!"

"Ah, stop yer damn scrappin'!"

The door of the Johnson home opened and Maggie looked out. Jimmie made a supreme cursing effort and hurled his mother into the room. He quickly followed and closed the door. The Rum Alley tenement swore disappointedly and retired.

The mother slowly gathered herself up from the floor. Her eyes glittered menacingly upon her children.

"Here, now," said Jimmie, "we've had enough of dis. Sit down, an' don' make no trouble."

He grasped her arm, and twisting it, forced her into a creaking chair.

"Keep yer hands off me," roared his mother again.

"Damn yer ol' hide," yelled Jimmie, madly. Maggie shrieked and ran into the other room. To her there came the sound of a storm of crashes and curses. There was a great final thump and Jimmie's voice cried: "Dere, damn yeh, stay still." Maggie opened the door now, and went warily out. "Oh, Jimmie."

He was leaning against the wall and swearing. Blood stood upon bruises on his knotty fore-arms where they had scraped against the floor or the walls in the scuffle. The mother lay screeching on the floor, the tears running down her furrowed face.

Maggie, standing in the middle of the room, gazed about her. The usual upheaval of the tables and chairs had taken place. Crockery was strewn broadcast in fragments. The stove had been disturbed on its legs, and now leaned idiotically to one side. A pail had been upset and water spread in all directions.

The door opened and Pete appeared. He shrugged his shoulders. "Oh, Gawd," he observed.

He walked over to Maggie and whispered in her ear. "Ah, what deh hell, Mag? Come ahn and we'll have a hell of a time."

The mother in the corner upreared her head and shook her tangled locks.

"Teh hell wid him and you," she said, glowering at her daughter in the gloom. Her eyes seemed to burn balefully. "Yeh've gone teh deh devil, Mag Johnson, yehs knows yehs have gone teh deh devil. Yer a disgrace teh yer people, damn yeh. An' now, git out an' go ahn wid dat doe-faced jude[1] of yours. Go teh hell wid him, damn yeh, an' a good riddance. Go teh hell an' see how yeh likes it."

Maggie gazed long at her mother.

"Go teh hell now, an' see how yeh likes it. Git out. I won't have sech as yehs in me house! Get out, d'yeh hear! Damn yeh, git out!"

The girl began to tremble.

At this instant Pete came forward. "Oh, what deh hell, Mag, see," whispered he softly in her ear. "Dis all blows over. See? Deh ol' woman 'ill be all right in deh mornin'. Come ahn out wid me! We'll have a hell of a time."

The woman on the floor cursed. Jimmie was intent upon his bruised fore-arms. The girl cast a glance about the room filled with a chaotic mass of debris, and at the red, writhing body of her mother.

"Go teh hell an' good riddance."

She went.

CHAPTER X

Jimmie had an idea it wasn't common courtesy for a friend to come to one's home and ruin one's sister. But he was not sure how much Pete knew about the rules of politeness.

---

[1] Dude, dandy.

The following night he returned home from work at rather a late hour in the evening. In passing through the halls he came upon the gnarled and leathery old woman who possessed the music box. She was grinning in the dim light that drifted through dust-stained panes. She beckoned to him with a smudged forefinger.

"Ah, Jimmie, what do yehs t'ink I got onto las' night. It was deh funnies' ting I ever saw," she cried, coming close to him and leering. She was trembling with eagerness to tell her tale. "I was by me door las' night when yer sister and her jude feller came in late, oh, very late. An' she, the dear, she was a-cryin' as if her heart would break, she was. It was deh funnies' t'ing I ever saw. An' right out here by me door she asked him did he love her, did he. An' she was a-cryin' as if her heart would break, poor t'ing. An' him, I could see by deh way what he said it dat she had been askin' orften, he says: 'Oh, hell, yes,' he says, says he, 'Oh, hell, yes.'"

Storm-clouds swept over Jimmie's face, but he turned from the leathery old woman and plodded on upstairs.

"Oh, hell, yes," called she after him. She laughed a laugh that was like a prophetic croak. "'Oh, hell, yes,' he says, says he, 'Oh, hell, yes.'"

There was no one in at home. The rooms showed that attempts had been made at tidying them. Parts of the wreckage of the day before had been repaired by an unskilful hand. A chair or two and the table, stood uncertainly upon legs. The floor had been newly swept. Too, the blue ribbons had been restored to the curtains, and the lambrequin, with its immense sheaves of yellow wheat and red roses of equal size, had been returned, in a worn and sorry state, to its position at the mantel. Maggie's jacket and hat were gone from the nail behind the door.

Jimmie walked to the window and began to look through the blurred glass. It occurred to him to vaguely wonder, for an instant, if some of the women of his acquaintance had brothers.

Suddenly, however, he began to swear.

"But he was me frien'! I brought 'im here! Dat's deh hell of it!"

He fumed about the room, his anger gradually rising to the furious pitch.

"I'll kill deh jay! Dat's what I'll do! I'll kill deh jay!"

He clutched his hat and sprang toward the door. But it opened and his mother's great form blocked the passage.

"What deh hell's deh matter wid yeh?" exclaimed she, coming into the rooms.

Jimmie gave vent to a sardonic curse and then laughed heavily.

"Well, Maggie's gone teh deh devil! Dat's what! See?"

"Eh?" said his mother.

"Maggie's gone teh deh devil! Are yehs deaf?" roared Jimmie, impatiently.

"Deh hell she has," murmured the mother, astounded.

Jimmie grunted, and then began to stare out at the window. His mother sat down in a chair, but a moment later sprang erect and delivered a maddened whirl of oaths. Her son turned to look at her as she reeled and swayed in the middle of the room, her fierce face convulsed with passion, her blotched arms raised high in imprecation.

"May Gawd curse her forever," she shrieked. "May she eat nothin' but stones and deh dirt in deh street. May she sleep in deh gutter an' never see deh sun shine agin. Deh damn—"

"Here, now," said her son. "Take a drop on yourself."

The mother raised lamenting eyes to the ceiling.

"She's deh devil's own chil', Jimmie," she whispered. "Ah, who would t'ink such a bad girl could grow up in our fambly, Jimmie, me son. Many deh hour I've spent in talk wid dat girl an' tol' her if she ever went on deh streets I'd see her damned. An' after all her bringin' up an' what I tol' her and talked wid her, she goes teh deh bad, like a duck teh water."

The tears rolled down her furrowed face. Her hands trembled.

"An' den when dat Sadie MacMallister next door to us was sent teh deh devil by dat feller what worked in deh soap-factory, didn't I tell our Mag dat if she—"

"Ah, dat's anuder story," interrupted the brother. "Of course, dat Sadie was nice an' all dat—but—see—it ain't dessame as if—well, Maggie was diff'ent—see—she was diff'ent."

He was trying to formulate a theory that he had always unconsciously held, that all sisters, excepting his own, could advisedly be ruined.

He suddenly broke out again. "I'll go t'ump hell outa deh mug what did her deh harm. I'll kill 'im! He t'inks he kin scrap, but when he gits me a-chasin' 'im he'll fin' out where he's wrong, deh damned duffer. I'll wipe up deh street wid 'im."

In a fury he plunged out of the doorway. As he vanished the mother raised her head and lifted both hands, entreating.

"May Gawd curse her forever," she cried.

In the darkness of the hallway Jimmie discerned a knot of women talking volubly. When he strode by they paid no attention to him.

"She allus was a bold thing," he heard one of them cry in an eager voice. "Dere wasn't a feller come teh deh house but she'd try teh mash 'im.[1] My Annie says deh shameless t'ing tried teh ketch her feller, her own feller, what we useter know his fader."

"I could a' tol' yehs dis two years ago," said a woman, in a key of triumph. "Yessir, it was over two years ago dat I says teh my ol' man, I says, 'Dat Johnson girl ain't straight,' I says. 'Oh, hell,' he says. 'Oh, hell.' 'Dat's all right,' I says, 'but I know what I knows,' I says, 'an' it 'ill come out later. You wait an' see,' I says, 'you see.'"

"Anybody what had eyes could see dat dere was somethin' wrong wid dat girl. I didn't like her actions."

On the street Jimmie met a friend. "What deh hell?" asked the latter.

Jimmie explained. "An' I'll t'ump 'im till he can't stand."

"Oh, what deh hell," said the friend. "What's deh use! Yeh'll git pulled in! Everybody 'ill be onto it! An' ten plunks![2] Gee!"

Jimmie was determined. "He t'inks he kin scrap, but he'll fin' out diff'ent."

"Gee," remonstrated the friend. "What deh hell?"

CHAPTER XI

On a corner a glass-fronted building shed a yellow glare upon the pavements. The open mouth of a saloon called seductively to passengers to enter and annihilate sorrow or create rage.

The interior of the place was papered in olive and bronze tints of imitation leather. A shining bar of counterfeit massiveness extended down the side of the room. Behind it a great mahogany-appearing sideboard reached the ceiling. Upon its shelves rested pyramids of

---

1 Flirt with him.
2 Dollars.

shimmering glasses that were never disturbed. Mirrors set in the face of the sideboard multiplied them. Lemons, oranges and paper napkins, arranged with mathematical precision, sat among the glasses. Many-hued decanters of liquor perched at regular intervals on the lower shelves. A nickel-plated cash register occupied a position in the exact centre of the general effect. The elementary senses of it all seemed to be opulence and geometrical accuracy.

Across from the bar a smaller counter held a collection of plates upon which swarmed frayed fragments of crackers, slices of boiled ham, dishevelled bits of cheese, and pickles swimming in vinegar. An odor of grasping, begrimed hands and munching mouths pervaded.

Pete, in a white jacket, was behind the bar bending expectantly toward a quiet stranger. "A beeh," said the man. Pete drew a foam-topped glassful and set it dripping upon the bar.

At this moment the light bamboo doors at the entrance swung open and crashed against the siding. Jimmie and a companion entered. They swaggered unsteadily but belligerently toward the bar and looked at Pete with bleared and blinking eyes.

"Gin," said Jimmie.

"Gin," said the companion.

Pete slid a bottle and two glasses along the bar. He bended his head sideways as he assiduously polished away with a napkin at the gleaming wood. He had a look of watchfulness upon his features.

Jimmie and his companion kept their eyes upon the bartender and conversed loudly in tones of contempt.

"He's a dindy masher,[1] ain't he, by Gawd?" laughed Jimmie.

"Oh, hell, yes," said the companion, sneering widely. "He's great, he is. Git onto deh mug on deh blokie. Dat's enough to make a feller turn hand-springs in 'is sleep."

The quiet stranger moved himself and his glass a trifle further away and maintained an attitude of oblivion.

"Gee! ain't he hot stuff!"

"Git onto his shape! Great Gawd!"

"Hey," cried Jimmie, in tones of command. Pete came along slowly, with a sullen dropping of the under lip.

"Well," he growled, "what's eatin' yehs?"

---

[1] A dandy, a flirt.

"Gin," said Jimmie.

"Gin," said the companion.

As Pete confronted them with the bottle and the glasses, they laughed in his face. Jimmie's companion, evidently overcome with merriment, pointed a grimy forefinger in Pete's direction.

"Say, Jimmie," demanded he, "what deh hell is dat behind deh bar?"

"Damned if I knows," replied Jimmie. They laughed loudly. Pete put down a bottle with a bang and turned a formidable face toward them. He disclosed his teeth and his shoulders heaved restlessly.

"You fellers can't guy¹ me," he said. "Drink yer stuff an' git out an' don' make no trouble." ↳ RIDICULE

Instantly the laughter faded from the faces of the two men and expressions of offended dignity immediately came.

"Who deh hell has said anyt'ing teh you," cried they in the same breath.

The quiet stranger looked at the door calculatingly.

"Ah, come off," said Pete to the two men. "Don't pick me up for no jay. Drink yer rum an' git out an' don' make no trouble."

"Oh, deh hell," airily cried Jimmie.

"Oh, deh hell," airily repeated his companion.

"We goes when we git ready! See!" continued Jimmie.

"Well," said Pete in a threatening voice, "don' make no trouble."

Jimmie suddenly leaned forward with his head on one side. He snarled like a wild animal. Naturalism

"Well, what if we does? See?" said he.

Dark blood flushed into Pete's face, and he shot a lurid glance at Jimmie.

"Well, den we'll see whose deh bes' man, you or me," he said.

The quiet stranger moved modestly toward the door.

Jimmie began to swell with valor. → more rordon

"Don' pick me up fer no tenderfoot.² When yeh tackles me yeh tackles one of deh bes' men in deh city. See? I'm a scrapper, I am. Ain't dat right, Billie?"

"Sure, Mike," responded his companion in tones of conviction.

"Oh, hell," said Pete, easily. "Go fall on yerself."

---

1 Ridicule.

2 Naïve person.

The two men again began to laugh.

"What deh hell is dat talkin'?" cried the companion.

"Damned if I knows," replied Jimmie with exaggerated contempt.

Pete made a furious gesture. "Git outa here now, an' don' make no trouble. See? Youse fellers er lookin' fer a scrap an' it's damn likely yeh'll fin' one if yeh keeps on shootin' off yer mout's. I know yehs! See? I kin lick better men dan yehs ever saw in yer lifes. Dat's right! See? Don' pick me up fer no stuff er yeh might be jolted out in deh street before yeh knows where yeh is. When I comes from behind dis bar, I t'rows yehs boat inteh deh street. See?"

"Oh, hell," cried the two men in chorus.

The glare of a panther came into Pete's eyes. "Dat's what I said! Unnerstan'?"

He came through a passage at the end of the bar and swelled down upon the two men. They stepped promptly forward and crowded close to him.   *argumentively*

They bristled like three roosters. They moved their heads pugnaciously and kept their shoulders braced. The nervous muscles about each mouth twitched with a forced smile of mockery.

"Well, what deh hell yer goin' teh do?" gritted Jimmie.

Pete stepped warily back, waving his hands before him to keep the men from coming too near.

"Well, what deh hell yer goin' teh do?" repeated Jimmie's ally. They kept close to him, taunting and leering. They strove to make him attempt the initial blow.

"Keep back, now! Don' crowd me," ominously said Pete.

Again they chorused in contempt. "Oh, hell!"

In a small, tossing group, the three men edged for positions like frigates contemplating battle.

"Well, why deh hell don' yeh try teh t'row us out?" cried Jimmie and his ally with copious sneers.

The bravery of bull-dogs sat upon the faces of the men. Their clenched fists moved like eager weapons.

The allied two jostled the bartender's elbows, glaring at him with feverish eyes and forcing him toward the wall.

Suddenly Pete swore redly. The flash of action gleamed from his eyes. He threw back his arm and aimed a tremendous, lightning-like blow at Jimmie's face. His foot swung a step forward and the weight

→ angry, embarrassed

of his body was behind his fist. Jimmie ducked his head, Bowery-like, with the quickness of a cat. The fierce, answering blows of him and his ally crushed on Pete's bowed head.

The quiet stranger vanished.

The arms of the combatants whirled in the air like flails. The faces of the men, at first flushed to flame-colored anger, now began to fade to the pallor of warriors in the blood and heat of a battle. Their lips curled back and stretched tightly over the gums in ghoul-like grins. Through their white, gripped teeth struggled hoarse whisperings of oaths. Their eyes glittered with murderous fire.

Each head was huddled between its owner's shoulders, and arms were swinging with marvelous rapidity. Feet scraped to and fro with a loud scratching sound upon the sanded floor. Blows left crimson blotches upon pale skin. The curses of the first quarter minute of the fight died away. The breaths of the fighters came wheezingly from their lips and the three chests were straining and heaving. Pete at intervals gave vent to low, labored hisses, that sounded like a desire to kill. Jimmie's ally gibbered at times like a wounded maniac. Jimmie was silent, fighting with the face of a sacrificial priest. The rage of fear shone in all their eyes and their blood-colored fists swirled.

At a tottering moment a blow from Pete's hand struck the ally and he crashed to the floor. He wriggled instantly to his feet and grasping the quiet stranger's beer glass from the bar, hurled it at Pete's head.

High on the wall it burst like a bomb, shivering fragments flying in all directions. Then missiles came to every man's hand. The place had heretofore appeared free of things to throw, but suddenly glass and bottles went singing through the air. They were thrown point blank at bobbing heads. The pyramid of shimmering glasses, that had never been disturbed, changed to cascades as heavy bottles were flung into them. Mirrors splintered to nothing.

The three frothing creatures on the floor buried themselves in a frenzy for blood. There followed in the wake of missiles and fists some unknown prayers, perhaps for death.

The quiet stranger had sprawled very pyrotechnically out on the sidewalk. A laugh ran up and down the avenue for the half of a block.

"Dey've t'rowed a bloke inteh deh street."

People heard the sound of breaking glass and shuffling feet within the saloon and came running. A small group, bending down to look under the bamboo doors, watching the fall of glass, and three pairs of violent legs, changed in a moment to a crowd.

A policeman came charging down the sidewalk and bounced through the doors into the saloon. The crowd bended and surged in absorbing anxiety to see.

Jimmie caught first sight of the on-coming interruption. On his feet he had the same regard for a policeman that, when on his truck, he had for a fire engine. He howled and ran for the side door.

The officer made a terrific advance, club in hand. One comprehensive sweep of the long night stick threw the ally to the floor and forced Pete to a corner. With his disengaged hand he made a furious effort at Jimmie's coat-tails. Then he regained his balance and paused.

"Well, well, you are a pair of pictures. What in hell yeh been up to?"

Jimmie, with his face drenched in blood, escaped up a side street, pursued a short distance by some of the more law-loving, or excited individuals of the crowd.

Later, from a corner safely dark, he saw the policeman, the ally and the bartender emerge from the saloon. Pete locked the doors and then followed up the avenue in the rear of the crowd-encompassed policeman and his charge.

On first thoughts Jimmie, with his heart throbbing at battle heat, started to go desperately to the rescue of his friend, but he halted.

"Ah, what deh hell?" he demanded of himself.

CHAPTER XII

In a hall of irregular shape sat Pete and Maggie drinking beer. A submissive orchestra dictated to by a spectacled man with frowsy hair and a dress suit, industriously followed the bobs of his head and the waves of his baton. A ballad singer, in a dress of flaming scarlet, sang in the inevitable voice of brass. When she vanished, men seated at the tables near the front applauded loudly, pounding the polished wood with their beer glasses. She returned attired in less gown, and sang again. She received another enthusiastic encore. She reappeared in still less gown and danced. The deafening rumble of glasses and clapping of hands that followed her exit indicated an overwhelming desire to have her come on for the fourth time, but the curiosity of the audience was not gratified.

Maggie was pale. From her eyes had been plucked all look of self-reliance. She leaned with a dependent air toward her companion. She was timid, as if fearing his anger or displeasure. She seemed to beseech tenderness of him.

Pete's air of distinguished valor had grown upon him until it threatened stupendous dimensions. He was infinitely gracious to the girl. It was apparent to her that his condescension was a marvel.

He could appear to strut even while sitting still and he showed that he was a lion of lordly characteristics by the air with which he spat.

With Maggie gazing at him wonderingly, he took pride in commanding the waiters who were, however, indifferent or deaf.

"Hi, you, git a russle on yehs! What deh hell yehs lookin' at? Two more beehs, d'yeh hear?"

He leaned back and critically regarded the person of a girl with a straw-colored wig who upon the stage was flinging her heels in somewhat awkward imitation of a well-known danseuse.[1]

At times Maggie told Pete long confidential tales of her former home life, dwelling upon the escapades of the other members of the family and the difficulties she had to combat in order to obtain a degree of comfort. He responded in tones of philanthropy. He pressed her arm with an air of reassuring proprietorship.

"Dey was damn jays," he said, denouncing the mother and brother.

The sound of the music which, by the efforts of the frowsy-headed leader, drifted to her ears through the smoke-filled atmosphere, made the girl dream. She thought of her former Rum Alley environment and turned to regard Pete's strong protecting fists. She thought of the collar and cuff manufactory and the eternal moan of the proprietor: "What een hell do you sink I pie fife dolla a week for? Play? No, py damn." She contemplated Pete's man-subduing eyes and noted that wealth and prosperity was indicated by his clothes. She imagined a future, rose-tinted, because of its distance from all that she previously had experienced.

As to the present she perceived only vague reasons to be miserable. Her life was Pete's and she considered him worthy of the

---

[1] A female ballet dancer.

charge. She would be disturbed by no particular apprehensions, so long as Pete adored her as he now said he did. She did not feel like a bad woman. To her knowledge she had never seen any better.

At times men at other tables regarded the girl furtively. Pete, aware of it, nodded at her and grinned. He felt proud.

"Mag, yer a bloomin' good-looker," he remarked, studying her face through the haze. The men made Maggie fear, but she blushed at Pete's words as it became apparent to her that she was the apple of his eye.

Grey-headed men, wonderfully pathetic in their dissipation, stared at her through clouds. Smooth-cheeked boys, some of them with faces of stone and mouths of sin, not nearly so pathetic as the grey heads, tried to find the girl's eyes in the smoke wreaths. Maggie considered she was not what they thought her. She confined her glances to Pete and the stage.

The orchestra played negro melodies and a versatile drummer pounded, whacked, clattered and scratched on a dozen machines to make noise.

Those glances of the men, shot at Maggie from under half-closed lids, made her tremble. She thought them all to be worse men than Pete.

"Come, let's go," she said.

As they went out Maggie perceived two women seated at a table with some men. They were painted and their cheeks had lost their roundness. As she passed them the girl, with a shrinking movement, drew back her skirts. ᴘʀᴏꜱᴛɪᴛᴜᴛɪᴏɴ?

CHAPTER XIII

Jimmie did not return home for a number of days after the fight with Pete in the saloon. When he did, he approached with extreme caution.

He found his mother raving. Maggie had not returned home. The parent continually wondered how her daughter could come to such a pass. She had never considered Maggie as a pearl dropped unstained into Rum Alley from Heaven, but she could not conceive how it was possible for her daughter to fall so low as to bring disgrace upon her family. She was terrific in denunciation of the girl's wickedness.

The fact that the neighbors talked of it, maddened her. When women came in, and in the course of their conversation casually asked, "Where's Maggie dese days?" the mother shook her fuzzy head at them and appalled them with curses. Cunning hints inviting confidence she rebuffed with violence.

"An' wid all deh bringin' up she had, how could she?" moaningly she asked of her son. "Wid all deh talkin' wid her I did an' deh t'ings I tol' her to remember? When a girl is bringed up deh way I bringed up Maggie, how kin she go teh deh devil?"

Jimmie was transfixed by these questions. He could not conceive how under the circumstances his mother's daughter and his sister could have been so wicked.

His mother took a drink from a squdgy[1] bottle that sat on the table. She continued her lament.

"She had a bad heart, dat girl did, Jimmie. She was wicked teh deh heart an' we never knowed it."

Jimmie nodded, admitting the fact.

"We lived in deh same house wid her an' I brought her up an' we never knowed how bad she was."

Jimmie nodded again.

"Wid a home like dis an' a mudder like me, she went teh deh bad," cried the mother, raising her eyes.

One day, Jimmie came home, sat down in a chair and began to wriggle about with a new and strange nervousness. At last he spoke shamefacedly.

"Well, look-a-here, dis t'ing queers us! See? We're queered! An' maybe it 'ud be better if I—well, I t'ink I kin look 'er up an'— maybe it 'ud be better if I fetched her home an'—"

The mother started from her chair and broke forth into a storm of passionate anger.

"What! Let 'er come an' sleep under deh same roof wid her mudder agin! Oh, yes, I will, won't I? Sure? Shame on yehs, Jimmie Johnson, fer sayin' such a t'ing teh yer own mudder—teh yer own mudder! Little did I t'ink when yehs was a babby playin' about me feet dat ye'd grow up teh say sech a t'ing teh yer mudder—yer own mudder. I never taut—"

---

[1] Squat.

Sobs choked her and interrupted her reproaches.

"Dere ain't nottin' teh raise sech hell about," said Jimmie. "I on'y says it 'ud be better if we keep dis t'ing dark, see? It queers us! See?"

His mother laughed a laugh that seemed to ring through the city and be echoed and re-echoed by countless other laughs. "Oh, yes, I will, won't I! Sure!"

"Well, yeh must take me fer a damn fool," said Jimmie, indignant at his mother for mocking him. "I didn't say we'd make 'er inteh a little tin angel, ner nottin', but deh way it is now she can queer us! Don' che see?"

"Aye, she'll git tired of deh life atter a while an' den she'll wanna be a-comin' home, won' she, deh beast! I'll let 'er in den, won' I?"

"Well, I didn' mean none of dis prod'gal bus'ness anyway," explained Jimmie.

"It wasn't no prod'gal dauter, yeh damn fool," said the mother. "It was prod'gal son, anyhow." BIBLICAL ALLUSION

"I know dat," said Jimmie.

For a time they sat in silence. The mother's eyes gloated on a scene her imagination could call before her. Her lips were set in a vindictive smile.

"Aye, she'll cry, won' she, an' carry on, an' tell how Pete, or some odder feller, beats 'er an' she'll say she's sorry an' all dat an' she ain't happy, she ain't, an' she wants to come home agin, she does."

With grim humor, the mother imitated the possible wailing notes of the daughter's voice.

"Den I'll take 'er in, won't I, deh beast. She kin cry 'er two eyes out on deh stones of deh street before I'll dirty deh place wid her. She abused an' ill-treated her own mudder—her own mudder what loved her an' she'll never git anodder chance dis side of hell."

Jimmie thought he had a great idea of women's frailty, but he could not understand why any of his kin should be victims.

"Damn her," he fervidly said.

Again he wondered vaguely if some of the women of his acquaintance had brothers. Nevertheless, his mind did not for an instant confuse himself with those brothers nor his sister with theirs. After the mother had, with great difficulty, suppressed the neighbors, she went among them and proclaimed her grief. "May Gawd forgive dat girl," was her continual cry. To attentive ears she recited the whole length and breadth of her woes.

"I bringed 'er up deh way a dauter oughta be bringed up an' dis is how she served me! She went teh deh devil deh first chance she got! May Gawd forgive her."

[When arrested for drunkenness she used the story of her daughter's downfall with telling effect upon the police-justices] Finally one of them said to her, peering down over his spectacles: ["Mary, the records of this and other courts show that you are the mother of forty-two daughters who have been ruined. The case is unparalleled in the annals of this court, and this court thinks—"

The mother went through life shedding large tears of sorrow. Her red face was a picture of agony.]

[Of course Jimmie publicly damned his sister that he might appear on a higher social plane. But, arguing with himself, stumbling about in ways that he knew not, he, once, almost came to a conclusion that his sister would have been more firmly good had she better known why. However, he felt that he could not hold such a view. He threw it hastily aside.]

ᴠᴸ CHAPTER XIV

In a hilarious hall there were twenty-eight tables and twenty-eight women and a crowd of smoking men. Valiant noise was made on a stage at the end of the hall by an orchestra composed of men who looked as if they had just happened in. Soiled waiters ran to and fro, swooping down like hawks on the unwary in the throng; clattering along the aisles with trays covered with glasses; stumbling over women's skirts and charging two prices for everything but beer, all with a swiftness that blurred the view of the cocoanut palms and dusty monstrosities painted upon the walls of the room. A bouncer, with an immense load of business upon his hands, plunged about in the crowd, dragging bashful strangers to prominent chairs, ordering waiters here and there and quarreling furiously with men who wanted to sing with the orchestra.

The usual smoke cloud was present, but so dense that heads and arms seemed entangled in it. The rumble of conversation was replaced by a roar. Plenteous oaths heaved through the air. The room rang with the shrill voices of women bubbling o'er with drink-laughter. The chief element in the music of the orchestra was speed. The musicians played in intent fury. A woman was singing and smiling upon the stage, but no one took notice of her. The rate at which the piano, cornet and violins were going, seemed to impart wildness to the half-drunken crowd. Beer glasses were emptied at a gulp and conversation became a rapid chatter. The smoke eddied and swirled like a shadowy river hurrying toward some unseen falls. Pete and Maggie entered the hall and took chairs at a table near the door. The woman who was seated there made an attempt to occupy Pete's attention and, failing, went away.

[Three weeks had passed since the girl had left home. The air of spaniel-like dependence had been magnified and showed its direct effect in the peculiar off-handedness and ease of Pete's ways toward her.]

She followed Pete's eyes with hers, anticipating with smiles gracious looks from him.

A woman of brilliance and audacity, accompanied by a mere boy, came into the place and took seats near them.

At once Pete sprang to his feet, his face beaming with glad surprise. "By Gawd, there's Nellie," he cried. Nellie = sized up from Maggie

He went over to the table and held out an eager hand to the woman.

"Why, hello, Pete, me boy, how are you," said she, giving him her fingers.

[Maggie took instant note of the woman.] She perceived that her black dress fitted her to perfection. Her linen collar and cuffs were spotless. Tan gloves were stretched over her well-shaped hands. A hat of a prevailing fashion perched jauntily upon her dark hair. She wore no jewelry and was painted with no apparent paint. She looked clear-eyed through the stares of the men.

"Sit down, and call your lady-friend over," she said cordially to Pete. At his beckoning Maggie came and sat between Pete and the mere boy.

"I thought yeh were gone away fer good," began Pete, at once. "When did yeh git back? How did dat Buff'lo bus'ness turn out?"

The woman shrugged her shoulders. "Well, he didn't have as

many stamps[1] as he tried to make out, so I shook him, that's all."

"Well, I'm glad teh see yehs back in deh city," said Pete, with awkward gallantry.

He and the woman entered into a long conversation, exchanging reminiscences of days together. Maggie sat still, unable to formulate an intelligent sentence upon the conversation and painfully aware of it.

She saw Pete's eyes sparkle as he gazed upon the handsome stranger. He listened smilingly to all she said. The woman was familiar with all his affairs, asked him about mutual friends, and knew the amount of his salary.

She paid no attention to Maggie, looking toward her once or twice and apparently seeing the wall beyond.

The mere boy was sulky. In the beginning he had welcomed with acclamations the additions.

"Let's all have a drink! What'll you take, Nell? And you, Miss what's-your-name. Have a drink, Mr. ——, you, I mean."

He had shown a sprightly desire to do the talking for the company and tell all about his family. In a loud voice he declaimed on various topics. He assumed a patronizing air toward Pete. As Maggie was silent, he paid no attention to her. He made a great show of lavishing wealth upon the woman of brilliance and audacity.

"Do keep still, Freddie! You gibber like an ape, dear," said the woman to him. She turned away and devoted her attention to Pete.

"We'll have many a good time together again, eh?"

"Sure, Mike," said Pete, enthusiastic at once.

"Say," whispered she, leaning forward, "let's go over to Billie's and have a heluva time."

"Well, it's dis way! See?" said Pete. I got dis lady frien' here."

"Oh, t'hell with her," argued the woman.

Pete appeared disturbed.

"All right," said she, nodding her head at him. "All right for you! We'll see the next time you ask me to go anywheres with you."

Pete squirmed.

"Say," he said, beseechingly, "come wid me a minit an' I'll tell yer why."

The woman waved her hand.

---

[1] Money.

"Oh, that's all right, you needn't explain, you know. You would-n't come merely because you wouldn't come, that's all there is of it."

To Pete's visible distress she turned to the mere boy, bringing him speedily from a terrific rage. He had been debating whether it would be the part of a man to pick a quarrel with Pete, or would he be justified in striking him savagely with his beer glass without warn-ing. But he recovered himself when the woman turned to renew her smilings. [He beamed upon her with an expression that was some-what tipsy and inexpressibly tender.]

"Say, shake that Bowery jay," requested he, in a loud whisper.

"Freddie, you are so droll," she replied.

Pete reached forward and touched the woman on the arm.

"Come out a minit while I tells yeh why I can't go wid yer. Yer doin' me dirt, Nell! I never taut ye'd do me dirt, Nell. Come on, will yer?" He spoke in tones of injury.

"Why, I don't see why I should be interested in your explana-tions," said the woman, with a coldness that seemed to reduce Pete to a pulp.

His eyes pleaded with her. "Come out a minit while I tells yeh."

The woman nodded slightly at Maggie and the mere boy, "'Scuse me."

The mere boy interrupted his loving smile and turned a shrivel-ling glare upon Pete. His boyish countenance flushed and he spoke, in a whine, to the woman:

"Oh, I say, Nellie, this ain't a square deal, you know. You aren't goin' to leave me and go off with that duffer, are you? I should think—"

"Why, you dear boy, of course I'm not," cried the woman, affec-tionately. She bended over and whispered in his ear. He smiled again and settled in his chair as if resolved to wait patiently.

As the woman walked down between the rows of tables, Pete was at her shoulder talking earnestly, apparently in explanation. The woman waved her hands with studied airs of indifference. The doors swung behind them, leaving Maggie and the mere boy seated at the table.

[Maggie was dazed. She could dimly perceive that something stupendous had happened.] She wondered why Pete saw fit to remonstrate with the woman, pleading for forgiveness with his eyes. She thought she noted an air of submission about her leonine Pete. She was astounded.

The mere boy occupied himself with cock-tails and a cigar. He was tranquilly silent for half an hour. Then he bestirred himself and spoke.

"Well," he said, sighing, "I knew this was the way it would be." There was another stillness. The mere boy seemed to be musing.

"She was pulling m'leg. That's the whole amount of it," he said, suddenly. "It's a bloomin' shame the way that girl does. Why, I've spent over two dollars in drinks to-night. And she goes off with that plug-ugly who looks as if he had been hit in the face with a coin-dye.[1] I call it rocky treatment for a fellah like me. Here, waiter, bring me a cock-tail and make it damned strong."

Maggie made no reply. She was watching the doors. "It's a mean piece of business," complained the mere boy. He explained to her how amazing it was that anybody should treat him in such a manner. "But I'll get square with her, you bet. She won't get far ahead of yours truly, you know," he added, winking. "I'll tell her plainly that it was bloomin' mean business. And she won't come it over me with any of her 'now-Freddie-dears.' She thinks my name is Freddie, you know, but of course it ain't. I always tell these people some name like that, because if they got onto your right name they might use it sometime. Understand? Oh, they don't fool me much."

Maggie was paying no attention, being intent upon the doors. \The mere boy relapsed into a period of gloom, during which he exterminated a number of cock-tails with a determined air, as if replying defiantly to fate. He occasionally broke forth into sentences composed of invectives joined together in a long string.

The girl was still staring at the doors. After a time the mere boy began to see cob-webs just in front of his nose. He spurred himself into being agreeable and insisted upon her having a charlotte-russe[2] and a glass of beer.

"They's gone," he remarked, "they's gone." He looked at her through the smoke wreaths. "Shay, lil' girl, we mightish well make bes' of it. You ain't such bad-lookin' girl, y'know. Not half bad. Can't come up to Nell, though. No, can't do it! Well, I should shay not! Nell fine-lookin' girl! F—i—n—ine. You look damn bad longsider her, but by y'self ain't so bad. Have to do anyhow. Nell gone. On'y you left. Not half bad, though."

---

1   A device for stamping coins from metal.
2   A sponge cake dessert with cream or custard filling.

Maggie stood up.

"I'm going home," she said.

The mere boy started.

"Eh? What? Home," he cried, struck with amazement. "I beg pardon, did hear say home?"

"I'm going home," she repeated.

"Great Gawd, what hava struck," demanded the mere boy of himself, stupefied.

In a semi-comatose state he conducted her on board an up-town car, ostentatiously paid her fare, leered kindly at her through the rear window and fell off the steps.

CHAPTER XV

A forlorn woman went along a lighted avenue. The street was filled with people desperately bound on missions. An endless crowd darted at the elevated station stairs and the horse cars were thronged with owners of bundles.

The pace of the forlorn woman was slow. She was apparently searching for some one. She loitered near the doors of saloons and watched men emerge from them. She scanned furtively the faces in the rushing stream of pedestrians. Hurrying men, bent on catching some boat or train, jostled her elbows, failing to notice her, their thoughts fixed on distant dinners.

The forlorn woman had a peculiar face. Her smile was no smile. But when in repose her features had a shadowy look that was like a sardonic grin, as if some one had sketched with cruel forefinger indelible lines about her mouth.

Jimmie came strolling up the avenue. The woman encountered him with an aggrieved air.

"Oh, Jimmie, I've been lookin' all over fer yehs—," she began.

Jimmie made an impatient gesture and quickened his pace.

"Ah, don't bodder me! Good Gawd!" he said, with the savageness of a man whose life is pestered.

The woman followed him along the sidewalk in somewhat the manner of a suppliant.

"But, Jimmie," she said, "yehs told me ye'd—"

Jimmie turned upon her fiercely as if resolved to make a last stand for comfort and peace.

"Say, fer Gawd's sake, Hattie, don' foller me from one end of deh city teh deh odder. Let up, will yehs! Give me a minute's res', can't yehs? Yehs makes me tired, allus taggin' me. See? Ain' yehs got no sense. Do yehs want people teh get onto me? Go chase yerself, fer Gawd's sake."

The woman stepped closer and laid her fingers on his arm. "But, look-a-here——"

Jimmie snarled. "Oh, go teh hell."

He darted into the front door of a convenient saloon and a moment later came out into the shadows that surrounded the side door. On the brilliantly lighted avenue he perceived the forlorn woman dodging about like a scout. Jimmie laughed with an air of relief and went away.

When he arrived home he found his mother clamoring. Maggie had returned. She stood shivering beneath the torrent of her mother's wrath.

"Well, I'm damned," said Jimmie in greeting.

His mother, tottering about the room, pointed a quivering forefinger.

"Lookut her, Jimmie, lookut her. Dere's yer sister, boy. Dere's yer sister. Lookut her! Lookut her!"

She screamed in scoffing laughter.

The girl stood in the middle of the room. She edged about as if unable to find a place on the floor to put her feet.

"Ha, ha, ha," bellowed the mother. "Dere she stands! Ain' she purty? Lookut her! Ain' she sweet, deh beast? Lookut her! Ha, ha, lookut her!"

She lurched forward and put her red and seamed hands upon her daughter's face. She bent down and peered keenly up into the eyes of the girl.

"Oh, she's jes' dessame as she ever was, ain' she? She's her mudder's purty darlin' yit, ain' she? Lookut her, Jimmie! Come here, fer Gawd's sake, and lookut her."

The loud, tremendous sneering of the mother brought the denizens of the Rum Alley tenement to their doors. Women came in the hallways. Children scurried to and fro.

"What's up? Dat Johnson party on anudder tear?"[1]

"Naw! Young Mag's come home!"

"Deh hell yeh say?"

Through the open door curious eyes stared in at Maggie. Children ventured into the room and ogled her, as if they formed the front row at a theatre. Women, without, bended toward each other and whispered, nodding their heads with airs of profound philosophy. A baby, overcome with curiosity concerning this object at which all were looking, sidled forward and touched her dress, cautiously, as if investigating a red-hot stove. Its mother's voice rang out like a warning trumpet. She rushed forward and grabbed her child, casting a terrible look of indignation at the girl.

Maggie's mother paced to and fro, addressing the doorful of eyes, expounding like a glib showman at a museum. Her voice rang through the building.

"Dere she stands," she cried, wheeling suddenly and pointing with dramatic finger. "Dere she stands! Lookut her! Ain' she a dindy? An' she was so good as to come home teh her mudder, she was! Ain' she a beaut'? Ain' she a dindy? Fer Gawd's sake!"

The jeering cries ended in another burst of shrill laughter.

The girl seemed to awaken. "Jimmie—"

He drew hastily back from her.

"Well, now, yer a hell of a t'ing, ain' yeh?" he said, his lips curling in scorn. Radiant virtue sat upon his brow and his repelling hands expressed horror of contamination.

Maggie turned and went.

The crowd at the door fell back precipitately. A baby falling down in front of the door, wrenched a scream like a wounded animal from its mother. Another woman sprang forward and picked it up, with a chivalrous air, as if rescuing a human being from an on-coming express train.

As the girl passed down through the hall, she went before open doors framing more eyes strangely microscopic, and sending broad beams of inquisitive light into the darkness of her path. On the second floor she met the gnarled old woman who possessed the music box.

---

1   Outburst, rampage.

"So," she cried, "'ere yehs are back again, are yehs? An' dey've kicked yehs out? Well, come in an' stay wid me teh-night. I ain' got no moral standin'."

[From above came an unceasing babble of tongues, over all of which rang the mother's derisive laughter.]

CHAPTER XVI

[Pete did not consider that he had ruined Maggie. If he had thought that her soul could never smile again, he would have believed the mother and brother, who were pyrotechnic over the affair, to be responsible for it.]

Besides, in his world, souls did not insist upon being able to smile. "What deh hell?"

He felt a trifle entangled. It distressed him. Revelations and scenes might bring upon him the wrath of the owner of the saloon, who insisted upon respectability of an advanced type.

"What deh hell do dey wanna raise such a smoke about it fer?" demanded he of himself, disgusted with the attitude of the family. He saw no necessity for anyone's losing their equilibrium merely because their sister or their daughter had stayed away from home.

Searching about in his mind for possible reasons for their conduct, he came upon the conclusion that Maggie's motives were correct, but that the two others wished to snare him. He felt pursued.

The woman of brilliance and audacity whom he had met in the hilarious hall showed a disposition to ridicule him.

"A little pale thing with no spirit," she said. "Did you note the expression of her eyes? There was something in them about pumpkin pie and virtue. That is a peculiar way the left corner of her mouth has of twitching, isn't it? Dear, dear, my cloud-compelling Pete, what are you coming to?"

Pete asserted at once that he never was very much interested in the girl. The woman interrupted him, laughing.

"Oh, it's not of the slightest consequence to me, my dear young man. You needn't draw maps for my benefit. Why should I be concerned about it?"

But Pete continued with his explanations. [If he was laughed at for his tastes in women, he felt obliged to say that they were only temporary or indifferent ones.]

The morning after Maggie had departed from home, Pete stood behind the bar. He was immaculate in white jacket and apron and his hair was plastered over his brow with infinite correctness. No customers were in the place. Pete was twisting his napkined fist slowly in a beer glass, softly whistling to himself and occasionally holding the object of his attention between his eyes and a few weak beams of sunlight that had found their way over the thick screens and into the shaded room.

With lingering thoughts of the woman of brilliance and audacity, the bartender raised his head and stared through the varying cracks between the swaying bamboo doors. Suddenly the whistling pucker faded from his lips. He saw Maggie walking slowly past. He gave a great start, fearing for the previously-mentioned eminent respectability of the place.

He threw a swift, nervous glance about him, all at once feeling guilty. No one was in the room.

He went hastily over to the side door. Opening it and looking out, he perceived Maggie standing, as if undecided, on the corner. She was searching the place with her eyes.

As she turned her face toward him Pete beckoned to her hurriedly, intent upon returning with speed to a position behind the bar and to the atmosphere of respectability upon which the proprietor insisted.

Maggie came to him, the anxious look disappearing from her face and a smile wreathing her lips.

"Oh, Pete—," she began brightly.

The bartender made a violent gesture of impatience.

"Oh, my Gawd," cried he, vehemently. "What deh hell do yeh wanna hang aroun' here fer? Do yeh wanna git me inteh trouble?" he demanded with an air of injury.

Astonishment swept over the girl's features. "Why, Pete! yehs tol' me—"

Pete glanced profound irritation. His countenance reddened with the anger of a man whose respectability is being threatened.

"Say, yehs makes me tired. See? What deh hell deh yeh wanna tag aroun' atter me fer? Yeh'll git me inteh trouble wid deh ol' man an' dey'll be hell teh pay! If he sees a woman roun' here he'll go crazy an' I'll lose me job! See? Ain' yehs got no sense? Don' be allus bodderin' me. See? Yer brudder come in here an' raised hell an' deh ol' man hada put up fer it! An' now I'm done! See? I'm done."

The girl's eyes stared into his face. "Pete, don't yeh remem—"

"Oh, hell," interrupted Pete, anticipating.

The girl seemed to have a struggle with herself. She was apparently bewildered and could not find speech. Finally she asked in a low voice: "But where kin I go?"

The question exasperated Pete beyond the powers of endurance. It was a direct attempt to give him some responsibility in a matter that did not concern him. In his indignation he volunteered information.

"Oh, go teh hell," cried he. He slammed the door furiously and returned, with an air of relief, to his respectability.

Maggie went away.

She wandered aimlessly for several blocks. She stopped once and asked aloud a question of herself: "Who?"

A man who was passing near her shoulder, humorously took the questioning word as intended for him.

"Eh? What? Who? Nobody! I didn't say anything," he laughingly said, and continued his way.

Soon the girl discovered that if she walked with such apparent aimlessness, some men looked at her with calculating eyes. She quickened her step, frightened. As a protection, she adopted a demeanor of intentness as if going somewhere.

After a time she left rattling avenues and passed between rows of houses with sternness and stolidity stamped upon their features. She hung her head for she felt their eyes grimly upon her.

Suddenly she came upon a stout gentleman in a silk hat and a chaste black coat, whose decorous row of buttons reached from his chin to his knees. The girl had heard of the Grace of God and she decided to approach this man.[1]

His beaming, chubby face was a picture of benevolence and kindheartedness. His eyes shone good-will.

But as the girl timidly accosted him, he gave a convulsive movement and saved his respectability by a vigorous side-step. He did not risk it to save a soul. For how was he to know that there was a soul before him that needed saving?

---

[1] He is apparently a clergyman.

CHAPTER XVII

Upon a wet evening, several months after the last chapter, two inter-minable rows of cars, pulled by slipping horses, jangled along a prominent side-street. A dozen cabs, with coat-enshrouded drivers, clattered to and fro. Electric lights, whirring softly, shed a blurred radiance. A flower dealer, his feet tapping impatiently, his nose and his wares glistening with rain-drops, stood behind an array of roses and chrysanthemums. Two or three theatres emptied a crowd upon the storm-swept pavements. Men pulled their hats over their eye-brows and raised their collars to their ears. Women shrugged impa-tient shoulders in their warm cloaks and stopped to arrange their skirts for a walk through the storm. People having been compara-tively silent for two hours burst into a roar of conversation, their hearts still kindling from the glowings of the stage.

The pavements became tossing seas of umbrellas. Men stepped forth to hail cabs or cars, raising their fingers in varied forms of polite request or imperative demand. An endless procession wended toward elevated stations. An atmosphere of pleasure and prosperity seemed to hang over the throng, born, perhaps, of good clothes and of having just emerged from a place of forgetfulness.

In the mingled light and gloom of an adjacent park, a handful of wet wanderers, in attitudes of chronic dejection, was scattered among the benches.

A girl of the painted cohorts of the city went along the street. She threw changing glances at men who passed her, giving smiling invita-tions to men of rural or untaught pattern and usually seeming sedately unconscious of the men with a metropolitan seal upon their faces.

Crossing glittering avenues, she went into the throng emerging from the places of forgetfulness. She hurried forward through the crowd as if intent upon reaching a distant home, bending forward in her handsome cloak, daintily lifting her skirts and picking for her well-shod feet the dryer spots upon the pavements.

The restless doors of saloons, clashing to and fro, disclosed animated rows of men before bars and hurrying barkeepers.

A concert hall gave to the street faint sounds of swift, machine-like music, as if a group of phantom musicians were hastening.

A tall young man, smoking a cigarette with a sublime air, strolled near the girl. He had on evening dress, a moustache, a chrysanthemum, and a look of ennui, all of which he kept carefully under his eye. Seeing the girl walk on as if such a young man as he was not in existence, he looked back transfixed with interest. He stared glassily for a moment, but gave a slight convulsive start when he discerned that she was neither new, Parisian, nor theatrical. He wheeled about hastily and turned his stare into the air, like a sailor with a search-light.

A stout gentleman, with pompous and philanthropic whiskers, went stolidly by, the broad of his back sneering at the girl.

A belated man in business clothes, and in haste to catch a car, bounced against her shoulder. "Hi, there, Mary, I beg your pardon! Brace up, old girl." He grasped her arm to steady her, and then was away running down the middle of the street.

The girl walked on out of the realm of restaurants and saloons. She passed more glittering avenues and went into darker blocks than those where the crowd travelled.

A young man in light overcoat and derby hat received a glance shot keenly from the eyes of the girl. He stopped and looked at her, thrusting his hands in his pockets and making a mocking smile curl his lips. "Come, now, old lady," he said, "you don't mean to tell me that you sized me up for a farmer?"

A laboring man marched along with bundles under his arms. To her remarks, he replied: "It's a fine evenin', ain't it?"

She smiled squarely into the face of a boy who was hurrying by with his hands buried in his overcoat, his blonde locks bobbing on his youthful temples, and a cheery smile of unconcern upon his lips. He turned his head and smiled back at her, waving his hands.

"Not this eve—some other eve!"

A drunken man, reeling in her pathway, began to roar at her. "I ain' ga no money, dammit," he shouted, in a dismal voice. He lurched on up the street, wailing to himself, "Dammit, I ain' ga no money. Damn ba' luck. Ain' ga no more money."

The girl went into gloomy districts near the river, where the tall black factories shut in the street and only occasional broad beams of light fell across the pavements from saloons. In front of one of these places, from whence came the sound of a violin vigorously scraped, the patter of feet on boards and the ring of loud laughter, there stood a man with blotched features.

"Ah, there," said the girl.

"I've got a date," said the man.

Further on in the darkness she met a ragged being with shifting, blood-shot eyes and grimy hands. "Ah, what deh hell? T'ink I'm a millionaire."

She went into the blackness of the final block. The shutters of the tall buildings were closed liked grim lips. The structures seemed to have eyes that looked over her, beyond her, at other things. Afar off the lights of the avenues glittered as if from an impossible distance. Street-car bells jingled with a sound of merriment.

When almost to the river the girl saw a great figure. On going forward she perceived it to be a huge fat man in torn and greasy garments. His grey hair straggled down over his forehead. His small, bleared eyes, sparkling from amidst great rolls of red fat, swept eagerly over the girl's upturned face. He laughed, his brown, disordered teeth gleaming under a grey, grizzled moustache from which beer-drops dripped. His whole body gently quivered and shook like that of a dead jelly fish. Chuckling and leering, he followed the girl of the crimson legions. ⟶ CREEPY

At their feet the river appeared a deathly black hue. Some hidden factory sent up a yellow glare, that lit for a moment the waters lapping oilily against timbers. The varied sounds of life, made joyous by distance and seeming unapproachableness, came faintly and died away to a silence.

CHAPTER XVIII

In a partitioned-off section of a saloon sat a man with a half dozen women, gleefully laughing, hovering about him. The man had arrived at that stage of drunkenness where affection is felt for the universe.

"I'm good f'ler, girls," he said, convincingly. "I'm damn good f'ler. An'body treats me right, I allus trea's zem right! See?"

The women nodded their heads approvingly. "To be sure," they cried in hearty chorus. "You're the kind of a man we like, Pete. You're outa sight! What yeh goin' to buy this time, dear?"

"An'thin' yehs wants, damn it," said the man in an abandonment of good will. His countenance shone with the true spirit of benevolence.

He was in the proper mode of missionaries. He would have frater-
nized with obscure Hottentots.[1] And above all, he was overwhelmed
in tenderness for his friends, who were all illustrious.

"An'thing yehs wants, damn it," repeated he, waving his hands with
beneficent recklessness. "I'm good f'ler, girls, an' if an'body treats me
right I—here," called he through an open door to a waiter, "bring girls
drinks, damn it. What 'ill yehs have, girls? An'thing yehs want, damn it!"

The waiter glanced in with the disgusted look of the man who
serves intoxicants for the man who takes too much of them. He
nodded his head shortly at the order from each individual, and went.

"Damn it," said the man, "we're havin' heluva time. I like you
girls! Damn'd if I don't! Yer right sort! See?"

He spoke at length and with feeling, concerning the excellencies
of his assembled friends.

"Don' try pull man's leg, but have a heluva time! Das right! Das
way teh do! Now, if I sawght yehs tryin' work me fer drinks, wouldn'
buy damn t'ing! But yer right sort, damn it! Yehs know how ter treat
a f'ler, an' I stays by yehs 'til spen' las' cent! Das right! I'm good f'ler
an' I knows when an'body treats me right!"

Between the times of the arrival and departure of the waiter, the
man discoursed to the women on the tender regard he felt for all
living things. He laid stress upon the purity of his motives in all dealings with men in the world and spoke of the fervor of his friendship for those who were amiable. Tears welled slowly from his eyes.
His voice quavered when he spoke to them.

Once when the waiter was about to depart with an empty tray,
the man drew a coin from his pocket and held it forth.

"Here," said he, quite magnificently, "here's quar'."

The waiter kept his hands on his tray.

"I don' want yer money," he said.

The other put forth the coin with tearful insistence.

"Here, damn it," cried he, "tak't! Yer damn goo' f'ler an' I wan'
yehs tak't!"

"Come, come, now," said the waiter, with the sullen air of a man
who is forced into giving advice. "Put yer mon in yer pocket! Yer
loaded an' yehs on'y makes a damn fool of yerself."

---

[1]   South Africans.

getting very drunk parting

As the latter passed out of the door the man turned pathetically to the women.

"He don' know I'm damn goo' f'ler," cried he, dismally.

"Never you mind, Pete, dear," said a woman of brilliance and audacity, laying her hand with great affection upon his arm. "Never you mind, old boy! We'll stay by you, dear!"

"Das ri'," cried the man, his face lighting up at the soothing tones of the woman's voice. "Das ri', I'm damn goo' f'ler an' w'en anyone trea's me ri', I treats zem ri'! Shee!"

"Sure!" cried the women. "And we're not goin' back on you, old man."

The man turned appealing eyes to the woman of brilliance and audacity. He felt that if he could be convicted of a contemptible action he would die.

"Shay, Nell, damn it, I allus trea's yehs shquare, didn' I? I allus been goo' f'ler wi' yehs, ain't I, Nell?"

"Sure you have, Pete," assented the woman. She delivered an oration to her companions. "Yessir, that's a fact. Pete's a square fellah, he is. He never goes back on a friend. He's the right kind an' we stay by him, don't we, girls?"

"Sure," they exclaimed. Looking lovingly at him they raised their glasses and drank his health.

"Girlsh," said the man, beseechingly, "I allus trea's yehs ri', didn' I? I'm goo' f'ler, ain' I, girlsh?"

"Sure," again they chorused.

"Well," said he finally, "le's have nozzer drink, zen."

"That's right," hailed a woman, "that's right. Yer no bloomin' jay! Yer spends yer money like a man. Dat's right."

The man pounded the table with his quivering fists.

"Yessir," he cried, with deep earnestness, as if someone disputed him. "I'm damn goo' f'ler, an' w'en anyone trea's me ri', I allus trea's—le's have nozzer drink."

He began to beat the wood with his glass.

"Shay," howled he, growing suddenly impatient. As the waiter did not then come, the man swelled with wrath.

"Shay," howled he again.

The waiter appeared at the door.

"Bringsh drinksh," said the man.

The waiter disappeared with the orders.

"Zat f'ler damn fool," cried the man. "He insul' me! I'm ge'man! Can' stan' be insul'! I'm goin' lickim when comes!"

"No, no," cried the women, crowding about and trying to subdue him. "He's all right! He didn't mean anything! Let it go! He's a good fellah!"

"Din' he insul' me?" asked the man earnestly.

"No," said they. "Of course he didn't! He's all right!"

"Sure he didn' insul' me?" demanded the man, with deep anxiety in his voice.

"No, no! We know him! He's a good fellah. He didn't mean anything."

"Well, zen," said the man, resolutely, "I'm go' 'pol'gize!"

When the waiter came, the man struggled to the middle of the floor.

"Girlsh shed you insul' me! I shay damn lie! I 'pol'gize!"

"All right," said the waiter.

The man sat down. He felt a sleepy but strong desire to straighten things out and have a perfect understanding with everybody.

"Nell, I allus trea's yeh shquare, din' I? Yeh likes me, don' yehs, Nell? I'm goo' f'ler?"

"Sure," said the woman of brilliance and audacity.

"Yeh knows I'm stuck on yehs, don' yehs, Nell?"

"Sure," she repeated, carelessly.

Overwhelmed by a spasm of drunken adoration, he drew two or three bills from his pocket, and, with the trembling fingers of an offering priest, laid them on the table before the woman.

"Yehs knows, damn it, yehs kin have all got, 'cause I'm stuck on yehs, Nell, damn't, I— I'm stuck on yehs, Nell—buy drinksh— damn't—we're havin' heluva time—w'en anyone trea's me ri'—I— damn't, Nell—we're havin' heluva—time."

Shortly he went to sleep with his swollen face fallen forward on his chest.

The women drank and laughed, not heeding the slumbering man in the corner. Finally he lurched forward and fell groaning to the floor.

The women screamed in disgust and drew back their skirts.

"Come ahn," cried one, starting up angrily, "let's get out of here."

The woman of brilliance and audacity stayed behind, taking up the bills and stuffing them into a deep, irregularly-shaped pocket. A guttural snore from the recumbent man caused her to turn and look down at him.

She laughed. "What a damn fool," she said, and went.

The smoke from the lamps settled heavily down in the little compartment, obscuring the way out. The smell of oil, stifling in its intensity, pervaded the air. The wine from an overturned glass dripped softly down upon the blotches on the man's neck.

CHAPTER XIX

In a room a woman sat at a table eating like a fat monk in a picture.

A soiled, unshaven man pushed open the door and entered.

"Well," said he, "Mag's dead."

"What?" said the woman, her mouth filled with bread.

"Mag's dead," repeated the man.

"Deh hell she is," said the woman. She continued her meal. When she finished her coffee she began to weep.

"I kin remember when her two feet was no bigger dan yer t'umb, and she weared worsted boots," moaned she.

"Well, whata dat?" said the man.

"I kin remember when she weared worsted boots," she cried.

The neighbors began to gather in the hall, staring in at the weeping woman as if watching the contortions of a dying dog. A dozen women entered and lamented with her. Under their busy hands the rooms took on that appalling appearance of neatness and order with which death is greeted.

Suddenly the door opened and a woman in a black gown rushed in with outstretched arms. "Ah, poor Mary," she cried, and tenderly embraced the moaning one.

"Ah, what ter'ble affliction is dis," continued she. Her vocabulary was derived from mission churches. "Me poor Mary, how I feel fer yehs! Ah, what a ter'ble affliction is a disobed'ent chile."

Her good, motherly face was wet with tears. She trembled in eagerness to express her sympathy. The mourner sat with bowed head, rocking her body heavily to and fro, and crying out in a high, strained voice that sounded like a dirge on some forlorn pipe.

"I kin remember when she weared worsted boots an' her two

feets was no bigger dan yer t'umb an' she weared worsted boots, Miss Smith," she cried, raising her streaming eyes.

"Ah, me poor Mary," sobbed the woman in black. With low, coddling cries, she sank on her knees by the mourner's chair, and put her arms about her. The other women began to groan in different keys.

"Yer poor misguided chil' is gone now, Mary, an' let us hope it's fer deh bes'. Yeh'll fergive her now, Mary, won't yehs, dear, all her disobed'ence? All her t'ankless behavior to her mudder an' all her badness? She's gone where her ter'ble sins will be judged."

The woman in black raised her face and paused. The inevitable sunlight came streaming in at the windows and shed a ghastly cheerfulness upon the faded hues of the room. Two or three of the spectators were sniffling, and one was loudly weeping. The mourner arose and staggered into the other room. In a moment she emerged with a pair of faded baby shoes held in the hollow of her hand.

"I kin remember when she used to wear dem," cried she. The women burst anew into cries as if they had all been stabbed. The mourner turned to the soiled and unshaven man.

"Jimmie, boy, go git yer sister! Go git yer sister an' we'll put deh boots on her feets!"

"Dey won't fit her now, yeh damn fool," said the man.

"Go git yer sister, Jimmie," shrieked the woman, confronting him fiercely.

The man swore sullenly. He went over to a corner and slowly began to put on his coat. He took his hat and went out, with a dragging, reluctant step.

The woman in black came forward and again besought the mourner.

"Yeh'll fergive her, Mary! Yeh'll fergive yer bad, bad, chil'! Her life was a curse an' her days were black an' yeh'll fergive yer bad girl? She's gone where her sins will be judged."

"She's gone where her sins will be judged," cried the other women, like a choir at a funeral.

"Deh Lord gives and deh Lord takes away," said the woman in black, raising her eyes to the sunbeams.

"Deh Lord gives and deh Lord takes away," responded the others.

"Yeh'll fergive her, Mary!" pleaded the woman in black. The mourner essayed to speak but her voice gave way. She shook her great shoulders frantically, in an agony of grief. Hot tears seemed to scald her quivering face. Finally her voice came and arose like a scream of pain.

"Oh, yes, I'll fergive her! I'll fergive her!"

Appendix A: Other New York Writings by Stephen Crane

[The stories included in this appendix are all set, like *Maggie*, in New York's Lower East Side. Maggie herself makes an appearance in *George's Mother*, a story that explores more fully than its more famous companion piece the complex interaction of violence, alcohol, and self-esteem in the Bowery. The other stories, "An Experiment in Misery," "An Experiment in Luxury," and "An Ominous Baby," demonstrate the symbiotic relationship between Crane's newspaper reporting of the slum and his fictional representations of it.]

1. *George's Mother* (New York: Edward Arnold, 1896)

In the swirling rain that came at dusk the broad avenue glistened with that deep bluish tint which is so widely condemned when it is put into pictures. There were long rows of shops, whose fronts shone with full, golden light. Here and there, from druggists' windows, or from the red street-lamps that indicated the positions of fire-alarm boxes, a flare of uncertain, wavering crimson was thrown upon the wet pavements.

The lights made shadows, in which the buildings loomed with a new and tremendous massiveness, like castles and fortresses. There were endless processions of people, mighty hosts, with umbrellas waving, banner-like, over them. Horse-cars, aglitter with new paint, rumbled in steady array between the pillars that supported the elevated railroad. The whole street resounded with the tinkle of bells, the roar of iron-shod wheels on the cobbles, the ceaseless trample of the hundreds of feet. Above all, too, could be heard the loud screams of the tiny newsboys, who scurried in all directions. Upon the corners, standing in from the dripping eaves, were many loungers, descended from the world that used to prostrate itself before pageantry.

A brown young man went along the avenue. He held a tin lunch-pail under his arm in a manner that was evidently uncomfortable. He was puffing at a corn-cob pipe. His shoulders had a self-reliant poise, and the hang of his arms and the raised veins of his hands showed him to be a man who worked with his muscles.

As he passed a street-corner a man in old clothes gave a shout of surprise, and rushing impetuously forward, grasped his hand.

"Hello, Kelcey, ol' boy," cried the man in old clothes. "How's th' boy, anyhow? Where in thunder yeh been fer th' last seventeen years? I'll be hanged if you ain't th' last man I ever expected t' see."

The brown youth put his pail to the ground and grinned. "Well, if it ain't ol' Charley Jones," he said, "How are yeh, anyhow? Where yeh been keepin' yerself? I ain't seen yeh fer a year!"

"Well, I should say so! Why, th' last time I saw you was up in Handyville!"

"Sure! On Sunday, we—"

"Sure! Out at Bill Sickles's place. Let's go get a drink!"

They made toward a little glass-fronted saloon that sat blinking jovially at the crowds. It engulfed them with a gleeful motion of its two widely smiling lips.

"What'll yeh take, Kelcey?"

"Oh, I guess I'll take a beer."

"Gimme little whiskey, John."

The two friends leaned against the bar and looked with enthusiasm upon each other.

"Well, well, I'm thunderin' glad t' see yeh," said Jones.

"Well, I guess," replied Kelcey. "Here's to yeh, ol' man."

"Let 'er go."

They lifted their glasses, glanced fervidly at each other, and drank.

"Yeh ain't changed much, on'y yeh've growed like th'devil," said Jones, reflectively, as he put down his glass. "I'd know yeh anywheres!"

"Certainly yeh would," said Kelcey. "An' I knew you, too, th' minute I saw yeh. Yer changed, though!"

"Yes," admitted Jones, with some complacency, "I s'pose I am." He regarded himself in the mirror that multiplied the bottles on the shelf back of the bar. He should have seen a grinning face with a rather pink nose. His derby was perched carelessly on the back part of his head. Two wisps of hair straggled down over his hollow temples. There was something very worldly and wise about him. Life did not seem to confuse him. Evidently he understood its complications. His hand thrust into his trousers' pocket, where he jingled keys, and his hat perched back on his head expressed a young man of vast knowledge. His extensive acquaintance with bartenders aided him materially in this habitual expression of wisdom. Having finished he turned to the barkeeper. "John, has any of th' gang been in t'-night yet?"

"No—not yet," said the barkeeper. "Ol' Bleecker was aroun' this afternoon about four. He said if I seen any of th' boys t' tell 'em he'd be up t'-night if he could get away. I saw Connor an' that other fellah goin' down th' avenyeh about an hour ago. I guess they'll be back after awhile."

"This is th' hang-out fer a great gang," said Jones, turning to Kelcey. "They're a great crowd, I tell yeh. We own th' place when we get started. Come aroun' some night. Any night, almost. T'-night, b' jiminy. They'll almost all be here, an' I'd like t' interduce yeh. They're a great gang! Gre-e-at!"

"I'd like teh," said Kelcey.

"Well, come ahead, then," cried the other, cordially. "Yeh'd like t' know 'em. It's an outa sight crowd. Come aroun' t'-night!"

"I will if I can."

"Well, yeh ain't got anything t' do, have yeh?" demanded Jones. "Well, come along, then. Yeh might just as well spend yer time with a good crowd 'a fellahs. An' it's a great gang. Great! Gre-e-at!"

"Well, I must make fer home now, anyhow," said Kelcey. "It's late as blazes. What'll yeh take this time, ol' man?"

"Gimme little more whiskey, John!"

"Guess I'll take another beer!"

Jones emptied the whiskey into his large mouth and then put the glass upon the bar. "Been in th' city long?" he asked. "Um—well, three years is a good deal fer a slick man. Doin' well? Oh, well, nobody's doin' well these days." He looked down mournfully at his shabby clothes. "Father's dead, ain't 'ee? Yeh don't say so? Fell off a scaffoldin', didn't 'ee? I heard it somewheres. Mother's livin', of course? I thought she was. Fine ol' lady—fi-i-ne. Well, you're th' last of her boys. Was five of yeh onct, wasn't there? I knew four m'self. Yes, five! I thought so. An' all gone but you, hey? Well, you'll have t' brace up an' be a comfort t' th' ol' mother. Well, well, well, who would 'a thought that on'y you'd be left out 'a all that mob 'a tow-headed kids. Well, well, well, it's a queer world, ain't it?

A contemplation of this thought made him sad. He sighed and moodily watched the other sip beer.

"Well, well, it's a queer world—a damn queer world."

"Yes," said Kelcey, "I'm th' on'y one left!" There was an accent of discomfort in his voice. He did not like this dwelling upon a sentiment that was connected with himself.

"How is th' ol' lady, anyhow?" continued Jones. "Th' last time I remember she was as spry as a little ol' cricket, an' was helpeltin' aroun' th' country lecturin' before W.C.T.U.'s[1] an' one thing an' another."

"Oh, she's pretty well," said Kelcey.

---

[1] Women's Christian Temperance Movement. Formed in 1874 by women concerned about the deleterious effects of alcohol consumption on domestic life, the movement advocated total abstinence.

"An' outa five boys you're th'on'y one she's got left? Well, well—have another drink before yeh go."

"Oh, I guess I've had enough."

A wounded expression came into Jones's eyes. "Oh, come on," he said. "Well, I'll take another beer!"

"Gimme little more whiskey, John!"

When they had concluded this ceremony, Jones went with his friend to the door of the saloon. "Good-by, ol' man," he said, genially. His homely features shone with friendliness. "Come aroun', now, sure. T'-night! See? They're a great crowd. Gre-e-at!"

II

A man with a red, mottled face put forth his head from a window and cursed violently. He flung a bottle high across two backyards at a window of the opposite tenement. It broke against the bricks of the house and the fragments fell crackling upon the stones below. The man shook his fist.

A bare-armed woman, making an array of clothes on a line in one of the yards, glanced casually up at the man and listened to his words. Her eyes followed his to the other tenement. From a distant window, a youth with a pipe, yelled some comments upon the poor aim. Two children, being in the proper yard, picked up the bits of broken glass and began to fondle them as new toys.

From the window at which the man raged came the sound of an old voice, singing. It quavered and trembled out into the air as if a sound-spirit had a broken wing.

"Should I be car-reed tew th' skies
O-on flow'ry beeds of ee-ease,
While others fought tew win th' prize
An' sailed through blood-ee seas."

The man in the opposite window was greatly enraged. He continued to swear.

A little old woman was the owner of the voice. In a fourth-story room of the red and black tenement she was trudging on a journey. In her arms she bore pots and pans, and sometimes a broom and dust-pan. She wielded them like weapons. Their weight seemed to have bended her back and crooked her arms until she walked with difficulty. Often she plunged her hands into water at a sink. She splashed about, the dwindled muscles working to and fro under the loose skin of her arms. She came from the sink, steaming and bedraggled as if she had crossed a flooded river.

There was the flurry of a battle in this room. Through the clouded dust or steam one could see the thin figure dealing mighty blows. Always her way seemed beset. Her broom was continually poised, lancewise, at dust demons. There came clashings and clangings as she strove with her tireless foes.

It was a picture of indomitable courage. And as she went on her way her voice was often raised in a long cry, a strange war-chant, a shout of battle and defiance, that rose and fell in harsh screams, and exasperated the ears of the man with the red, mottled face.

"Should I be car-reed tew th' skies
O-on flow'ry be-eds of ee-ease———"

Finally she halted for a moment. Going to the window she sat down and mopped her face with her apron. It was a lull, a moment of respite. Still it could be seen that she even then was planning skirmishes, charges, campaigns. She gazed thoughtfully about the room and noted the strength and position of her enemies. She was very alert.

At last, she turned to the mantel. "Five o'clock," she murmured, scrutinizing a little, swaggering, nickel-plated clock.

She looked out at chimneys growing thickly on the roofs. A man at work on one seemed like a bee. In the intricate yards below, vine-like lines had strange leaves of cloth. To her ears there came the howl of the man with the red, mottled face. He was engaged in a furious altercation with the youth who had called attention to his poor aim. They were like animals in a jungle.

In the distance an enormous brewery towered over the other buildings. Great gilt letters advertised a brand of beer. Thick smoke came from funnels and spread near it like vast and powerful wings. The structure seemed a great bird, flying. The letters of the sign made a chain of gold hanging from its neck. The little old woman looked at the brewery. It vaguely interested her, for a moment, as a stupendous affair, a machine of mighty strength.

Presently she sprang from her rest and began to buffet with her shrivelled arms. In a moment the battle was again in full swing. Terrific blows were given and received. There arose the clattering uproar of a new fight. The little intent warrior never hesitated nor faltered. She fought with a strong and relentless will. Beads and lines of perspiration stood upon her forehead.

Three blue plates were leaning in a row on the shelf back of the stove. The little old woman had seen it done somewhere. In front of them swaggered the round nickel-plated clock. Her son had stuck many cigarette pictures in the rim of a looking-glass that hung near. Occasional chromos[1] were tacked upon the yellowed walls of the room. There was one in a gilt frame. It was quite an affair, in reds and greens. They all seemed like trophies.

It began to grow dark. A mist came winding. Rain plashed softly upon the window-sill. A lamp had been lighted in the opposite tenement; the strong orange glare revealed the man with a red, mottled face. He was seated by a table, smoking and reflecting.

The little old woman looked at the clock again. "Quarter 'a six." She had paused for a moment, but she now hurled herself fiercely at the stove that lurked in the gloom, red-eyed, like a dragon. It hissed, and there was renewed clangor of blows. The little old woman dashed to and fro.

III

As it grew toward seven o'clock the little old woman became nervous. She often would drop into a chair and sit staring at the little clock.

"I wonder why he don't come," she continually repeated. There was a small, curious note of despair in her voice. As she sat thinking and staring at the clock the expressions of her face changed swiftly. All manner of emotions flickered in her eyes and about her lips. She was evidently perceiving in her imagination the journey of a loved person. She dreamed for him mishaps and obstacles. Something tremendous and irritating was hindering him from coming to her.

She had lighted an oil-lamp. It flooded the room with vivid yellow glare. The table, in its oil-cloth covering, had previously appeared like a bit of bare, brown desert. It now was a white garden, growing the fruits of her labor.

"Seven o'clock," she murmured, finally. She was aghast.

Then suddenly she heard a step upon the stair. She sprang up and began to bustle about the room. The little fearful emotions passed at once from her face. She seemed now to be ready to scold.

---

[1] Short for chromolithograph, a coloured lithographic picture.

Young Kelcey entered the room. He gave a sigh of relief, and dropped his pail in a corner. He was evidently greatly wearied by a hard day of toil.

The little old woman hobbled over to him and raised her wrinkled lips. She seemed on the verge of tears and an outburst of reproaches.

"Hello!" he cried, in a voice of cheer. "Been gettin' anxious?"

"Yes," she said, hovering about him. "Where yeh been, George? What made yeh so late? I've been waitin' th' longest while. Don't throw your coat down there. Hang it up behind th' door."

The son put his coat on the proper hook, and then went to splatter water in a tin wash-basin at the sink.

"Well, yeh see, I met Jones—you remember Jones? Ol' Handyville fellah. An' we had t' stop an' talk over ol' times. Jones is quite a boy."

The little old woman's mouth set in a sudden straight line. "Oh, that Jones," she said. "I don't like him."

The youth interrupted a flurry of white towel to give a glance of irritation. "Well, now, what's th' use of talkin' that way?" he said to her. "What do yeh know' bout 'im? Ever spoke to 'im in yer life?"

"Well, I don't know as I ever did since he grew up," replied the little old woman. "But I know he ain't th' kind 'a man I'd like t' have you go around with. He ain't a good man. I'm sure he ain't. He drinks."

Her son began to laugh. "Th' dickens he does?" He seemed amazed, but not shocked at this information.

She nodded her head with the air of one who discloses a dreadful thing. "I'm sure of it! Once I saw 'im comin' outa Simpson's Hotel, up in Handyville, an' he could hardly walk. He drinks! I'm sure he drinks!"

"Holy smoke!" said Kelcey.

They sat down at the table and began to wreck the little white garden. The youth leaned back in his chair, in the manner of a man who is paying for things. His mother bended alertly forward, apparently watching each mouthful. She perched on the edge of her chair, ready to spring to her feet and run to the closet or the stove for anything that he might need. She was as anxious as a young mother with a babe. In the careless and comfortable attitude of the son there was denoted a great deal of dignity.

"Yeh ain't eatin' much t'-night, George?"

"Well, I ain't very hungry, t' tell th' truth."

"Don't yeh like yer supper, dear? Yeh must eat somethin', chile. Yeh mustn't go without."

"Well, I'm eatin' somethin', ain't I?"

He wandered aimlessly through the meal. She sat over behind the little blackened coffee-pot and gazed affectionately upon him.

After a time she began to grow agitated. Her worn fingers were gripped. It could be seen that a great thought was within her. She was about to venture something. She had arrived at a supreme moment. "George," she said, suddenly, "come t' prayer-meetin' with me t'-night."

The young man dropped his fork. "Say, you must be crazy," he said, in amazement.

"Yes, dear," she continued, rapidly, in a small pleading voice, "I'd like t' have yeh go with me onct in a while. Yeh never go with me any more, dear, an' I'd like t' have yeh go. Yeh ain't been anywheres at all with me in th' longest while."

"Well," he said, "well, but what th' blazes——"

"Ah, come on," said the little old woman. She went to him and put her arms about his neck. She began to coax him with caresses.

The young man grinned. "Thunderation!" he said, "what would I do at a prayer-meetin'?"

The mother considered him to be consenting. She did a little antique caper.

"Well, yeh can come an' take care 'a yer mother," she cried, gleefully. "It's such a long walk every Thursday night alone, an' don't yeh s'pose that when I have such a big, fine, strappin' boy, I want 'im t' beau me aroun' some? Ah, I knew ye'd come."

He smiled for a moment, indulgent of her humor. But presently his face turned a shade of discomfort. "But——" he began, protesting.

"Ah, come on," she continually repeated.

He began to be vexed. He frowned into the air. A vision came to him of dreary blackness arranged in solemn rows. A mere dream of it was depressing.

"But——" he said again. He was obliged to make great search for an argument. Finally he concluded, "But what th'blazes would I do at prayer-meetin'?"

In his ears was the sound of a hymn, made by people who tilted their heads at a prescribed angle of devotion. It would be too apparent that they were all better than he. When he entered they would turn their heads and regard him with suspicion. This would be an enormous aggravation, since he was certain that he was as good as they.

"Well, now, y' see," he said, quite gently, "I don't wanta go, an' wouldn't do me no good t' go if I didn't wanta go."

His mother's face swiftly changed. She breathed a huge sigh, the counterpart of ones he had heard upon like occasions. She put a tiny black bonnet on her head, and wrapped her figure in an old shawl. She cast a martyr-like glance upon her son and went mournfully away. She resembled a limited funeral procession.

The young man writhed under it to an extent. He kicked moodily at a table-leg. When the sound of her footfalls died away he felt distinctly relieved.

IV

That night, when Kelcey arrived at the little smiling saloon, he found his friend Jones standing before the bar engaged in a violent argument with a stout man.

"Oh, well," this latter person was saying, "you can make a lot of noise, Charlie, for a man that never says anything—let's have a drink!"

Jones was waving his arms and delivering splintering blows upon some distant theories. The stout man chuckled fatly and winked at the bartender.

The orator ceased for a moment to say, "Gimme little whiskey, John." At the same time he perceived young Kelcey. He sprang forward with a welcoming cry. "Hello, ol' man, didn't much think ye'd come." He led him to the stout man.

"Mr. Bleecker—my friend Mr. Kelcey!"

"How d'yeh do!"

"Mr. Kelcey, I'm happy to meet you, sir; have a drink."

They drew up in line and waited. The busy hands of the bartender made glasses clink. Mr. Bleecker, in a very polite way, broke the waiting silence.

"Never been here before, I believe, have you, Mr. Kelcey?"

The young man felt around for a high-bred reply. "Er—no—I've never had tha—er—pleasure," he said.

After a time the strained and wary courtesy of their manners wore away. It became evident to Bleecker that his importance slightly dazzled the young man. He grew warmer. Obviously, the youth was one whose powers of perception were developed. Directly, then, he launched forth into a tale of by-gone days, when the world was better. He had known all the great men of that age. He reproduced his conversations with them. There were traces of pride and of mournfulness in his voice. He rejoiced at the glory of the world of dead spirits. He grieved at the youth and flippancy of the present one. He lived with his head in the clouds of the past, and he seemed obliged to talk of what he saw there.

Jones nudged Kelcey ecstatically in the ribs. "You've got th' ol' man started in great shape," he whispered.

Kelcey was proud that the prominent character of the place talked at him, glancing into his eyes for appreciation of fine points.

Presently they left the bar, and going into a little rear room, took seats about a table. A gas-jet with a colored globe shed a crimson radiance. The polished wood of walls and furniture gleamed with faint rose-colored reflections. Upon the floor sawdust was thickly sprinkled.

Two other men presently came. By the time Bleecker had told three tales of the grand past, Kelcey was slightly acquainted with everybody.

He admired Bleecker immensely. He developed a brotherly feeling for the others, who were all gentle-spoken. He began to feel that he was passing the happiest evening of his life. His companions were so jovial and good-natured; and everything they did was marked by such courtesy.

For a time the two men who had come in late did not presume to address him directly. They would say: "Jones, won't your friend have so and so, or so and so?" And Bleecker would begin his orations: "Now, Mr. Kelcey, don't you think?"

Presently he began to believe that he was a most remarkably fine fellow, who had at last found his place in a crowd of most remarkably fine fellows.

Jones occasionally breathed comments into his ear.

"I tell yeh, Bleecker's an ol'-timer. He was a husky guy in his day, yeh can bet. He was one 'a th' best known men in N' York onct. Yeh ought to hear him tell about——"

Kelcey listened intently. He was profoundly interested in the intimate tales of men who had gleamed in the rays of old suns.

"That O'Connor's a damn fine fellah," interjected Jones once, referring to one of the others. "He's one 'a th' best fellahs I ever knowed. He's always on th' dead level. An' he's always jest th'same as yeh see 'im now—good-natured an' grinnin'."

Kelcey nodded. He could well believe it.

When he offered to buy drinks there came a loud volley of protests. "No, no, Mr. Kelcey," cried Bleecker, "no, no. Tonight you are our guest. Some other time——"

"Here," said O'Connor, "it's my turn now."

He called and pounded for the bartender. He then sat with a coin in his hand warily eying the others. He was ready to frustrate them if they offered to pay.

After a time Jones began to develop qualities of great eloquence and wit. His companions laughed. "It's the whiskey talking now," said Bleecker.

He grew earnest and impassioned. He delivered speeches on various subjects. His lectures were to him very imposing. The force of his words thrilled him. Sometimes he was overcome.

The others agreed with him in all things. Bleecker grew almost tender, and considerately placed words here and there for his use. As Jones became fiercely energetic the others became more docile in agreeing. They soothed him with friendly interjections.

His mood changed directly. He began to sing popular airs with enthusiasm. He congratulated his companions upon being in society. They were excited by his frenzy. They began to fraternize in jovial fashion. It was understood that they were true and tender spirits. They had come away from a grinding world filled with men who were harsh.

When one of them chose to divulge some place where the world had pierced him, there was a chorus of violent sympathy. They rejoiced at their temporary isolation and safety.

Once a man, completely drunk, stumbled along the floor of the saloon. He opened the door of the little room and made a show of entering. The men sprang instantly to their feet. They were ready to throttle any invader of their island. They elbowed each other in rivalry as to who should take upon himself the brunt of an encounter.

"Oh!" said the drunken individual, swaying on his legs and blinking at the party, "oh! thish private room?"

"That's what it is, Willie," said Jones. "An' you git outa here er we'll throw yeh out."

"That's what we will," said the others.

"Oh," said the drunken man. He blinked at them aggrievedly for an instant and then went away.

They sat down again. Kelcey felt, in a way, that he would have liked to display his fidelity to the others by whipping the intruder.

The bartender came often. "Gee, you fellahs er tanks," he said, in a jocular manner, as he gathered empty glasses and polished the table with his little towel.

Through the exertions of Jones the little room began to grow clamorous. The tobacco-smoke eddied about the forms of the men in ropes and wreaths. Near the ceiling there was a thick gray cloud.

Each man explained, in his way, that he was totally out of place in the before-mentioned world. They were possessed of various virtues which were unappreciated by those with whom they were commonly obliged to mingle; they were fitted for a tree-shaded land, where everything was peace. Now that five of them had congregated it gave them happiness to speak their inmost thoughts without fear of being misunderstood.

As he drank more beer Kelcey felt his breast expand with manly feeling. He knew that he was capable of sublime things. He wished that some day one of his present companions would come to him for relief. His mind pictured a little scene. In it he was magnificent in his friendship.

He looked upon the beaming faces and knew that if at that instant there should come a time for a great sacrifice he would blissfully make it. He would pass tranquilly into the unknown, or into bankruptcy, amid the ejaculations of his companions upon his many virtues.

They had no bickerings during the evening. If one chose to momentarily assert himself, the others instantly submitted.

They exchanged compliments. Once old Bleecker stared at Jones for a few moments. Suddenly he broke out: "Jones, you're one of the finest fellows I ever knew!" A flush of pleasure went over the other's face, and then he made a modest gesture, the protest of an humble man. "Don't flim-flam me, ol' boy," he said, with earnestness. But Bleecker roared that he was serious about it. The two men arose and shook hands emotionally. Jones bunted against the table and knocked off a glass.

Afterward a general hand-shaking was inaugurated. Brotherly sentiments flew about the room. There was an uproar of fraternal feeling.

Jones began to sing. He beat time with precision and dignity. He gazed into the eyes of his companions, trying to call music from their souls. O'Connor joined in heartily, but with another tune. Off in a corner old Bleecker was making a speech.

The bartender came to the door. "Gee, you fellahs er making a row. It's time fer me t' shut up th' front th' place, an' you mugs better sit on yerselves. It's one o'clock."

They began to argue with him. Kelcey, however, sprang to his feet. "One o'clock," he said. "Holy smoke, I mus' be flyin'!"

There came protesting howls from Jones. Bleecker ceased his oration. "My dear boy—" he began. Kelcey searched for his hat. "I've gota go t' work at seven," he said.

The others watched him with discomfort in their eyes. "Well," said O'Connor, "if one goes we might as well all go." They sadly took their hats and filed out.

The cold air of the street filled Kelcey with vague surprise. It made his head feel hot. As for his legs, they were like willow-twigs.

A few yellow lights blinked. In front of an all-night restaurant a huge red electric lamp hung and sputtered. Horse-car bells jingled far down the street. Overhead a train thundered on the elevated road.

On the sidewalk the men took fervid leave. They clutched hands with extraordinary force and proclaimed, for the last time, ardent and admiring friendships.

When he arrived at his home Kelcey proceeded with caution. His mother had left a light burning low. He stumbled once in his voyage across the floor. As he paused to listen he heard the sound of little snores coming from her room.

He lay awake for a few moments and thought of the evening. He had a pleasurable consciousness that he had made a good impression upon those fine fellows. He felt that he had spent the most delightful evening of his life.

V

Kelcey was cross in the morning. His mother had been obliged to shake him a great deal, and it had seemed to him a most unjust thing. Also, when he, blinking his eyes, had entered the kitchen, she had said: "Yeh left th' lamp burnin' all night last night, George. How many times must I tell yeh never t' leave th' lamp burnin'?"

He ate the greater part of his breakfast in silence, moodily stirring his coffee and glaring at a remote corner of the room with eyes that felt as if they had been baked. When he moved his eyelids there was a sensation that they were cracking. In his mouth there was a singular taste. It seemed to him that he had been sucking the end of a wooden spoon. Moreover, his temper was rampant within him. It sought something to devour.

Finally he said, savagely: "Damn these early hours!"

His mother jumped as if he had flung a missile at her. "Why, George—" she began.

Kelcey broke in again. "Oh, I know all that—but this gettin' up in th' mornin' so early makes me sick. Jest when a man is gettin' his mornin' nap he's gota get up. I—"

"George, dear," said his mother, "yeh know how I hate yeh t' swear, dear. Now please don't." She looked beseechingly at him.

He made a swift gesture. "Well, I ain't swearin', am I?" he demanded.

"I was on'y sayin' that this gettin'-up business gives me a pain, wasn't I?"

"Well, yeh know how swearin' hurts me," protested the little old woman. She seemed about to sob. She gazed off retrospectively. She apparently was recalling persons who had never been profane.

"I don't see where yeh ever caught this way a' swearin' out at every-thing," she continued, presently. "Fred, ner John, ner Willie never swore a bit. Ner Tom neither, except when he was real mad."

The son made another gesture. It was directed into the air, as if he saw there a phantom injustice. "Oh, good thunder," he said, with an accent of despair. Thereupon, he relapsed into a mood of silence. He sombrely regarded his plate.

This demeanor speedily reduced his mother to meekness. When she spoke again it was in a conciliatory voice. "George, dear, won't yeh bring some sugar home t'-night?" It could be seen that she was asking for a crown of gold.

Kelcey aroused from his semi-slumber. "Yes, if I kin remember it," he said.

The little old woman arose to stow her son's lunch into the pail. When he had finished his breakfast he stalked for a time about the room in a dignified way. He put on his coat and hat, and taking his lunch-pail went to the door. There he halted, and without turning his head, stiffly said: "Well, good-by!"

The little old woman saw that she had offended her son. She did not seek an explanation. She was accustomed to these phenomena. She made haste to surrender.

"Ain't yeh goin' t' kiss me good-by," she asked in a little woful voice.

The youth made a pretence of going on, deaf-heartedly. He wore the dignity of an injured monarch.

Then the little old woman called again in forsaken accents: "George—George—ain't yeh goin' t' kiss me good by?" When he moved he found that she was hanging to his coattails.

He turned eventually with a murmur of a sort of tenderness. "Why, 'a course I am," he said. He kissed her. Withal there was an undertone of superiority in his voice, as if he were granting an astonishing suit. She looked at him with reproach and gratitude and affection.

She stood at the head of the stairs and watched his hand sliding along the rail as he went down. Occasionally she could see his arm and part of his shoulder. When he reached the first floor she called to him: "Good-by!"

The little old woman went back to her work in the kitchen with a frown of perplexity upon her brow. "I wonder what was th' matter with George this mornin'," she mused. "He didn't seem a bit like himself!"

As she trudged to and fro at her labor she began to speculate. She was much worried. She surmised in a vague way that he was a sufferer from a great internal disease. It was something no doubt that devoured the kidneys or quietly fed upon the lungs. Later, she imagined a woman, wicked and fair, who had fascinated him and was turning his life into a bitter thing. Her mind created many wondrous influences that were swooping like green dragons at him. They were changing him to a morose man, who suffered silently. She longed to discover them, that she might go bravely to the rescue of her heroic son. She knew that he, generous in his pain, would keep it from her. She racked her mind for knowledge.

However, when he came home at night he was extraordinarily blithe. He seemed to be a lad of ten. He capered all about the room. When she was bringing the coffee-pot from the stove to the table, he made show of waltzing with her so that she spilled some of the coffee. She was obliged to scold him.

All through the meal he made jokes. She occasionally was compelled to laugh, despite the fact that she believed that she should not laugh at her own son's jokes. She uttered reproofs at times, but he did not regard them.

"Golly," he said once, "I feel fine as silk. I didn't think I'd get over feelin' bad so quick. It—" He stopped abruptly.

During the evening he sat content. He smoked his pipe and read from an evening paper. She bustled about at her work. She seemed utterly happy with him there, lazily puffing out little clouds of smoke and giving frequent brilliant dissertations upon the news of the day. It seemed to her that she must be a model mother to have such a son, one who came home to her at night and sat contented, in a languor of the muscles after a good day's toil. She pondered upon the science of her management.

The week thereafter, too, she was joyous, for he stayed at home each night of it, and was sunny-tempered. She became convinced that she was a perfect mother, rearing a perfect son. There came often a love-light into her eyes. The wrinkled, yellow face frequently warmed into a smile of the kind that a maiden bestows upon him who to her is first and perhaps last.

VI

The little old woman habitually discouraged all outbursts of youthful vanity upon the part of her son. She feared that he would get to think too much of himself, and she knew that nothing could do more harm. Great self-esteem was always passive, she thought, and if he grew to regard his qualities of mind as forming a dazzling constellation, he would tranquilly sit still and not do those wonders she expected of him. So she was constantly on the alert to suppress even a shadow of such a thing. As for him he ruminated with the savage, vengeful bitterness of a young man, and decided that she did not comprehend him.

But despite her precautions he often saw that she believed him to be the most marvellous young man on the earth. He had only to look at those two eyes that became lighted with a glow from her heart whenever he did some excessively brilliant thing. On these occasions he could see her glance triumphantly at a neighbor, or whoever happened to be present. He grew to plan for these glances. And then he took a vast satisfaction in detecting and appropriating them.

Nevertheless, he could not understand why, directly after a scene of this kind, his mother was liable to call to him to hang his coat on the hook under the mantel, her voice in a key of despair as if he were negligent and stupid in what was, after all, the only important thing in life.

"If yeh'll only get in the habit of doin' it, it'll be jest as easy as throwin' it down anywheres," she would say to him. "When yeh pitch it down anywheres, somebody's got t' pick it up, an' that'll most likely be your poor ol' mother. Yeh can hang it up yerself, if yeh'll on'y think." This was intolerable. He usually went then and hurled his coat savagely at the hook. The correctness of her position was maddening.

It seemed to him that anyone who had a son of his glowing attributes should overlook the fact that he seldom hung up his coat. It was impossible to explain this situation to his mother. She was unutterably narrow. He grew sullen.

There came a time, too, that, even in all his mother's tremendous admiration for him, he did not entirely agree with her. He was delighted that she liked his great wit. He spurred himself to new and flashing effort because of this appreciation. But for the greater part he could see that his mother took pride in him in quite a different way from that in which he took pride in himself. She rejoiced at qualities in him that indicated that he was going to become a white and looming king among men. From these she made pictures in which he appeared as a benign personage, blessed by the filled hands of the poor, one whose brain could hold massive thoughts and awe certain men about whom she had read. She was fêted as the mother of this enormous man. These dreams were her solace. She spoke of them to no one because she knew that, worded, they would be ridiculous. But she dwelt with them, and they shed a radiance of gold upon her long days, her sorry labor. Upon the dead altars of her life she had builded the little fires of hope for another.

He had a complete sympathy for as much as he understood of these thoughts of his mother. They were so wise that he admired her foresight. As for himself, however, most of his dreams were of a nearer time. He had many of the distant future when he would be a man with a cloak of coldness concealing his gentleness and his faults, and of whom the men and, more particularly, the women, would think with reverence. He agreed with his mother that at that time he would go through the obstacles to other men like a flung stone. And then he would have power and he would enjoy having his bounty and his wrath alike fall swiftly upon those below. They would be awed. And above all he would mystify them.

But then his nearer dreams were a multitude. He had begun to look at the great world revolving near to his nose. He had a vast curiosity concerning this city in whose complexities he was buried. It was an impenetrable mystery, this city. It was a blend of many enticing colors. He longed to comprehend it completely, that he might walk understandingly in its greatest marvels, its mightiest march of life, its sin. He dreamed of a comprehension whose pay was the admirable attitude of a man of knowledge. He remembered Jones. He could not help but admire a man who knew so many bartenders.

VII

An indefinite woman was in all of Kelcey's dreams. As a matter of fact it was not he whom he pictured as wedding her. It was a vision of himself greater, finer, more terrible. It was himself as he expected to be. In scenes which he took mainly from pictures, this vision conducted a courtship, strutting, posing, and lying through a drama which was magnificent from glow of purple. In it he was icy, self-possessed; but she, the dreamgirl, was consumed by wild, torrential passion. He went to the length of having her display it before the people. He saw them wonder at his tranquillity. It amazed them infinitely to see him remain cold before the glory of this peerless woman's love. She was to him as beseeching for affection as a pet animal, but still he controlled appearances and none knew of his deep abiding love. Some day, at the critical romantic time, he was going to divulge it. In these long dreams there were accessories of castle-like houses, wide lands, servants, horses, clothes.

They began somewhere in his childhood. When he ceased to see himself as a stern general pointing a sword at the nervous and abashed horizon, he became this sublime king of a vague woman's heart. Later when he had read some books, it all achieved clearer expression. He was told in them that there was a goddess in the world whose business it was to wait until he should exchange a glance with her. It became a creed, subtly powerful. It saved discomfort for him and for several women who flitted by him. He used her as a standard.

Often he saw the pathos of her long wait, but his faith did not falter. The world was obliged to turn gold in time. His life was to be fine and heroic, else he would not have been born. He believed that the common-place lot was the sentence, the doom of certain people who did not know how to feel. His blood was a tender current of life. He thought that the usual should fall to others whose nerves were of lead. Occasionally be wondered how fate was going to begin in making an enormous figure of him; but he had no doubt of the result. A chariot of pink clouds was coming for him. His faith was his reason for existence. Meanwhile he could dream of the indefinite woman and the fragrance of roses that came from her hair.

One day he met Maggie Johnson on the stairs. She had a pail of beer in one hand and a brown-paper parcel under her arm. She glanced at him. He discovered that it would wither his heart to see another man signally successful in the smiles of her. And the glance that she gave him was so indifferent and so unresponsive to the sudden vivid admiration in his own eyes that he immediately concluded that she was magnificent in two ways.

As she came to the landing, the light from a window passed in a silver gleam over the girlish roundness of her cheek. It was a thing that he remembered.

He was silent for the most part at supper that night. He was particularly unkind when he did speak. His mother, observing him apprehensively, tried in vain to picture the new terrible catastrophe. She eventually concluded that he did not like the beef-stew. She put more salt in it.

He saw Maggie quite frequently after the meeting upon the stairs. He reconstructed his dreams and placed her in the full glory of that sun. The dream-woman, the goddess, pitched from her pedestal, lay prostrate, unheeded, save when he brought her forth to call her insipid and childish in the presence of his new religion.

He was relatively happy sometimes when Maggie's mother would get drunk and make terrific uproars. He used then to sit in the dark and make scenes in which he rescued the girl from her hideous environment.

He laid clever plans by which he encountered her in the halls, at the door, on the street. When he succeeded in meeting her he was always overcome by the thought that the whole thing was obvious to her. He could feel the shame of it burn his face and neck. To prove to her that she was mistaken he would turn away his head or regard her with a granite stare.

After a time he became impatient of the distance between them. He saw looming princes who would aim to seize her. Hours of his leisure and certain hours of his labor he spent in contriving. The shade of this girl was with him continually. With her he builded his grand dramas so that he trod in clouds, the matters of his daily life obscured and softened by a mist.

He saw that he need only break down the slight conventional barriers and she would soon discover his noble character. Sometimes he could see it all in his mind. It was very skilful. But then his courage flew away at the supreme moment. Perhaps the whole affair was humorous to her. Perhaps she was watching his mental contortions. She might laugh. He felt that he would then die or kill her. He could not approach the dread moment. He sank often from the threshold of knowledge. Directly after these occasions, it was his habit to avoid her to prove that she was a cipher to him.

He reflected that if he could only get a chance to rescue her from something, the whole tragedy would speedily unwind.

He met a young man in the halls one evening who said to him: "Say, me frien', where d' d' Johnson birds live in heh? I can't fin' me feet in dis bloomin' joint. I been battin' round heh fer a half-hour."

"Two flights up," said Kelcey stonily. He had felt a sudden quiver of his heart. The grandeur of the clothes, the fine worldly air, the experience, the self-reliance, the courage that shone in the countenance of this other young man made him suddenly sink to the depths of woe. He stood listening in the hall, flushing and ashamed of it, until he heard them coming down-stairs together. He slunk away then. It would have been a horror to him if she had discovered him there. She might have felt sorry for him.

They were going out to a show, perhaps. That pig of the world in his embroidered cloak was going to dazzle her with splendor. He mused upon how unrighteous it was for other men to dazzle women with splendor.

As he appreciated his handicap he swore with savage, vengeful bitterness. In his home his mother raised her voice in a high key of monotonous irritability. "Hang up yer coat, can't yeh, George?" she cried at him. "I can't go round after yeh all th' time. It's jest as easy t' hang it up as it is t' throw it down that way. Don't yeh ever git tired 'a hearin' me yell at yeh!"

"Yes," he exploded. In this word he put a profundity of sudden anger. He turned toward his mother a face, red, seamed, hard with hate and rage. They stared a moment in silence. Then she turned and staggered toward her room. Her hip struck violently against the corner of the table during this blind passage. A moment later the door closed.

Kelcey sank down in a chair with his legs thrust out straight and his hands deep in his trousers' pockets. His chin was forward upon his breast and his eyes stared before him. There swept over him all the self-pity that comes when the soul is turned back from a road.

VIII

During the next few days Kelcey suffered from his first gloomy conviction that the earth was not grateful to him for his presence upon it. When sharp words were said to him, he interpreted them with what seemed to be a lately acquired insight. He could now perceive that the universe hated him. He sank to the most sublime depths of despair.

One evening of this period he met Jones. The latter rushed upon him with enthusiasm. "Why, yer jest th' man I wanted t' see! I was comin' round t' your place t'-night. Lucky I met yeh! Ol' Bleecker's goin' t' give a blow-out t'-morrah night. Anything yeh want t' drink' All th' boys'll be there an' everything. He tol' me expressly that he wanted yeh t' be there. Great time! Great! Can yeh come?"

Kelcey grasped the other's hand with fervor. He felt now that there was some solacing friendship in space. "You bet I will, ol' man," he said, huskily. "I'd like nothin' better in th' world!"

As he walked home he thought that he was a very grim figure. He was about to taste the delicious revenge of a partial self-destruction. The universe would regret its position when it saw him drunk.

He was a little late in getting to Bleecker's lodging. He was delayed while his mother read aloud a letter from an old uncle, who wrote in one place: "God bless the boy! Bring him up to be the man his father was." Bleecker lived in an old three-storied house on a side-street. A Jewish tailor lived and worked in the front parlor, and old Bleecker lived in the back parlor. A German, whose family took care of the house, occupied the basement. Another German, with a wife and eight children, rented the dining-room. The two upper floors were inhabited by tailors, dressmakers, a pedler, and mysterious people who were seldom seen. The door of the little hall bedroom, at the foot of the second flight, was always open, and in there could be seen two bended men who worked at mending opera-glasses. The German woman in the dining-room was not friends with the little dressmaker in the rear room of the third floor, and frequently they yelled the vilest names up and down between the balusters. Each part of the woodwork was scratched and rubbed by the contact of innumerable persons. In one wall there was a long slit with chipped edges, celebrating the time when a man had thrown a hatchet at his wife. In the lower hall there was an eternal woman, with a rag and a pail of suds, who knelt over the worn oil-cloth. Old Bleecker felt that he had quite respectable and high-class apartments. He was glad to invite his friends.

Bleecker met Kelcey in the hall. He wore a collar that was cleaner and higher than his usual one. It changed his appearance greatly. He was now formidably aristocratic. "How are yeh, ol' man?" he shouted. He grasped Kelcey's arm, and, babbling jovially, conducted him down the hall and into the ex-parlor.

A group of standing men made vast shadows in the yellow glare of the lamp. They turned their heads as the two entered. "Why, hello, Kelcey, ol' man," Jones exclaimed, coming rapidly forward. "Good fer you! Glad yeh come! Yeh know O'Connor, 'a course! An' Schmidt! an' Woods! Then there's Zeusentell! Mr. Zeusentell—my friend Mr. Kelcey! Shake hands—both good fellows, damnitall! Then here is—oh, gentlemen, my friend Mr. Kelcey! A good fellow, he is, too! I've known 'im since I was a kid! Come, have a drink!" Everybody was excessively amiable. Kelcey felt that he had social standing. The strangers were cautious and respectful.

"By all means," said old Bleecker. "Mr. Kelcey, have a drink! An' by th' way, gentlemen, while we're about it, let's all have a drink!" There was much laughter. Bleecker was so droll at times.

With mild and polite gesturing they marched up to the table. There were upon it a keg of beer, a long row of whiskey bottles, a little heap of corn-cob pipes, some bags of tobacco, a box of cigars, and a mighty collection of glasses, cups, and mugs. Old Bleecker had arranged them so deftly that they resembled a primitive bar. There was considerable scuffling for possession of the cracked cups. Jones politely but vehemently insisted upon drinking from the worst of the assortment. He was quietly opposed by others. Everybody showed that they were awed by Bleecker's lavish hospitality. Their demeanors expressed their admiration at the cost of this entertainment.

Kelcey took his second mug of beer away to a corner and sat down with it. He wished to socially reconnoitre. Over in a corner a man was telling a story, in which at intervals he grunted like a pig. A half dozen men were listening. Two or three others sat alone in isolated places. They looked expectantly bright, ready to burst out cordially if anyone should address them. The row of bottles made quaint shadows upon the table, and upon a side-wall the keg of beer created a portentous black figure that reared toward the ceiling, hovering over the room and its inmates with spectral stature. Tobacco-smoke lay in lazy cloud-banks overhead.

Jones and O'Connor stayed near the table, occasionally being affable in all directions. Kelcey saw old Bleecker go to them and heard him whisper: "Come, we must git th' thing started. Git th' thing started." Kelcey saw that the host was fearing that all were not having a good time. Jones conferred with O'Connor and then O'Connor went to the man named Zeusentell. O'Connor evidently proposed something. Zeusentell refused at once. O'Connor beseeched. Zeusentell remained implacable. At last O'Connor broke off his argument, and going to the centre of the room, held up his hand. "Gentlemen," he shouted loudly, "we will now have a recitation by Mr. Zeusentell, entitled 'Patrick Clancy's Pig'!" He then glanced triumphantly at Zeusentell and said: "Come on!" Zeusentell had been twisting and making pantomimic appeals. He said, in a reproachful whisper: "You son of a gun."

The men turned their heads to glance at Zeusentell for a moment and then burst into a sustained clamor. "Hurray! Let 'er go! Come— give it t' us! Spring it! Spring it! Let it come!" As Zeusentell made no advances, they appealed personally. "Come, ol' man, let 'er go! Whatter yeh 'fraid of? Let 'er go! Go ahn! Hurry up!"

Zeusentell was protesting with almost frantic modesty. O'Connor took him by the lapel and tried to drag him; but he leaned back, pulling at his coat and shaking his head. "No, no, I don't know it, I tell yeh! I can't! I don't know it! I tell yeh I don't know it! I've forgotten it, I tell yeh! No—no—no—no. Ah, say, lookahere, le' go me, can't yeh? What's th' matter with yeh? I tell yeh I don't know it!" The men applauded violently. O'Connor did not relent. A little battle was waged until all of a sudden Zeusentell was seen to grow wondrously solemn. A hush fell upon the men. He was about to begin. He paused in the middle of the floor and nervously adjusted his collar and cravat. The audience became grave. "'Patrick Clancy's Pig,'" announced Zeusentell in a shrill, dry, unnatural tone. And then he began in rapid singsong:

"Patrick Clancy had a pig
Th' pride uv all th' nation,
The half uv him was half as big
As half uv all creation——"

When he concluded the others looked at each other to convey their appreciation. They then wildly clapped their hands or tinkled their glasses. As Zeusentell went toward his seat a man leaned over and asked: "Can yeh tell me where I kin git that." He had made a great success. After an enormous pressure he was induced to recite two more tales. Old Bleecker finally led him forward and pledged him in a large drink. He declared that they were the best things he had ever heard.

The efforts of Zeusentell imparted a gayety to the company. The men having laughed together were better acquainted, and there was now a universal topic. Some of the party, too, began to be quite drunk.

The invaluable O'Connor brought forth a man who could play the mouth-organ. The latter, after wiping his instrument upon his coat-sleeve, played all the popular airs. The men's heads swayed to and fro in the clouded smoke. They grinned and beat time with their feet. A valor, barbaric and wild, began to show in their poses and in their faces, red and glistening from perspiration. The conversation resounded in a hoarse roar. The beer would not run rapidly enough for Jones, so he remained behind to tilt the keg. This caused the black shadow on the wall to retreat and advance, sinking mystically to loom forward again with sudden menace, a huge dark figure controlled, as by some unknown emotion. The glasses, mugs, and cups travelled swift and regular, catching orange reflections from the lamp-light. Two or three men were grown so careless that they were continually spilling their drinks. Old Bleecker, cackling with pleasure, seized time to glance triumphantly at Jones. His party was going to be a success.

IX

Of a sudden Kelcey felt the buoyant thought that he was having a good time. He was all at once an enthusiast, as if he were at a festival of a religion. He felt that there was something fine and thrilling in this affair isolated from a stern world, and from which the laughter arose like incense. He knew that old sentiment of brotherly regard for those about him. He began to converse tenderly with them. He was not sure of his drift of thought, but he knew that he was immensely sympathetic. He rejoiced at their faces, shining red and wrinkled with smiles. He was capable of heroisms.

His pipe irritated him by going out frequently. He was too busy in amiable conversations to attend to it. When he arose to go for a match he discovered that his legs were a trifle uncertain under him. They bended and did not precisely obey his intent. At the table he lit a match and then, in laughing at a joke made near him, forgot to apply it to the bowl of his pipe. He succeeded with the next match after annoying trouble. He swayed so that the match would appear first on one side of the bowl and then on the other. At last he happily got it directly over the tobacco. He had burned his fingers. He inspected them, laughing vaguely.

Jones came and slapped him on the shoulder. "Well, ol' man, let's take a drink fer ol' Handyville's sake!"

Kelcey was deeply affected. He looked at Jones with moist eyes. "I'll go yeh," he said. With an air of profound melancholy, Jones poured out some whiskey. They drank reverently. They exchanged a glistening look of tender recollections and then went over to where Bleecker was telling a humorous story to a circle of giggling listeners. The old man sat like a fat, jolly god. "——and just at that moment th' old woman put her head out of th' window an' said: 'Mike, yez lezy divil, fer phwat do yez be slapin' in me new geranium bid?' An' Mike woke up an' said: 'Domn a wash-woman thot do niver wash her own bidclues. Here do I be slapin' in nothin' but dhirt an' wades.'" The men slapped their knees, roaring loudly. They begged him to tell another. A clamor of comment arose concerning the anecdote, so that when old Bleecker began a fresh one nobody was heeding.

It occurred to Jones to sing. Suddenly he burst forth with a ballad that had a rippling waltz movement, and seizing Kelcey, made a furious attempt to dance. They sprawled over a pair of outstretched legs and pitched headlong. Kelcey fell with a yellow crash. Blinding lights flashed before his vision. But he arose immediately, laughing. He did not feel at all hurt. The pain in his head was rather pleasant.

Old Bleecker, O'Connor, and Jones, who now limped and drew breath through his teeth, were about to lead him with much care and tenderness to the table for another drink, but he laughingly pushed them away and went unassisted. Bleecker told him: "Great Gawd, your head struck hard enough t' break a trunk."

He laughed again, and with a show of steadiness and courage he poured out an extravagant portion of whiskey. With cold muscles he put it to his lips and drank it. It chanced that this addition dazed him like a powerful blow. A moment later it affected him with blinding and numbing power. Suddenly unbalanced, he felt the room sway. His blurred sight could only distinguish a tumbled mass of shadow through which the beams from the light ran like swords of flame. The sound of the many voices was to him like the roar of a distant river. Still, he felt that if he could only annul the force of these million winding fingers that gripped his senses, he was capable of most brilliant and entertaining things.

He was at first of the conviction that his feelings were only temporary. He waited for them to pass away, but the mental and physical pause only caused a new reeling and swinging of the room. Chasms with inclined approaches were before him; peaks leaned toward him. And withal he was blind and numb with surprise. He understood vaguely in his stupefaction that it would disgrace him to fall down a chasm.

At last he perceived a shadow, a form, which he knew to be Jones. The adorable Jones, the supremely wise Jones, was walking in this strange land without fear or care, erect and tranquil. Kelcey murmured in admiration and affection, and fell toward his friend. Jones's voice sounded as from the shores of the unknown. "Come, come, ol' man, this will never do. Brace up." It appeared after all that Jones was not wholly wise. "Oh, I'm—all ri' Jones! I'm all ri'! I wan' shing song! Tha's all! I wan' shing song!"

Jones was stupid. "Come now, sit down an' shut up."

It made Kelcey burn with fury. "Jones, le' me alone, I tell yeh! Le' me alone! I wan' shing song er te' story! G'l'm'n, I lovsh girl live down my shtreet. Thash reason 'm drunk, 'tis! She——"

Jones seized him and dragged him toward a chair. He heard him laugh. He could not endure these insults from his friend. He felt blazing desire to strangle his companion. He threw out his hand violently, but Jones grappled him close and he was no more than dried leaf. He was amazed to find that Jones possessed the strength of twenty horses. He was forced skilfully to the floor.

As he lay, he reflected in great astonishment upon Jones's muscle. It was singular that he had never before discovered it. The whole incident had impressed him immensely. An idea struck him that he might denounce Jones for it. It would be a sage thing. There would be a thrilling and dramatic moment in which he would dazzle all the others. But at this moment he was assailed by a mighty desire to sleep. Sombre and soothing clouds of slumber were heavily upon him. He closed his eyes with a sigh that was yet like that of a babe.

When he awoke, there was still the battleful clamor of the revel. He half arose with a plan of participating, when O'Connor came and pushed him down again, throwing out his chin in affectionate remonstrance and saying, "Now, now," as to a child.

The change that had come over these men mystified Kelcey in great degree. He had never seen anything so vastly stupid as their idea of his state. He resolved to prove to them that they were dealing with one whose mind was very clear. He kicked and squirmed in O'Connor's arms, until, with a final wrench, he scrambled to his feet and stood tottering in the middle of the room. He would let them see that he had a strangely lucid grasp of events. "G'l'm'n, I lovsh girl! I ain' drunker'n yeh all are! She——"

He felt them hurl him to a corner of the room and pile chairs and tables upon him until he was bundled beneath a stupendous mountain. Far above, as up a mine's shaft, there were voices, lights, and vague figures. He was not hurt physically, but his feelings were unutterably injured. He, the brilliant, the good, the sympathetic had been thrust fiendishly from the party. They had had the comprehension of red lobsters. It was an unspeakable barbarism. Tears welled piteously from his eyes. He planned long diabolical explanations!

X

At first the gray lights of dawn came timidly into the room, remaining near the windows, afraid to approach certain sinister corners. Finally, mellow streams of sunshine poured in, undraping the shadows to disclose the putrefaction, making pitiless revelation. Kelcey awoke with a groan of undirected misery. He tossed his stiffened arms about his head for a moment and then leaning heavily upon his elbow stared blinking at his environment. The grim truthfulness of the day showed disaster and death. After the tumults of the previous night the interior of this room resembled a decaying battle-field. The air hung heavy and stifling with the odors of tobacco, men's breaths, and beer half filling forgotten glasses. There was ruck of broken tumblers, pipes, bottles, spilled tobacco, cigar stumps. The chairs and tables were pitched this way and that way, as after some terrible struggle. In the midst of it all lay old Bleecker stretched upon a couch in deepest sleep, as abandoned in attitude, as motionless, as ghastly as if it were a corpse that had been flung there.

A knowledge of the thing came gradually into Kelcey's eyes. He looked about him with an expression of utter woe, regret, and loathing. He was compelled to lie down again. A pain above his eyebrows was like that from an iron-clamp.

As he lay pondering, his bodily condition created for him a bitter philosophy, and he perceived all the futility of a red existence. He saw his life problems confronting him like granite giants and he was no longer erect to meet them. He had made a calamitous retrogression in his war. Spectres were to him now as large as clouds.

Inspired by the pitiless ache in his head, he was prepared to reform and live a white life. His stomach informed him that a good man was the only being who was wise. But his perception of his future was hopeless. He was aghast at the prospect of the old routine. It was impossible. He trembled before its exactions.

Turning toward the other way, he saw that the gold portals of vice no longer enticed him. He could not hear the strains of alluring music. The beckoning sirens of drink had been killed by this pain in his head. The desires of his life suddenly lay dead like mullein stalks.[1] Upon reflection, he saw, therefore, that he was perfectly willing to be virtuous if somebody would come and make it easy for him.

When he stared over at old Bleecker, he felt a sudden contempt and dislike for him. He considered him to be a tottering old beast. It was disgusting to perceive aged men so weak in sin. He dreaded to see him awaken lest he should be required to be somewhat civil to him.

Kelcey wished for a drink of water. For some time he had dreamed of the liquid, deliciously cool. It was an abstract, uncontained thing that poured upon him and tumbled him, taking away his pain like a kind of surgery. He arose and staggered slowly toward a little sink in a corner of the room. He understood that any rapid movement might cause his head to split.

The little sink was filled with a chaos of broken glass and spilled liquids. A sight of it filled him with horror, but he rinsed a glass with scrupulous care, and filling it, took an enormous drink. The water was an intolerable disappointment. It was insipid and weak to his scorched throat and not at all cool. He put down the glass with a gesture of despair. His face became fixed in the stony and sullen expression of a man who waits for the recuperative power of morrows.

---

[1] A plant with woolly leaves and tall yellow flowers.

Old Bleecker awakened. He rolled over and groaned loudly. For awhile he thrashed about in a fury of displeasure at his bodily stiffness and pain. Kelcey watched him as he would have watched a death agony. "Good Gawd," said the old man, "beer an' whiskey make th' devil of a mix. Did yeh see th' fight?"

"No," said Kelcey, stolidly.

"Why, Zeusentell an' O'Connor had a great old mill. They were scrappin' all over th' place. I thought we were all goin' t' get pulled. Thompson, that fellah over in th' corner, though, he sat down on th' whole business. He was a dandy! He had t' poke Zeusentell! He was a bird! Lord, I wish I had a Manhattan!"[1]

Kelcey remained in bitter silence while old Bleecker dressed. "Come an' get a cocktail," said the latter briskly. This was part of his aristocracy. He was the only man of them who knew much about cocktails. He perpetually referred to them. "It'll brace yeh right up! Come along! Say, you get full too soon. You oughter wait until later, me boy! You're too speedy!" Kelcey wondered vaguely where his companion had lost his zeal for polished sentences, his iridescent mannerisms.

"Come along," said Bleecker.

Kelcey made a movement of disdain for cocktails, but he followed the other to the street. At the corner they separated. Kelcey attempted a friendly parting smile and then went on up the street. He had to reflect to know that he was erect and using his own muscles in walking. He felt like a man of paper, blown by the winds. Withal, the dust of the avenue was galling to his throat, eyes, and nostrils, and the roar of traffic cracked his head. He was glad, however, to be alone, to be rid of old Bleecker. The sight of him had been as the contemplation of a disease.

His mother was not at home. In his little room he mechanically undressed and bathed his head, arms, and shoulders. When he crawled between the two white sheets he felt a first lifting of his misery. His pillow was soothingly soft. There was an effect that was like the music of tender voices.

When he awoke again his mother was bending over him giving vent to alternate cries of grief and joy. Her hands trembled so that they were useless to her. "Oh, George, George, where have yeh been? What has happened t' yeh? Oh, George, I've been so worried! I didn't sleep a wink all night."

Kelcey was instantly wide awake. With a moan of suffering he turned his face to the wall before he spoke. "Never mind, mother, I'm all right.

---

[1] A cocktail made from vermouth and a spirit.

Don't fret now! I was knocked down by a truck last night in th' street, an' they took me t' th' hospital; but it's all right now. I got out jest a little while ago. They told me I'd better go home an' rest up."

His mother screamed in pity, horror, joy, and self-reproach for something unknown. She frenziedly demanded the details. He sighed with unutterable weariness. "Oh—wait—wait—wait," he said shutting his eyes as from the merciless monotony of a pain. "Wait—wait—please wait. I can't talk now. I want t' rest."

His mother condemned herself with a little cry. She adjusted his pillow, her hands shaking with love and tenderness. "There, there don't mind, dearie! But yeh can't think how worried I was—an' crazy. I was near frantic. I went down t' th' shop, an' they said they hadn't seen anything 'a yeh there. The foreman was awful good t' me. He said he'd come up this afternoon t' see if yeh had come home yet. He tol' me not t' worry. Are yeh sure yer all right? Ain't there anythin' I kin git fer yeh? What did th' docter say?"

Kelcey's patience was worn. He gestured, and then spoke querulously. "Now—now—mother, it's all right, I tell yeh! All I need is a little rest an' I'll be as well as ever. But it makes it all th' worse if yeh stand there an' ask me questions an' make me think. Jest leave me alone fer a little while, an' I'll be as well as ever. Can't yeh do that?"

The little old woman puckered her lips funnily. "My, what an old bear th' boy is!" She kissed him blithely. Presently she went out, upon her face a bright and glad smile that must have been a reminiscence of some charming girlhood.

XI

At one time Kelcey had a friend who was struck in the head by the pole of a truck and knocked senseless. He was taken to the hospital, from which he emerged in the morning an astonished man, with rather a dim recollection of the accident. He used to hold an old brier-wood pipe in his teeth in a manner peculiar to himself, and, with a brown derby hat tilted back on his head, recount his strange sensations. Kelcey had always remembered it as a bit of curious history. When his mother cross-examined him in regard to the accident, he told this story with barely a variation. Its truthfulness was incontestable.

At the shop he was welcomed on the following day with considerable enthusiasm. The foreman had told the story and there were already jokes created concerning it. Mike O'Donnell, whose wit was famous, had planned a humorous campaign, in which he made charges against Kelcey, which were, as a matter of fact, almost the exact truth. Upon hearing it, Kelcey looked at him suddenly from the corners of his eyes, but otherwise remained imperturbable. O'Donnell eventually despaired. "Yez can't goiy[1] that kid! He tekes ut all loike mate an' dhrink." Kelcey often told the story, his pipe held in his teeth peculiarly, and his derby tilted back on his head.

He remained at home for several evenings, content to read the papers and talk with his mother. She began to look around for the tremendous reason for it. She suspected that his nearness to death in the recent accident had sobered his senses and made him think of high things. She mused upon it continually. When he sat moodily pondering she watched him. She said to herself that she saw the light breaking in upon his spirit. She felt that it was a very critical period of his existence. She resolved to use all her power and skill to turn his eyes toward the lights in the sky. Accordingly she addressed him one evening. "Come, go t' prayer-meetin' t'-night with me, will yeh, George?" It sounded more blunt than she intended.

He glanced at her in sudden surprise. "Huh?"

As she repeated her request, her voice quavered. She felt that it was a supreme moment. "Come, go t' prayer-meetin' t' night, won't yeh?"

He seemed amazed. "Oh, I don't know," he began. He was fumbling in his mind for a reason for refusing. "I don't wanta go. I'm tired as th' dickens!" His obedient shoulders sank down languidly. His head mildly drooped.

The little old woman, with a quick perception of her helplessness, felt a motherly rage at her son. It was intolerable that she could not impart motion to him in a chosen direction. The waves of her desires were puny against the rocks of his indolence. She had a great wish to beat him. "I don't know what I'm ever goin' t' do with yeh," she told him, in a choking voice. "Yeh won't do anything I ask yeh to. Yeh never pay th' least bit 'a attention t' what I say. Yeh don't mind me any more than yeh would a fly. Whatever am I goin' t' do with yeh?" She faced him in a battleful way, her eyes blazing with a sombre light of despairing rage.

He looked up at her ironically. "I don't know," he said, with calmness. "What are yeh?" He had traced her emotions and seen her fear of his rebellion. He thrust out his legs in the easy scorn of a rapier-bravo. "What are yeh?"

---

[1]   Guy, ridicule.

The little old woman began to weep. They were tears without a shame of grief. She allowed them to run unheeded down her cheeks. As she stared into space her son saw her regarding there the powers and influences that she had held in her younger life. She was in some way acknowledging to fate that she was now but withered grass, with no power but the power to feel the winds. He was smitten with a sudden shame. Besides, in the last few days he had gained quite a character for amiability. He saw something grand in relenting at this point. "Well," he said, trying to remove a sulky quality from his voice, "well, if yer bound t' have me go, I s'pose I'll have t' go."

His mother, with strange, immobile face, went to him and kissed him on the brow. "All right, George!" There was in her wet eyes an emotion which he could not fathom.

She put on her bonnet and shawl, and they went out together. She was unusually silent, and made him wonder why she did not appear gleeful at his coming. He was resentful because she did not display more appreciation of his sacrifice. Several times he thought of halting and refusing to go farther, to see if that would not wring from her some acknowledgment.

In a dark street the little chapel sat humbly between two towering apartment-houses. A red street-lamp stood in front. It threw a marvellous reflection upon the wet pavements. It was like the death-stain of a spirit. Farther up the brilliant lights of an avenue made a span of gold across the black street. A roar of wheels and a clangor of bells came from this point, interwoven into a sound emblematic of the life of the city. It seemed somehow to affront this solemn and austere little edifice. It suggested an approaching barbaric invasion. The little church, pierced, would die with a fine, illimitable scorn for its slayers.

When Kelcey entered with his mother he felt a sudden quaking. His knees shook. It was an awesome place to him. There was a menace in the red padded carpet and the leather doors, studded with little brass tacks that penetrated his soul with their pitiless glances. As for his mother, she had acquired such a new air that he would have been afraid to address her. He felt completely alone and isolated at this formidable time.

There was a man in the vestibule who looked at them blandly. From within came the sound of singing. To Kelcey there was a million voices. He dreaded the terrible moment when the doors should swing back. He wished to recoil, but at that instant the bland man pushed the doors aside and he followed his mother up the center aisle of the little chapel. To him there was a riot of lights that made him transparent. The multitudinous pairs of eyes that turned toward him were implacable in their cool valuations.

They had just ceased singing. He who conducted the meeting motioned that the services should wait until the new-comers found seats. The little old woman went slowly on toward the first rows. Occasionally she paused to scrutinize vacant places, but they did not seem to meet her requirements. Kelcey was in agony. He thought the moment of her decision would never come. In his unspeakable haste he walked a little faster than his mother. Once she paused to glance in her calculating way at some seats and he forged ahead. He halted abruptly and returned, but by that time she had resumed her thoughtful march up the aisle. He could have assassinated her. He felt that everybody must have seen his torture, during which his hands were to him like monstrous swollen hides. He was wild with a rage in which his lips turned slightly livid. He was capable of doing some furious, unholy thing.

When the little old woman at last took a seat, her son sat down beside her slowly and stiffly. He was opposing his strong desire to drop.

When from the mists of his shame and humiliation the scene came before his vision, he was surprised to find that all eyes were not fastened upon his face. The leader of the meeting seemed to be the only one who saw him. He stared gravely, solemnly, regretfully. He was a pale-faced, but plump young man in a black coat that buttoned to his chin. It was evident to Kelcey that his mother had spoken of him to the young clergyman, and that the latter was now impressing upon him the sorrow caused by the contemplation of his sin. Kelcey hated the man.

A man seated alone over in a corner began to sing. He closed his eyes and threw back his head. Others, scattered sparsely throughout the innumerable light-wood chairs, joined him as they caught the air. Kelcey heard his mother's frail, squeaking soprano. The chandelier in the centre was the only one lighted, and far at the end of the room one could discern the pulpit swathed in gloom, solemn and mystic as a bier. It was surrounded by vague shapes of darkness on which at times was the glint of brass, or of glass that shone like steel, until one could feel there the presence of the army of the unknown, possessors of the great eternal truths, and silent listeners at this ceremony. High up, the stained-glass windows loomed in leaden array like dull-hued banners, merely catching occasional splashes of dark wine-color from the lights. Kelcey fell to brooding concerning this indefinable presence which he felt in a church.

One by one people arose and told little tales of their religious faith. Some were tearful and others calm, emotionless, and convincing. Kelcey listened closely for a time. These people filled him with a great curiosity. He was not familiar with their types.

At last the young clergyman spoke at some length. Kelcey was amazed, because, from the young man's appearance, he would not have suspected him of being so glib; but the speech had no effect on Kelcey, excepting to prove to him again that he was damned.

XII

Kelcey sometimes wondered whether he liked beer. He had been obliged to cultivate a talent for imbibing it. He was born with an abhorrence which he had steadily battled until it had come to pass that he could drink from ten to twenty glasses of beer without the act of swallowing causing him to shiver. He understood that drink was an essential to joy, to the coveted position of a man of the world and of the streets. The saloons contained the mystery of a street for him. When he knew its saloons he comprehended the street. Drink and its surroundings were the eyes of a superb green dragon to him. He followed a fascinating glitter, and the glitter required no explanation.

Directly after old Bleecker's party he almost reformed. He was tired and worn from the tumult of it, and he saw it as one might see a skeleton emerged from a crimson cloak. He wished then to turn his face away. Gradually, however, he recovered his mental balance. Then he admitted again by his point of view that the thing was not so terrible. His headache had caused him to exaggerate. A drunk was not the blight which he had once remorsefully named it. On the contrary, it was a mere unpleasant incident. He resolved, however, to be more cautious.

When prayer-meeting night came again his mother approached him hopefully. She smiled like one whose request is already granted. "Well, will yeh go t' prayer-meetin' with me t'-night again?"

He turned toward her with eloquent suddenness, and then riveted his eyes upon a corner of the floor. "Well, I guess not," he said.

His mother tearfully tried to comprehend his state of mind. "What has come over yeh?" she said, tremblingly. "Yeh never used t' be this way, George. Yeh never used t' be so cross an' mean t'me——"

"Oh, I ain't cross an' mean t' yeh," he interpolated, exasperated and violent.

"Yes, yeh are, too! I ain't hardly had a decent word from yeh in ever so long. Yet as cross an' as mean as yeh can be. I don't know what t' make of it. It can't be——" There came a look in her eyes that told that she was going to shock and alarm him with her heaviest sentence—"it can't be that yeh've got t' drinkin'."

Kelcey grunted with disgust at the ridiculous thing. "Why, what an old goose yer gettin' t' be."

She was compelled to laugh a little, as a child laughs between tears at a hurt. She had not been serious. She was only trying to display to him how she regarded his horrifying mental state. "Oh, of course, I didn't mean that, but I think yeh act jest as bad as if yeh did drink. I wish yeh would do better, George!"

She had grown so much less frigid and stern in her censure that Kelcey seized the opportunity to try to make a joke of it. He laughed at her, but she shook her head and continued: "I do wish yeh would do better. I don't know what's t' become 'a yeh, George. Yeh don't mind what I say no more 'n if I was th' wind in th' chimbly. Yeh don't care about nothin' 'cept goin' out nights. I can't ever get yeh t' prayer-meetin' ner church; yeh never go out with me anywheres unless yeh can't get out of it; yeh swear an' take on sometimes like everything, yeh never——"

He gestured wrathfully in interruption. "Say, lookahere, can't yeh think 'a something I do?"

She ended her oration then in the old way. "An' I don't know what's goin' t' become 'a yeh."

She put on her bonnet and shawl and then came and stood near him, expectantly. She imparted to her attitude a subtle threat of unchangeableness. He pretended to be engrossed in his newspaper. The little swaggering clock on the mantel became suddenly evident, ticking with loud monotony. Presently she said, firmly: "Well, are yeh comin'?"

He was reading.

"Well, are yeh comin'?"

He threw his paper down, angrily. "Oh, why don't yeh go on an' leave me alone?" he demanded in supreme impatience. "What do yeh wanta pester me fer? Yeh'd think there was robbers. Why can't yeh go alone er else stay home? You wanta go an' I don't wanta go, an' yeh keep all time tryin' t' drag me. Yeh know I don't wanta go." He concluded in a last defiant wounding of her. "What do I care 'bout those ol' bags-'a-wind anyhow? They gimme a pain!"

His mother turned her face and went from him. He sat staring with a mechanical frown. Presently he went and picked up his newspaper.

Jones told him that night that everybody had had such a good time at old Bleecker's party that they were going to form a club. They waited at the little smiling saloon, and then amid much enthusiasm all signed a membership-roll. Old Bleecker, late that night, was violently elected president. He made speeches of thanks and gratification during the remainder of the meeting. Kelcey went home rejoicing. He felt that at any rate he would have true friends. The dues were a dollar for each week.

He was deeply interested. For a number of evenings he fairly gobbled his supper in order that he might be off to the little smiling saloon to discuss the new organization. All the men were wildly enthusiastic. One night the saloon-keeper announced that he would donate half the rent of quite a large room over his saloon. It was an occasion for great cheering. Kelcey's legs were like whalebone when he tried to go upstairs upon his return home, and the edge of each step was moved curiously forward.

His mother's questions made him snarl. "Oh, nowheres!" At other times he would tell her: "Oh, t' see some friends 'a mine! Where d' yeh s'pose?"

Finally, some of the women of the tenement concluded that the little old mother had a wild son. They came to condole with her. They sat in the kitchen for hours. She told them of his wit, his cleverness, his kind heart.

XIII

At a certain time Kelcey discovered that some young men who stood in the cinders between a brick wall and the pavement, and near the side-door of a corner saloon, knew more about life than other people. They used to lean there smoking and chewing, and comment upon events and persons. They knew the neighborhood extremely well. They debated upon small typical things that transpired before them until they had extracted all the information that existence contained. They sometimes inaugurated little fights with foreigners or well-dressed men. It was here that Sapristi Glielmi, the pedler, stabbed Pete Brady to death, for which he got a life-sentence. Each patron of the saloon was closely scrutinized as he entered the place.

Sometimes they used to throng upon the heels of a man and in at the bar assert that he had asked them in to drink. When he objected, they would claim with one voice that it was too deep an insult and gather about to thrash him. When they had caught chance customers and absolute strangers, the barkeeper had remained in stolid neutrality, ready to serve one or seven, but two or three times they had encountered the wrong men. Finally, the proprietor had come out one morning and told them, in the fearless way of his class, that their pastime must cease. "It quits right here! See? Right here! Th' nex' time yeh try t' work it, I come with th' bung-starter, an' th' mugs I miss with it git pulled. See? It quits!" Infrequently, however, men did ask them in to drink.

The policeman of that beat grew dignified and shrewd whenever he approached this corner. Sometimes he stood with his hands behind his back and cautiously conversed with them. It was understood on both sides that it was a good thing to be civil.

In winter this band, a trifle diminished in numbers, huddled in their old coats and stamped little flat places in the snow, their faces turned always toward the changing life in the streets. In the summer they became more lively. Sometimes, then, they walked out to the curb to look up and down the street. Over in a trampled vacant lot, surrounded by high tenement-houses, there was a sort of a den among some bowlders. An old truck was made to form a shelter. The small hoodlums of that vicinity all avoided the spot. So many of them had been thrashed upon being caught near it. It was the summer-time lounging-place of the band from the corner.

They were all too clever to work. Some of them had worked, but these used their experiences as stores from which to draw tales. They were like veterans with their wars. One lad in particular used to recount how he whipped his employer, the proprietor of a large grain and feed establishment. He described his victim's features and form and clothes with minute exactness. He bragged of his wealth and social position. It had been a proud moment of the lad's life. He was like a savage who had killed a great chief.

Their feeling for contemporaneous life was one of contempt. Their philosophy taught that in a large part the whole thing was idle and a great bore. With fine scorn they sneered at the futility of it. Work was done by men who had not the courage to stand still and let the skies clap together if they willed.

The vast machinery of the popular law indicated to them that there were people in the world who wished to remain quiet. They awaited the moment when they could prove to them that a riotous upheaval, a cloud-burst of destruction would be a delicious thing. They thought of their fingers buried in the lives of these people. They longed dimly for a time when they could run through decorous streets with crash and roar of war, an army of revenge for pleasures long possessed by others, a wild sweeping compensation for their years without crystal and gilt, women and wine. This thought slumbered in them, as the image of Rome might have lain small in the hearts of the barbarians.

Kelcey respected these youths so much that he ordinarily used the other side of the street. He could not go near to them, because if a passerby minded his own business he was a disdainful prig and had insulted them; if he showed that he was aware of them they were likely to resent his not minding his own business and prod him into a fight if the opportunity were good. Kelcey longed for their acquaintance and friendship, for with it came social safety and ease; they were respected so universally.

Once in another street Fidsey Corcoran was whipped by a short, heavy man. Fidsey picked himself up, and in the fury of defeat hurled pieces of brick at his opponent. The short man dodged with skill and then pursued Fidsey for over a block. Sometimes he got near enough to punch him. Fidsey raved in maniacal fury. The moment the short man would attempt to resume his own affairs, Fidsey would turn upon him again, tears and blood upon his face, with the lashed rage of a vanquished animal. The short man used to turn about, swear madly, and make little dashes. Fidsey always ran and then returned as pursuit ceased. The short man apparently wondered if this maniac was ever going to allow him to finish whipping him. He looked helplessly up and down the street. People were there who knew Fidsey, and they remonstrated with him; but he continued to confront the short man, gibbering like a wounded ape, using all the eloquence of the street in his wild oaths.

Finally the short man was exasperated to black fury. He decided to end the fight. With low snarls, ominous as death, he plunged at Fidsey.

Kelcey happened there then. He grasped the short man's shoulder. He cried out in the peculiar whine of the man who interferes. "Oh, hol' on! Yeh don't wanta hit 'im any more! Yeh've done enough to 'im now! Leave 'im be!"

The short man wrenched and tugged. He turned his face until his teeth were almost at Kelcey's cheek: "Le' go me! Le' go me, you——" The rest of his sentence was screamed curses.

Kelcey's face grew livid from fear, but he somehow managed to keep his grip. Fidsey, with but an instant's pause, plunged into the new fray.

They beat the short man. They forced him against a high boardfence where for a few seconds their blows sounded upon his head in swift thuds. A moment later Fidsey descried a running policeman. He made off, fleet as a shadow. Kelcey noted his going. He ran after him.

Three or four blocks away they halted. Fidsey said: "I'd 'a licked dat big stuff in 'bout a minute more," and wiped the blood from his eyes.

At the gang's corner, they asked: "Who soaked yeh, Fidsey?" His description was burning. Everybody laughed. "Where is 'e now?" Later they began to question Kelcey. He recited a tale in which he allowed himself to appear prominent and redoubtable. They looked at him then as if they thought he might be quite a man.

Once when the little old woman was going out to buy something for her son's supper, she discovered him standing at the side-door of the saloon engaged intimately with Fidsey and the others. She slunk away, for she understood that it would be a terrible thing to confront him and his pride there with youths who were superior to mothers.

When he arrived home he threw down his hat with a weary sigh, as if he had worked long hours, but she attacked him before he had time to complete the falsehood. He listened to her harangue with a curled lip. In defence he merely made a gesture of supreme exasperation. She never understood the advanced things in life. He felt the hopelessness of ever making her comprehend. His mother was not modern.

XIV

The little old woman arose early and bustled in the preparation of breakfast. At times she looked anxiously at the clock. An hour before her son should leave for work she went to his room and called him in the usual tone of sharpness, "George! George!"

A sleepy growl came to her.

"Come, come it's time t' git up," she continued. "Come now, git right up!"

Later she went again to the door. "George, are yeh gittin' up?"

"Huh?"

"Are yeh gittin' up?"

"Yes, I'll git right up!" He had introduced a valor into his voice which she detected to be false. She went to his bedside and took him by the shoulder. "George—George—git up!"

From the mist-lands of sleep he began to protest incoherently. "Oh, le' me be, won' yeh? 'M sleepy!"

She continued to shake him. "Well, it's time t' git up. Come—come—come on, now."

Her voice, shrill with annoyance, pierced his ears in a slender, piping thread of sound. He turned over on the pillow to bury his head in his arms. When he expostulated, his tones came half-smothered. "Oh le' me be, can't yeh? There's plenty 'a time! Jest fer ten minutes! 'M sleepy!"

She was implacable. "No, yeh must git up now! Yeh ain't got more 'n time enough t' eat yer breakfast an' git t' work."

Eventually he arose, sullen and grumbling. Later he came to his breakfast, blinking his dry eyelids, his stiffened features set in a mechanical scowl.

Each morning his mother went to his room, and fought a battle to arouse him. She was like a soldier. Despite his pleadings, his threats, she remained at her post, imperturbable and unyielding.

These affairs assumed large proportions in his life. Sometimes he grew beside himself with a bland, unformulated wrath. The whole thing was a consummate imposition. He felt that he was being cheated of his sleep. It was an injustice to compel him to arise morning after morning with bitter regularity, before the sleep-gods had at all loosened their grasp. He hated that unknown force which directed his life.

One morning he swore a tangled mass of oaths, aimed into the air, as if the injustice poised there. His mother flinched at first; then her mouth set in the little straight line. She saw that the momentous occasion had come. It was the time of the critical battle. She turned upon him valorously. "Stop your swearin', George Kelcey. I won't have yeh talk so before me! I won't have it! Stop this minute! Not another word! Do yeh think I'll allow yeh t' swear b'fore me like that? Not another word! I won't have it! I declare I won't have it another minute!"

At first her projected words had slid from his mind as if striking against ice, but at last he heeded her. His face grew sour with passion and misery. He spoke in tones dark with dislike. "Th' 'ell yeh won't? Whatter yeh goin' t' do 'bout it?" Then, as if he considered that he had not been sufficiently impressive, he arose and slowly walked over to her. Having arrived at point-blank range he spoke again. "Whatter yeh goin't' do 'bout it?" He regarded her then with an unaltering scowl, albeit his mien was as dark and cowering as that of a condemned criminal.

She threw out her hands in the gesture of an impotent one. He was acknowledged victor. He took his hat and slowly left her.

For three days they lived in silence. He brooded upon his mother's agony and felt a singular joy in it. As opportunity offered, he did little despicable things. He was going to make her abject. He was now uncontrolled, ungoverned; he wished to be an emperor. Her suffering was all a sort of compensation for his own dire pains.

She went about with a gray, impassive face. It was as if she had survived a massacre in which all that she loved had been torn from her by the brutality of savages.

One evening at six he entered and stood looking at his mother as she peeled potatoes. She had hearkened to his coming listlessly, without emotion, and at his entrance she did not raise her eyes.

"Well, I'm fired," he said, suddenly.

It seemed to be the final blow. Her body gave a convulsive movement in the chair. When she finally lifted her eyes, horror possessed her face. Her under jaw had fallen. "Fired? Outa work? Why—George?" He went over to the window and stood with his back to her. He could feel her gray stare upon him.

"Yep! Fired!"

At last she said, "Well—whatter yeh goin' t' do?"

He tapped the pane with his finger-nail. He answered in a tone made hoarse and unnatural by an assumption of gay carelessness, "Oh, nothin'!"

She began, then, her first weeping. "Oh—George—George— George——"

He looked at her scowling. "Ah, whatter yeh givin' us? Is this all I git when I come home f'm being fired? Anybody 'ud think it was my fault. I couldn't help it."

She continued to sob in a dull, shaking way. In the pose of her head there was an expression of her conviction that comprehension of her pain was impossible to the universe. He paused for a moment, and then, with his usual tactics, went out, slamming the door. A pale flood of sunlight, imperturbable at its vocation, streamed upon the little old woman, bowed with pain, forlorn in her chair.

XV

Kelcey was standing on the corner next day when three little boys came running. Two halted some distance away, and the other came forward. He halted before Kelcey, and spoke importantly. "Hey, your ol' woman's sick." "What?"

"Your ol' woman's sick."

"Git out!"

"She is, too!"

"Who tol' yeh?"

"Mis' Callahan. She said fer me t' run an' tell yeh. Dey want yeh." A swift dread struck Kelcey. Like flashes of light little scenes from the past shot through his brain. He had thoughts of a vengeance from the clouds. As he glanced about him the familiar view assumed a meaning that was ominous and dark. There was prophecy of disaster in the street, the buildings, the sky, the people. Something tragic and terrible in the air was known to his nervous, quivering nostrils. He spoke to the little boy in a tone that quavered. "All right!"

Behind him he felt the sudden contemplative pause of his companions of the gang. They were watching him. As he went rapidly up the street he knew that they had come out to the middle of the walk and were staring after him. He was glad that they could not see his face, his trembling lips, his eyes wavering in fear. He stopped at the door of his home and stared at the panel as if he saw written thereon a word. A moment later he entered. His eye comprehended the room in a frightened glance.

His mother sat gazing out at the opposite walls and windows. She was leaning her head upon the back of the chair. Her face was overspread with a singular pallor, but the glance of her eyes was strong and the set of her lips was tranquil.

He felt an unspeakable thrill of thanksgiving at seeing her seated there calmly. "Why, mother, they said yeh was sick," he cried, going toward her impetuously. "What's th' matter?"

She smiled at him. "Oh, it ain't nothin'! I on'y got kinda dizzy, that's all." Her voice was sober and had the ring of vitality in it.

He noted her common-place air. There was no alarm or pain in her tones, but the misgivings of the street, the prophetic twinges of his nerves made him still hesitate. "Well—are you sure it ain't? They scared me 'bout t' death."

"No, it ain't anything, on'y some sorta dizzy feelin'. I fell down b'hind th' stove. Missis Callahan, she came an' picked me up. I must 'a laid there fer quite a while. Th' docter said he guessed I'd be all right in a couple 'a hours. I don't feel nothin'!"

Kelcey heaved a great sigh of relief. "Lord, I was scared." He began to beam joyously, since he was escaped from his fright. "Why, I couldn't think what had happened," he told her.

"Well, it ain't nothin'," she said.

He stood about awkwardly, keeping his eyes fastened upon her in a sort of surprise, as if he had expected to discover that she had vanished. The reaction from his panic was a thrill of delicious contentment. He took a chair and sat down near her, but presently he jumped up to ask: "There ain't nothin' I can git fer yeh, is ther?" He looked at her eagerly.

In his eyes shone love and joy. If it were not for the shame of it he would have called her endearing names.

"No, ther ain't nothin'," she answered. Presently she continued, in a conversational way, "Yeh ain't found no work yit, have yeh?"

The shadow of his past fell upon him then and he became suddenly morose. At last he spoke in a sentence that was a vow, a declaration of change. "No, I ain't, but I'm goin' t' hunt fer it hard, you bet."

She understood from his tone that he was making peace with her. She smiled at him gladly. "Yer a good boy, George!" A radiance from the stars lit her face.

Presently she asked, "D' yeh think yer old boss would take yeh on ag'in if I went t' see him?"

"No," said Kelcey, at once. "It wouldn't do no good! They got all th' men they want. There ain't no room there. It wouldn't do no good." He ceased to beam for a moment as he thought of certain disclosures. "I'm goin' t' try to git work everywheres. I'm goin' t' make a wild break t' git a job, an' if there's one anywheres I'll git it."

She smiled at him again. "That's right, George!"

When it came supper-time he dragged her in her chair over to the table and then scurried to and fro to prepare a meal for her. She laughed gleefully at him. He was awkward and densely ignorant. He exaggerated his helplessness sometimes until she was obliged to lean back in her chair to laugh. Afterward they sat by the window. Her hand rested upon his hair.

XVI

When Kelcey went to borrow money from old Bleecker, Jones and the others, he discovered that he was below them in social position. Old Bleecker said gloomily that he did not see how he could loan money at that time. When Jones asked him to have a drink, his tone was careless. O'Connor recited at length some bewildering financial troubles of his own. In them all he saw that something had been reversed. They remained silent upon many occasions, when they might have grunted in sympathy for him.

As he passed along the street near his home he perceived Fidsey Corcoran and another of the gang. They made eloquent signs. "Are yeh wid us?"

He stopped and looked at them. "What's wrong with yeh?"

"Are yeh wid us er not," demanded Fidsey. "New barkeep'! Big can! We got it over in d' lot. Big can, I tell yeh." He drew a picture in the air, so to speak, with his enthusiastic fingers.

Kelcey turned dejectedly homeward. "Oh, I guess not, this roun'."

"What's d' matter wi'che?" said Fidsey. "Yer gittin' t' be a reg'lar willie! Come ahn, I tell yeh! Youse gits one smoke at d' can b'cause yeh b'longs t' d'gang, an' yeh don't wanta give it up widout er scrap! See? Some udder John'll git yet smoke. Come ahn!"

When they arrived at the place among the bowlders in the vacant lot, one of the band had a huge and battered tin-pail tilted afar up. His throat worked convulsively. He was watched keenly and anxiously by five or six others. Their eyes followed carefully each fraction of distance that the pail was lifted. They were very silent.

Fidsey burst out violently as he perceived what was in progress. "Heh, Tim, yeh big sojer,[1] le' go d' can! What'a yeh t'ink! Wese er in dis! Le'go dat!"

He who was drinking made several angry protesting contortions of his throat. Then he put down the pail and swore. "Who's a big sojer? I ain't gittin' more 'n me own smoke! Yet too bloomin' swift! Yeh'd t'ink yeh was d' on'y mug what owned dis can! Close yer face while I gits me smoke!"

He took breath for a moment and then returned the pail to its tilted position. Fidsey went to him and worried and clamored. He interfered so seriously with the action of drinking that the other was obliged to release the pail again for fear of choking.

Fidsey grabbed it and glanced swiftly at the contents. "Dere! Dat's what I was hollerin' at! Lookut d' beer! Not 'nough t' wet yer t'roat! Yehs can't have not'in' on d' level wid youse damn' tanks! Youse was a reg'lar resevoiy, Tim Connigan! Look what yeh lef' us! Ah, say, youse was a dandy! What 'a yeh t'ink we ah? Willies? Don' we want no smoke? Say, lookut dat can! It's drier'n hell! What 'a yeh t'ink?"

Tim glanced in at the beer. Then he said: "Well, d' mug what come b'fore me, he on'y lef' me dat much. Blue Billee, he done d' swallerin'! I on'y had a tas'e!"

Blue Billie, from his seat near, called out in wrathful protest: "Yeh lie, Tim. I never had more'n a mouf-ful!" An inspiration evidently came to him then, for his countenance suddenly brightened, and, arising, he

---

[1] In the nineteenth century to "soger" or "sojer" was to malinger, to feign illness, or make merely a show of working.

went toward the pail. "I ain't had me reg'lar smoke yit! Guess I come in aheader Fidsey, don' I?"

Fidsey, with a sardonic smile, swung the pail behind him. "I guess nit! Not dis minnet! Youse hadger smoke. If yeh ain't, yeh don't git none. See?"

Blue Billie confronted Fidsey determinedly. "D' 'ell I don't!"

"Nit," said Fidsey.

Billie sat down again.

Fidsey drank his portion. Then he manoeuvred skilfully before the crowd until Kelcey and the other youth took their shares. "Youse er a mob 'a tanks," he told the gang. "Nobodyud git not'in' if dey wasn't on t' yehs!"

Blue Billie's soul had been smouldering in hate against Fidsey. "Ah, shut up! Youse ain't gota take care 'a dose two mugs, dough. Youse hadger smoke, ain't yeh? Den yer tr'u. G' home!"

"Well, I hate t' see er bloke use 'imself fer a tank," said Fidsey. "But youse don't wanta go jollyin' 'round 'bout d' can, Blue, er youse'll git done."

"Who'll do me?" demanded Blue Billie, casting his eye about him.

"Kel' will," said Fidsey, bravely.

"D' 'ell he will?"

"Dat's what he will!"

Blue Billie made the gesture of a warrior. "He never saw d' day 'a his life dat he could do me little finger. If 'e says much t' me, I'll push 'is face all over d' lot."

Fidsey called to Kelcey. "Say, Kel, hear what dis mug is chewin'?"

Kelcey was apparently deep in other matters. His back was half-turned.

Blue Billie spoke to Fidsey in a battleful voice. "Did 'e ever say 'e could do me?"

Fidsey said: "Soitenly 'e did. Youse is dead easy, 'e says. He says he kin punch holes in you, Blue!"

"When did 'e say it?"

"Oh—any time. Youse is a cinch, Kel' says."

Blue Billie walked over to Kelcey. The others of the band followed him exchanging joyful glances.

"Did youse say yeh could do me?"

Kelcey slowly turned, but he kept his eyes upon the ground. He heard Fidsey darting among the others telling of his prowess, preparing them for the downfall of Blue Billie. He stood heavily on one foot and moved his hands nervously. Finally he said, in a low growl, "Well, what if I did?"

The sentence sent a happy thrill through the band. It was the formidable question. Blue Billie braced himself. Upon him came the responsibility of the next step. The gang fell back a little upon all sides. They looked expectantly at Blue Billie.

He walked forward with a deliberate step until his face was close to Kelcey.

"Well, if you did," he said, with a snarl between his teeth, "I'm goin' t' t'ump d' life outa yeh right heh!"

A little boy, wild of eye and puffing, came down the slope as from an explosion. He burst out in a rapid treble, "Is dat Kelcey feller here? Say, yeh ol' woman's sick again. Dey want yeh! Yehs better run! She's awful sick!"

The gang turned with loud growls. "Ah, git outa here!" Fidsey threw a stone at the little boy and chased him a short distance, but he continued to clamor, "Youse better come, Kelcey feller! She's awful sick! She was hollerin'! Dey been lookin' fer yeh over'n hour!" In his eagerness he returned part way, regardless of Fidsey!

Kelcey had moved away from Blue Billie. He said: "I guess I'd better go!" They howled at him. "Well," he continued, "I can't—I don't want—I don't wanta leave me mother be—she—"

His words were drowned in the chorus of their derision. "Well, looka-here"—he would begin and at each time their cries and screams ascended. They dragged at Blue Billie. "Go fer 'im, Blue! Slug 'im! Go ahn!"

Kelcey went slowly away while they were urging Blue Billie to do a decisive thing. Billie stood fuming and blustering and explaining himself. When Kelcey had achieved a considerable distance from him, he stepped forward a few paces and hurled a terrible oath. Kelcey looked back darkly.

XVII

When he entered the chamber of death, he was brooding over the recent encounter and devising extravagant revenges upon Blue Billie and the others.

The little old woman was stretched upon her bed. Her face and hands were of the hue of the blankets. Her hair, seemingly of a new and wondrous grayness, hung over her temples in whips and tangles. She was sickeningly motionless, save for her eyes, which rolled and swayed in maniacal glances.

A young doctor had just been administering medicine. "There," he said, with a great satisfaction, "I guess that'll do her good!" As he went briskly toward the door he met Kelcey. "Oh," he said. "Son?"

Kelcey had that in his throat which was like fur. When he forced his voice, the words came first low and then high as if they had broken through something. "Will she—will she——"

The doctor glanced back at the bed. She was watching them as she would have watched ghouls, and muttering. "Can't tell," he said. "She's wonderful woman! Got more vitality than you and I together! Can't tell! May—may not! Good-day! Back in two hours."

In the kitchen Mrs. Callahan was feverishly dusting the furniture, polishing this and that. She arranged everything in decorous rows. She was preparing for the coming of death. She looked at the floor as if she longed to scrub it.

The doctor paused to speak in an undertone to her, glancing at the bed. When he departed she labored with a renewed speed.

Kelcey approached his mother. From a little distance he called to her. "Mother—mother——" He proceeded with caution lest this mystic being upon the bed should clutch at him.

"Mother—mother—don't yeh know me?" He put forth apprehensive, shaking fingers and touched her hand.

There were two brilliant steel-colored points upon her eyeballs. She was staring off at something sinister.

Suddenly she turned to her son in a wild babbling appeal. "Help me! Help me! Oh, help me! I see them coming."

Kelcey called to her as to a distant place. "Mother! Mother!" She looked at him, and then there began within her a struggle to reach him with her mind. She fought with some implacable power whose fingers were in her brain. She called to Kelcey in stammering, incoherent cries for help.

Then she again looked away. "Ah, there they come! There they come! Ah, look—look—loo—" She arose to a sitting posture without the use of her arms.

Kelcey felt himself being choked. When her voice pealed forth in a scream he saw crimson curtains moving before his eyes. "Mother—oh, mother—there's nothin'—there's nothin'——"

She was at a kitchen-door with a dish-cloth in her hand. Within there had just been a clatter of crockery. Down through the trees of the orchard she could see a man in a field ploughing. "Bill—o-o-oh, Bill— have yeh seen Georgie? Is he out there with you? Georgie! Georgie! Come right here this minnet! Right—this—minnet!"

She began to talk to some people in the room. "I want t' know what yeh want here! I want yeh t' git out! I don't want yeh here! I don't feel good t'-day, an' I don't want yeh here! I don't feel good t'-day! I want yeh t' git out!" Her voice became peevish. "Go away! Go away! Go away!"

Kelcey lay in a chair. His nerveless arms allowed his fingers to sweep the floor. He became so that he could not hear the chatter from the bed, but he was always conscious of the ticking of the little clock out on the kitchen shelf.

When he aroused, the pale-faced but plump young clergyman was before him.

"My poor lad——" began this latter.

The little old woman lay still with her eyes closed. On the table at the head of the bed was a glass containing a water-like medicine. The reflected lights made a silver star on its side. The two men sat side by side, waiting. Out in the kitchen Mrs. Callahan had taken a chair by the stove and was waiting.

Kelcey began to stare at the wall-paper. The pattern was clusters of brown roses. He felt them like hideous crabs crawling upon his brain.

Through the door-way he saw the oil-cloth covering of the table catching a glimmer from the warm afternoon sun. The window disclosed a fair, soft sky, like blue enamel, and a fringe of chimneys and roofs, resplendent here and there. An endless roar, the eternal trample of the marching city, came mingled with vague cries. At intervals the woman out by the stove moved restlessly and coughed.

Over the transom from the hall-way came two voices.

"Johnnie!"

"Wot!"

"You come right here t' me! I want yehs t' go t' d' store fer me!"

"Ah, ma, send Sally!"

"No, I will not! You come right here!"

"All right, in a minnet!"

"Johnnie!"

"In a minnet, I tell yeh!"

"Johnnie——" There was the sound of a heavy tread, and later a boy squealed. Suddenly the clergyman started to his feet. He rushed forward and peered. The little old woman was dead.

2. An Experiment in Misery, New York Press (22 April 1894)

[*The Open Boat and Other Tales of Adventure* (1898). First published in the *New York Press*, the story carried a long introductory passage and a concluding paragraph, which Crane later omitted. The excised material is reprinted at the end of the story in the present edition.]

It was late at night, and a fine rain was swirling softly down, causing the pavements to glisten with hue of steel and blue and yellow in the rays of the innumerable lights. A youth was trudging slowly, without enthusiasm, with his hands buried deep in his trousers' pockets, toward the downtown places where beds can be hired for coppers. He was clothed in an aged and tattered suit, and his derby was a marvel of dust-covered crown and torn rim. He was going forth to eat as the wanderer may eat, and sleep as the homeless sleep. By the time he had reached City Hall Park he was so completely plastered with yells of "bum" and "hobo," and with various unholy epithets that small boys had applied to him at intervals, that he was in a state of the most profound dejection. The sifting rain saturated the old velvet collar of his overcoat, and as the wet cloth pressed against his neck, he felt that there no longer could be pleasure in life. He looked about him searching for an outcast of highest degree that they two might share miseries. But the lights threw a quivering glare over rows and circles of deserted benches that glistened damply, showing patches of wet sod behind them. It seemed that their usual freights had fled on this night to better things. There were only squads of well-dressed Brooklyn people who swarmed toward the Bridge.

The young man loitered about for a time and then went shuffling off down Park Row. In the sudden descent in style of the dress of the crowd he felt relief, and as if he were at last in his own country. He began to see tatters that matched his tatters. In Chatham Square there were aimless men strewn in front of saloons and lodging-houses, standing sadly, patiently, reminding one vaguely of the attitudes of chickens in a storm. He aligned himself with these men, and turned slowly to occupy himself with the flowing life of the great street.

Through the mists of the cold and storming night, the cable cars went in silent procession, great affairs shining with red and brass, moving with formidable power, calm and irresistible, dangerful and gloomy, breaking silence only by the loud fierce cry of the gong. Two rivers of people swarmed along the sidewalks, spattered with black mud, which made each shoe leave a scar-like impression. Overhead elevated trains with a shrill grinding of the wheels stopped at the station, which upon its leg-like pillars seemed to resemble some monstrous kind of crab squatting over the street. The quick fat puffings of the engines could be heard. Down an alley there were sombre curtains of purple and black, on which street lamps dully glittered like embroidered flowers.

A saloon stood with a voracious air on a corner. A sign leaning against the front of the doorpost announced: "Free hot soup tonight." The swing doors snapping to and fro like ravenous lips, made gratified smacks as the saloon gorged itself with plump men, eating with astounding and endless appetite, smiling in some indescribable manner as the men came from all directions like sacrifices to a heathenish superstition.

Caught by the delectable sign, the young man allowed himself to be swallowed. A bartender placed a schooner of dark and portentous beer on the bar. Its monumental form upreared until the froth a-top was above the crown of the young man's brown derby.

"Soup over there, gents," said the bartender, affably. A little yellow man in rags and the youth grasped their schooners and went with speed toward a lunch counter, where a man with oily but imposing whiskers ladled genially from a kettle until he had furnished his two mendicants with a soup that was steaming hot, and in which there were little floating suggestions of chicken. The young man, sipping his broth, felt the cordiality expressed by the warmth of the mixture, and he beamed at the man with oily but imposing whiskers, who was presiding like a priest behind an altar. "Have some more, gents?" he inquired of the two sorry figures before him. The little yellow man accepted with a swift gesture, but the youth shook his head and went out, following a man whose wondrous seediness promised that he would have a knowledge of cheap lodging-houses.

On the side-walk he accosted the seedy man. "Say, do you know a cheap place t' sleep?"

The other hesitated for a time, gazing sideways. Finally he nodded in the direction of up the street. "I sleep up there," he said, "when I've got th' price."

"How much?"

"Ten cents."

The young man shook his head dolefully. "That's too rich for me."

At that moment there approached the two a reeling man in strange garments. His head was a fuddle of bushy hair and whiskers from which his eyes peered with a guilty slant. In a close scrutiny it was possible to distinguish the cruel lines of a mouth, which looked as if its lips had just closed with satisfaction over some tender and piteous morsel. He appeared like an assassin steeped in crimes performed awkwardly.

But at this time his voice was tuned to the coaxing key of an affectionate puppy. He looked at the men with wheedling eyes and began to sing a little melody for charity.

"Say, gents, can't yeh give a poor feller a couple of cents t' git a bed. I got five an' I gits anudder two I gits me a bed. Now, on th' square, gents, can't yeh jest gimme two cents t' git a bed. Now, yeh know how a respecter'ble gentlem'n feels when he's down on his luck an' I——"

The seedy man, staring with imperturbable countenance at a train which clattered overhead, interrupted in an expressionless voice: "Ah, go t' h——!"

But the youth spoke to the prayerful assassin in tones of astonishment and inquiry. "Say, you must be crazy! Why don't yeh strike somebody that looks as if they had money?"

The assassin, tottering about on his uncertain legs, and at intervals brushing imaginary obstacles from before his nose, entered into a long explanation of the psychology of the situation. It was so profound that it was unintelligible.

When he had exhausted the subject, the young man said to him: "Let's see th' five cents."

The assassin wore an expression of drunken woe at this sentence, filled with suspicion of him. With a deeply pained air he began to fumble in his clothing, his red hands trembling. Presently he announced in a voice of bitter grief, as if he had been betrayed: "There's on'y four."

"Four," said the young man thoughtfully. "Well, look-a-here, I'm a stranger here, an' if ye'll steer me to your cheap joint I'll find the other three."

The assassin's countenance became instantly radiant with joy. His whiskers quivered with the wealth of his alleged emotions. He seized the young man's hand in a transport of delight and friendliness.

"B' gawd," he cried, "if ye'll do that, b' gawd, I'd say yeh was a damned good feller, I would, an' I'd remember yeh all m' life, I would, b' gawd, an' if I ever got a chance I'd return the compliment,"—he spoke with drunken dignity—"b'gawd, I'd treat yeh white, I would, an' I'd allus remember yeh——"

The young man drew back, looking at the assassin coldly. "Oh, that's all right," he said. "You show me th' joint—that's all you've got t' do."

The assassin, gesticulating gratitude, led the young man along a dark street. Finally he stopped before a little dusty door. He raised his hand impressively. "Look-a-here," he said, and there was a thrill of deep and ancient wisdom upon his face, "I've brought yeh here, an' that's my part, ain't it? If th' place don't suit yeh, yeh needn't git mad at me, need yeh? There won't be no bad feelin', will there?"

"No," said the young man.

The assassin waved his arm tragically and led the march up the steep stairway. On the way the young man furnished the assassin with three pennies. At the top a man with benevolent spectacles looked at them through a hole in the board. He collected their money, wrote some names on a register, and speedily was leading the two men along a gloom-shrouded corridor.

Shortly after the beginning of this journey the young man felt his liver turn white, for from the dark and secret places of the building there suddenly came to his nostrils strange and unspeakable odors that assailed him like malignant diseases with wings. They seemed to be from human bodies closely packed in dens; the exhalations from a hundred pairs of reeking lips; the fumes from a thousand bygone debauches; the expression of a thousand present miseries.

A man, naked save for a little snuff-colored undershirt, was parading sleepily along the corridor. He rubbed his eyes, and, giving vent to a prodigious yawn, demanded to be told the time.

"Half past one."

The man yawned again. He opened a door, and for a moment his form was outlined against a black, opaque interior. To this door came the three men, and as it was again opened the unholy odors rushed out like fiends, so that the young man was obliged to struggle as against an overpowering wind.

It was some time before the youth's eyes were good in the intense gloom within, but the man with benevolent spectacles led him skilfully, pausing but a moment to deposit the limp assassin upon a cot. He took the youth to a cot that lay tranquilly by the window, and, showing him a tall locker for clothes that stood near the head with the ominous air of a tombstone, left him.

The youth sat on his cot and peered about him. There was a gas-jet in a distant part of the room, that burned a small flickering orange-hued flame. It caused vast masses of tumbled shadows in all parts of the place, save where, immediately about it, there was a little gray haze. As the young man's eyes became used to the darkness he could see upon the cots that thickly littered the floor the forms of men sprawled out, lying in death-like silence or heaving and snoring with tremendous effort, like stabbed fish.

The youth locked his derby and his shoes in the mummy-case near him and then lay down with an old and familiar coat around his shoulders. A blanket he handled gingerly, drawing it over part of the coat. The cot was covered with leather and cold as melting snow. The youth was obliged to shiver for some time on this affair, which was like a slab. Presently, however, his chill gave him peace, and during this period of leisure from it he turned his head to stare at his friend the assassin, whom he could dimly discern where he lay sprawled on a cot in the abandon of a man filled with drink. He was snoring with incredible vigor. His wet hair and beard dimly glistened and his inflamed nose shone with subdued luster like a red light in a fog.

Within reach of the youth's hand was one who lay with yellow breast and shoulders bare to the cold drafts. One arm hung over the side of the cot and the fingers lay full length upon the wet cement floor of the room. Beneath the inky brows could be seen the eyes of the man exposed by the partly opened lids. To the youth it seemed that he and this corpse-like being were exchanging a prolonged stare and that the other threatened with his eyes. He drew back, watching his neighbor from the shadows of his blanket-edge. The man did not move once through the night, but lay in this stillness as of death, like a body stretched out, expectant of the surgeon's knife.

And all through the room could be seen the tawny hues of naked flesh, limbs thrust into the darkness, projecting beyond the cots; upreared knees; arms hanging, long and thin, over the cot-edges. For the most part they were statuesque, carven, dead. With the curious lockers standing all about like tombstones there was a strange effect of a graveyard, where bodies were merely flung.

Yet occasionally could be seen limbs wildly tossing in fantastic, nightmare gestures, accompanied by guttural cries, grunts, oaths. And there was one fellow off in a gloomy corner, who in his dreams was oppressed by some frightful calamity, for of a sudden he began to utter long wails that went almost like yells from a hound, echoing wailfully and weird through this chill place of tombstones, where men lay like the dead.

The sound, in its high piercing beginnings that dwindled to final melancholy moans, expressed a red and grim tragedy of the unfathomable possibilities of the man's dreams. But to the youth these were not merely the shrieks of a vision-pierced man. They were an utterance of the meaning of the room and its occupants. It was to him the protest of the wretch who feels the touch of the imperturbable granite wheels and who then cries with an impersonal eloquence, with a strength not from him, giving voice to the wail of a whole section, a class, a people. This, weaving into the young man's brain and mingling with his views of the vast and somber shadows that like mighty black fingers curled around the naked bodies, made the young man so that he did not sleep, but lay carving the biographies for these men from his meager experience. At times the fellow in the corner howled in a writhing agony of his imaginations.

Finally a long lance-point of gray light shot through the dusty panes of the window. Without, the young man could see roofs drearily white in the dawning. The point of light yellowed and grew brighter, until the golden rays of the morning sun came in bravely and strong. They touched with radiant color the form of a small, fat man who snored in stuttering fashion. His round and shiny bald head glowed suddenly with the velour of a decoration. He sat up, blinked at the sun, swore fretfully and pulled his blanket over the ornamental splendors of his head.

The youth contentedly watched this rout of the shadows before the bright spears of the sun and presently he slumbered. When he awoke he heard the voice of the assassin raised in valiant curses. Putting up his head he perceived his comrade seated on the side of the cot engaged in scratching his neck with long finger nails that rasped like files.

"Hully Jee dis is a new breed. They've got can-openers on their feet," he continued in a violent tirade.

The young man hastily unlocked his closet and took out his shoes and hat. As he sat on the side of the cot, lacing his shoes, he glanced about and saw that daylight had made the room comparatively commonplace and uninteresting. The men, whose faces seemed stolid, serene or absent, were engaged in dressing, while a great crackle of bantering conversation arose.

A few were parading in unconcerned nakedness. Here and there were men of brawn, whose skins shone clear and ruddy. They took splendid poses, standing massively, like chiefs. When they had dressed in their ungainly garments there was an extraordinary change. They then showed bumps and deficiencies of all kinds.

There were others who exhibited many deformities. Shoulders were slanting, humped, pulled this way and pulled that way. And notable among these latter men was the little fat man who had refused to allow his head to be glorified. His pudgy form, builded like a pear, bustled to and fro, while he swore in fishwife fashion. It appeared that some article of his apparel had vanished.

The young man, attired speedily, went to his friend, the assassin. At first the latter looked dazed at the sight of the youth. This face seemed to be appealing to him through the cloud-wastes of his memory. He scratched his neck and reflected. At last he grinned, a broad smile gradually spreading until his countenance was a round illumination. "Hello, Willie," he cried, cheerily.

"Hello," said the young man "Are yeh ready t' fly?"

"Sure." The assassin tied his shoe carefully with some twine and came ambling.

When he reached the street the young man experienced no sudden relief from unholy atmospheres. He had forgotten all about them, and had been breathing naturally and with no sensation of discomfort or distress.

He was thinking of these things as he walked along the street, when he was suddenly startled by feeling the assassin's hand, trembling with excitement, clutching his arm, and when the assassin spoke, his voice went into quavers from a supreme agitation.

"I'll be hully, bloomin' blowed, if there wasn't a feller with a night-shirt on up there in that joint!"

The youth was bewildered for a moment, but presently he turned to smile indulgently at the assassin's humor.

"Oh, you're a d—— liar," he merely said.

Whereupon the assassin began to gesture extravagantly and take oath by strange gods. He frantically placed himself at the mercy of remarkable fates if his tale were not true. "Yes, he did! I cross m' heart thousan' times!" he protested, and at the time his eyes were large with amazement, his mouth wrinkled in unnatural glee. "Yessir! A nightshirt! A hully[1] white nightshirt!"

"You lie!"

"Nosir! I hope ter die b'fore I kin git anudder ball if there wasn't a jay wid a hully, bloomin' white nightshirt!"

His face was filled with the infinite wonder of it. "A hully white nightshirt," he continually repeated.

The young man saw the dark entrance to a basement restaurant. There was a sign which read, "No mystery about our hash," and there were other age-stained and world-battered legends which told him that the place was within his means. He stopped before it and spoke to the assassin. "I guess I'll git somethin' t' eat."

[1] Holy.

At this the assassin, for some reason, appeared to be quite embarrassed. He gazed at the seductive front of the eating place for a moment. Then he started slowly up the street. "Well, good-by, Willie," he said bravely.

For an instant the youth studied the departing figure. Then he called out, "Hol' on a minnet." As they came together he spoke in a certain fierce way, as if he feared that the other would think him to be charitable. "Look-a-here, if yeh wanta git some breakfas' I'll lend yeh three cents t' do it with. But say, look-a-here, you've gotta git out an' hustle. I ain't goin' t' support yeh, or I'll go broke b'fore night. I ain't no millionaire."

"I take me oath, Willie," said the assassin earnestly, "th' on'y thing I really needs is a ball.[1] Me t'roat feels like a fryin' pan. But as I can't get a ball, why, th' next bes' thing is breakfast, an' if yeh do that for me, b' gawd, I say yeh was th' whitest lad I ever see."

They spent a few moments in dexterous exchanges of phrases, in which they each protested that the other was, as the assassin had originally said, "a respecter'ble gentlem'n." And they concluded with mutual assurances that they were the souls of intelligence and virtue. Then they went into the restaurant.

There was a long counter, dimly lighted from hidden sources. Two or three men in soiled white aprons rushed here and there.

The youth bought a bowl of coffee for two cents and a roll for one cent. The assassin purchased the same. The bowls were webbed with brown seams, and the tin spoons wore an air of having emerged from the first pyramid. Upon them were black, moss-like encrustations of age, and they were bent and scarred from the attacks of long-forgotten teeth. But over their repast the wanderers waxed warm and mellow. The assassin grew affable as the hot mixture went soothingly down his parched throat, and the young man felt courage flow in his veins.

Memories began to throng in on the assassin, and he brought forth long tales, intricate, incoherent, delivered with a chattering swiftness as from an old woman. "——great job out 'n Orange.[2] Boss keep yeh hustlin', though, all time. I was there three days, and then I went an' ask 'im t' lend me a dollar. 'G-g-go ter the devil,' he ses, an' I lose me job.

——"South no good. Damn niggers work for twenty-five an' thirty cents a day. Run white man out. Good grub, though. Easy livin'.

---

[1]   A drink, probably of brandy.
[2]   Orange County, New York.

———"Yas; useter work little in Toledo,[1] raftin' logs. Make two or three dollars er day in the spring. Lived high. Cold as ice, though, in the winter———

"I was raised in northern N'York. O-o-o-oh, yeh jest ough to live there. No beer ner whisky, though, way off in the woods. But all th' good hot grub yeh can eat. B' gawd, I hung around there long as I could till th' ol' man fired me. 'Git t'hell outa here, yeh wuthless skunk, git t'hell outa here an' go die,' he ses. 'You're a hell of a father,' I says, 'you are,' an' I quit 'im."

As they were passing from the dim eating-place they encountered an old man who was trying to steal forth with a tiny package of food, but a tall man with an indomitable moustache stood dragon-fashion, barring the way of escape. They heard the old man raise a plaintive protest. "Ah, you always want to know what I take out, and you never see that I usually bring a package in here from my place of business."

As the wanderers trudged slowly along Park Row, the assassin began to expand and grow blithe. "B'gawd, we've been livin' like kings," he said, smacking appreciative lips.

"Look out, or we'll have t' pay fer it t'-night," said the youth, with gloomy warning.

But the assassin refused to turn his gaze toward the future. He went with a limping step, into which he injected a suggestion of lamb-like gambols. His mouth was wreathed in a red grin.

In City Hall Park the two wanderers sat down in the little circle of benches sanctified by traditions of their class. They huddled in their old garments, slumbrously conscious of the march of the hours which for them had no meaning.

The people of the street hurrying hither and thither made a blend of black figures, changing, yet frieze-like. They walked in their good clothes as upon important missions, giving no gaze to the two wanderers seated upon the benches. They expressed to the young man his infinite distance from all he valued. Social position, comfort, the pleasures of living were unconquerable kingdoms. He felt a sudden awe.

And in the background a multitude of buildings, of pitiless hues and sternly high, were to him emblematic of a nation forcing its regal head into the clouds, throwing no downward glances; in the sublimity of its aspirations ignoring the wretches who may flounder at its feet. The roar of the city in his ear was to him the confusion of strange tongues,

---

[1]   A city in Ohio.

babbling heedlessly; it was the clink of coin, the voice of the city's hopes which were to him no hopes.

He confessed himself an outcast, and his eyes from under the lowered rim of his hat began to glance guiltily, wearing the criminal expression that comes with certain convictions.

Material deleted from **An Experiment in Misery**

Opening paragraphs

Two men stood regarding a tramp.

"I wonder how he feels," said one, reflectively. "I suppose he is homeless, friendless, and has, at the most, only a few cents in his pocket. And if this is so, I wonder how he feels." The other being the elder, spoke with an air of authoritative wisdom. "You can tell nothing of it unless you are in that condition yourself. It is idle to speculate about it from this distance."

"I suppose so," said the younger man, and then he added as from an inspiration: "I think I'll try it. Rags and tatters, you know, a couple of dimes, and hungry, too, if possible. Perhaps I could discover his point of view or something near it."

"Well, you might," said the other, and from those words begins this veracious narrative of an experiment in misery.

The youth went to the studio of an artist friend, who, from his store, rigged him out in an aged suit and a brown derby hat that had been made long years before. And then the youth went forth to try to eat as the tramp may eat, and sleep as the wanderers sleep. It was late at night, and a fine rain was swirling softly down, covering the pavements with a bluish luster. He began a weary trudge toward the downtown places, where beds can be hired for coppers. By the time he had reached City Hall Park he was so completely plastered with yells of "bum" and "hobo," and with various unholy epithets that small boys had applied to him at intervals that he was in a state of profound dejection, and looking searchingly for an outcast of high degree that the two might share miseries. But the lights threw a quivering glare over rows and circles of deserted benches that glistened damply, showing patches of wet sod behind them. It seemed that their usual freights of sorry humanity had fled on this night to better things. There were only squads of well dressed Brooklyn people, who swarmed toward the Bridge.

The young man loitered about for a time, and then went shuffling off down Park row. In the sudden descent in style of the dress of the crowd he felt relief. He began to see others whose tatters matched his tatters. In Chatham square there were aimless men strewn in front of saloons and lodging houses. He aligned himself with these men, and turned slowly to occupy himself with the pageantry of the street.

The mists of the cold and damp night made an intensely blue haze, through which the gaslights in the windows of stores and saloons shone with a golden radiance. The street cars rumbled softly, as if going upon carpet stretched in the aisle made by the pillars of the elevated road. Two interminable processions of people went along the wet pavements, spattered with black mud that made each shoe leave a scar-like impression. The high buildings lurked a-back, shrouded in shadows. Down a side street there were mystic curtains of purple and black, on which lamps dully glittered like embroidered flowers.

Concluding paragraphs

"Well," said the friend, "did you discover his point of view?"

"I don't know that I did," replied the young man; "but at any rate I think mine own has undergone a considerable alteration."

3. *An Experiment in Luxury, New York Press* (19 April 1894)

"If you accept this invitation you will have an opportunity to make another social study," said the old friend.

The youth laughed. "If they caught me making a study of them they'd attempt a murder. I would be pursued down Fifth avenue by the entire family."

"Well," persisted the old friend who could only see one thing at a time, "it would be very interesting. I have been told all my life that millionaires have no fun, and I know that the poor are always assured that the millionaire is a very unhappy person. They are informed that miseries swarm around all wealth, that all crowned heads are heavy with care, and——"

"But still——" began the youth.

"And, in the irritating, brutalizing, enslaving environment of their poverty, they are expected to solace themselves with these assurances," continued the old friend. He extended his gloved palm and began to tap it impressively with a finger of his other hand. His legs were spread apart in a fashion peculiar to his oratory. "I believe that it is mostly false. It is true that wealth does not release a man from many things from which he would gladly purchase release. Consequences cannot be bribed. I suppose that every man believe steadfastly that he has a private tragedy which makes him yearn for other existences. But it is impossible for me to believe that these things equalize themselves; that there are burrs under all rich cloaks and benefits in all ragged jackets, and the preaching of it seems wicked to me. There are those who have opportunities; there are those who are robbed of——"

"But look here," said the young man; "what has this got to do with my paying Jack a visit?"

"It has got a lot to do with it," said the old friend sharply. "As I said, there are those who have opportunities; there are those who are robbed——"

"Well, I won't have you say Jack ever robbed anybody of anything, because he's as honest a fellow as ever lived," interrupted the youth, with warmth. "I have known him for years, and he is a perfectly square fellow. He doesn't know about these infernal things. He isn't criminal because you say he is benefited by a condition which other men created."

"I didn't say he was," retorted the old friend. "Nobody is responsible for anything. I wish to Heaven somebody was, and then we could all jump on him. Look here, my boy, our modern civilization is——"

"Oh, the deuce!" said the young man.

The old friend then stood very erect and stern. "I can see by your frequent interruptions that you have not yet achieved sufficient pain in life. I hope one day to see you materially changed. You are yet——"

"There he is now," said the youth, suddenly. He indicated a young man who was passing. He went hurriedly toward him, pausing once to gesture adieu to his old friend.

———

The house was broad and brown and stolid like the face of a peasant. It had an inanity of expression, an absolute lack of artistic strength that was in itself powerful because it symbolized something. It stood, a homely pile of stone, rugged, grimly self reliant, asserting its quality as a fine thing when in reality the beholder usually wondered why so much money had been spent to obtain a complete negation. Then from another point of view it was important and mighty because it stood as a fetich, formidable because of traditions of worship.

When the great door was opened the youth imagined that the footman who held a hand on the knob looked at him with a quick, strange stare. There was nothing definite in it; it was all vague and elusive, but a suspicion was certainly denoted in some way. The youth felt that he, one of the outer barbarians, had been detected to be a barbarian by the guardian of the portal, he of the refined nose, he of the exquisite sense, he who must be more atrociously aristocratic than any that he serves. And the youth, detesting himself for it, found that he would rejoice to take a frightful revenge upon this lackey who, with a glance of his eyes, had called him a name. He would have liked to have been for a time a dreadful social perfection whose hand, waved lazily, would cause hordes of the idolatrous imperfect to be smitten in the eyes. And in the tumult of his imagination he did not think it strange that he should plan in his vision to come around to this house and with the power of his new social majesty, reduce this footman to ashes.

He had entered with an easy feeling of independence, but after this incident the splendor of the interior filled him with awe. He was a wanderer in a fairy land, and who felt that his presence marred certain effects. He was an invader with a shamed face, a man who had come to steal certain colors, forms, impressions that were not his. He had a dim thought that some one might come to tell him to begone.

His friend, unconscious of this swift drama of thought, was already upon the broad staircase. "Come on," he called. When the youth's foot struck from a thick rug and changed upon the tiled floor he was almost frightened.

There was cool abundance of gloom. High up stained glass caught the sunlight, and made it into marvelous hues that in places touched the dark walls. A broad bar of yellow gilded the leaves of lurking plants. A softened crimson glowed upon the head and shoulders of a bronze swordsman, who perpetually strained in a terrific lunge, his blade thrust at random into the shadow, piercing there an unknown something.

An immense fireplace was at one end, and its furnishings gleamed until it resembled a curious door of a palace, and on the threshold, where one would have to pass a fire burned redly. From some remote place came the sound of a bird twittering busily. And from behind heavy portieres came a subdued noise of the chatter of three, twenty or a hundred women.

He could not relieve himself of this feeling of awe until he had reached his friend's room. There they lounged carelessly and smoked pipes. It was an amazingly comfortable room. It expressed to the visitor that he could do supremely as he chose, for it said plainly that in it the owner did supremely as he chose. The youth wondered if there had not been some domestic skirmishing to achieve so much beautiful disorder. There were various articles left about defiantly, as if the owner openly flaunted the feminine ideas of precision. The disarray of a table that stood prominently defined the entire room. A set of foils, a set of boxing gloves, a lot of illustrated papers, an inkstand and a hat lay entangled upon it. Here was surely a young man, who, when his menacing mother, sisters or servants knocked, would open a slit in the door like a Chinaman in an opium joint, and tell them to leave him to his beloved devices. And yet, withal, the effect was good, because the disorder was not necessary, and because there are some things that when flung down, look to have been flung by an artist. A baby can create an effect with a guitar. It would require genius to deal with the piled up dishes in a Cherry Street sink.

The youth's friend lay back upon the broad seat that followed the curve of the window and smoked in blissful laziness. Without one could see the windowless wall of a house overgrown with a green, luxuriant vine. There was a glimpse of a side street. Below were the stables. At intervals a little fox terrier ran into the court and barked tremendously.

The youth, also blissfully indolent, kept up his part of the conversation on the recent college days, but continually he was beset by a stream of sub-conscious reflection. He was beginning to see a vast wonder in it that they two lay sleepily chatting with no more apparent responsibility than rabbits, when certainly there were men, equally fine perhaps, who were being blackened and mashed in the churning life of the lower places. And all this had merely happened; the great secret hand had guided them here and had guided others there. The eternal mystery of social condition exasperated him at this time. He wondered if incomprehensible justice were the sister of open wrong.

And, above all, why was he impressed, awed, overcome by a mass of materials, a collection of the trophies of wealth, when he knew that to him their dominant meaning was that they represented a lavish expenditure? For what reason did his nature so deeply respect all this? Perhaps his ancestors had been peasants bowing heads to the heel of appalling pomp of princes or rows of little men who stood to watch a king kill a flower with his cane. There was one side of him that said there were finer things in life, but the other side did homage.

Presently he began to feel that he was a better man than many entitled to a great pride. He stretched his legs like a man in a garden, and he thought that he belonged to the garden. Hues and forms had smothered certain of his comprehensions. There had been times in his life when little voices called to him continually from the darkness; he heard them now as an idle, half-smothered babble on the horizon edge. It was necessary that it should be so, too. There was the horizon, he said, and, of course, there should be a babble of pain on it. Thus it was written; it was a law, he thought. And, anyway, perhaps it was not so bad as those who babbled tried to tell.

In this way and with this suddenness he arrived at a stage. He was become a philosopher, a type of the wise man who can eat but three meals a day, conduct a large business and understand the purposes of infinite power. He felt valuable. He was sage and important.

There were influences, knowledges that made him aware that he was idle and foolish in his new state, but he inwardly reveled like a barbarian in his environment. It was delicious to feel so high and mighty, to feel that the unattainable could be purchased like a penny bun. For a time, at any rate, there was no impossible. He indulged in monarchical reflections.

As they were dressing for dinner his friend spoke to him in this wise: "Be sure not to get off anything that resembles an original thought before my mother. I want her to like you, and I know that when any one says a thing cleverly before her he ruins himself with her forever. Confine your talk to orthodox expressions. Be dreary and unspeakably commonplace in the true sense of the word. Be damnable."

"It will be easy for me to do as you say," remarked the youth.

"As far as the old man goes," continued the other, "he's a blooming good fellow. He may appear like a sort of a crank if he happens to be in that mood, but he's all right when you come to know him. And besides he doesn't dare do that sort of thing with me, because I've got nerve enough to bully him. Oh, the old man is all right."

On their way down the youth lost the delightful mood that he had enjoyed in his friend's rooms. He dropped it like a hat on the stairs. The splendor of color and form swarmed upon him again. He bowed before the strength of this interior; it said a word to him which he believed he should despise, but instead he crouched. In the distance shone his enemy, the footman.

"There will be no people here to-night, so you may see the usual evening row between my sister Mary and me, but don't be alarmed or uncomfortable, because it is quite an ordinary matter," said his friend, as they were about to enter a little drawing room that was well apart from the grander rooms.

The head of the family, the famous millionaire, sat on a low stool before the fire. He was deeply absorbed in the gambols of a kitten who was plainly trying to stand on her head that she might use all four paws in grappling with an evening paper with which her playmate was poking her ribs. The old man chuckled in complete glee. There was never such a case of abstraction, of want of care. The man of millions was in a far land where mechanics and bricklayers go, a mystic land of little, universal emotions, and he had been guided to it by the quaint gestures of a kitten's furry paws.

His wife, who stood near, was apparently not at all a dweller in thought lands. She was existing very much in the present. Evidently she had been wishing to consult with her husband on some tremendous domestic question, and she was in a state of rampant irritation, because he refused to acknowledge at this moment that she or any such thing as a tremendous domestic question was in existence. At intervals she made savage attempts to gain his attention.

As the youth saw her she was in a pose of absolute despair. And her eyes expressed that she appreciated all the tragedy of it. Ah, they said, hers was a life of terrible burden, of appalling responsibility; her pathway was beset with unsolved problems, her horizon was lined with tangled difficulties, while her husband—the man of millions—continued to play with the kitten. Her expression was an admission of heroism.

The youth saw that here at any rate was one denial of his oratorical old friend's statement. In the face of this woman there was no sign that life was sometimes a joy. It was impossible that there could be any pleasure in living for her. Her features were as lined and creased with care and worriment as those of an apple woman. It was as if the passing of each social obligation, of each binding form of her life had left its footprints, scarring her face.

Somewhere in her expression there was terrible pride, that kind of pride which, mistaking the form for the real thing, worships itself because of its devotion to the form.

In the lines of the mouth and the set of the chin could be seen the might of a grim old fighter. They denoted all the power of machination of a general, veteran of a hundred battles. The little scars at the corners of her eyes made a wondrously fierce effect, baleful, determined, without regard somehow to ruck of pain. Here was a savage, a barbarian, a spear woman of the Philistines, who fought battles to excel in what are thought to be the refined and worthy things in life; here was a type of Zulu[1] chieftainess who scuffled and scrambled for place before the white altars of social excellence. And woe to the socially weaker who should try to barricade themselves against that dragon.

---

[1]   A south African people, largely from KwaZulu/Natal province.

It was certain that she never rested in the shade of the trees. One could imagine the endless churning of that mind. And plans and other plans coming forth continuously, defeating a rival here, reducing a family there, bludgeoning a man here, a maid there. Woe and wild eyes followed like obedient sheep upon her trail.

Too, the youth thought he could see that here was the true abode of conservatism—in the mothers, in those whose ears displayed their diamonds instead of their diamonds displaying their ears, in the ancient and honorable controllers who sat in remote corners and pulled wires and respected themselves with a magnitude of respect that heaven seldom allows on earth. There lived tradition and superstition. They were perhaps ignorant of that which they worshiped, and, not comprehending it at all, it naturally followed that the fervor of their devotion could set the sky ablaze.

As he watched, he saw that the mesmeric power of a kitten's waving paws was good. He rejoiced in the spectacle of the little fuzzy cat trying to stand on its head, and by this simple antic defeating some intention of a great domestic Napoleon.[1]

The three girls of the family were having a musical altercation over by the window. Then and later the youth thought them adorable. They were wonderful to him in their charming gowns. They had time and opportunity to create effects, to be beautiful. And it would have been a wonder to him if he had not found them charming, since making themselves so could but be their principal occupation.

Beauty requires certain justices, certain fair conditions. When in a field no man can say: "Here should spring up a flower; here one should not." With incomprehensible machinery and system, nature sends them forth in places both strange and proper, so that, somehow, as we see them each one is a surprise to us. But at times, at places, one can say: "Here no flower can flourish." The youth wondered then why he had been sometimes surprised at seeing women fade, shrivel, their bosoms flatten, their shoulders crook forward, in the heavy swelter and wrench of their toil. It must be difficult, he thought, for a woman to remain serene and uncomplaining when she contemplated the wonder and the strangeness of it.

The lights shed marvelous hues of softened rose upon the table. In the encircling shadows the butler moved with a mournful, deeply solemn air. Upon the table there was color of pleasure, of festivity, but this servant in the background went to and fro like a slow religious procession.

---

[1] Napoleon Bonaparte (1796–1821), emperor of France.

The youth felt considerable alarm when he found himself involved in conversation with his hostess. In the course of this talk he discovered the great truth that when one submits himself to a thoroughly conventional conversation he runs risks of being most amazingly stupid. He was glad that no one cared to overhear it.

The millionaire, deprived of his kitten, sat back in his chair and laughed at the replies of his son to the attacks of one of the girls. In the rather good wit of his offspring he took an intense delight, but he laughed more particularly at the words of the son.

Indicated in this light chatter about the dinner table there was an existence that was not at all what the youth had been taught to see. Theologians had for a long time told the poor man that riches did not bring happiness, and they had solemnly repeated this phrase until it had come to mean that misery was commensurate with dollars, that each wealthy man was inwardly a miserable wretch. And when a wail of despair or rage had come from the night of the slums they had stuffed this epigram down the throat of he who cried out and told him that he was a lucky fellow. They did this because they feared.

The youth, studying this family group, could not see that they had great license to be pale and haggard. They were no doubt fairly good, being not strongly induced toward the by-paths. Various worlds turned open doors toward them. Wealth in a certain sense is liberty. If they were fairly virtuous he could not see why they should be so persistently pitied.

And no doubt they would dispense their dollars like little seeds upon the soil of the world if it were not for the fact that since the days of the ancient great political economist, the more exalted forms of virtue have grown to be utterly impracticable.

4. *An Ominous Baby*, *Arena* (9 May 1894); reprinted in *The Open Boat and Other Tales of Adventure* (1898)

A baby was wandering in a strange country. He was a tattered child with a frowsled wealth of yellow hair. His dress, of a checked stuff, was soiled and showed the marks of many conflicts like the chain-shirt of a warrior. His sun-tanned knees shone above wrinkled stockings which he pulled up occasionally with an impatient movement when they entangled his feet. From a gaping shoe there appeared an array of tiny toes.

He was toddling along an avenue between rows of stolid, brown houses. He went slowly, with a look of absorbed interest on his small, flushed face. His blue eyes stared curiously. Carriages went with a musical rumble over the smooth asphalt. A man with a chrysanthemum was going up steps. Two nursery-maids chatted as they walked slowly, while their charges hob-nobbed amiably between perambulators. A truck wagon roared thunderously in the distance.

The child from the poor district made way along the brown street filled with dull gray shadows. High up, near the roofs, glancing sun-rays changed cornices to blazing gold and silvered the fronts of windows. The wandering baby stopped and stared at the two children laughing and playing in their carriages among the heaps of rugs and cushions. He braced his legs apart in an attitude of earnest attention. His lower jaw fell and disclosed his small even teeth. As they moved on, he followed the carriages with awe in his face as if contemplating a pageant. Once one of the babies, with twittering laughter, shook a gorgeous rattle at him. He smiled jovially in return.

Finally a nursery maid ceased conversation and, turning, made a gesture of annoyance.

"Go 'way, little boy," she said to him. "Go 'way. You're all dirty."

He gazed at her with infant tranquility for a moment and then went slowly off, dragging behind him a bit of rope he had acquired in another street. He continued to investigate the new scenes. The people and houses struck him with interest as would flowers and trees. Passengers had to avoid the small, absorbed figure in the middle of the sidewalk. They glanced at the intent baby face covered with scratches and dust as with scars and powder smoke.

After a time, the wanderer discovered upon the pavement, a pretty child in fine clothes playing with a toy. It was a tiny fire engine painted brilliantly in crimson and gold. The wheels rattled as its small owner dragged it uproariously about by means of a string. The babe with his bit of rope trailing behind him paused and regarded the child and the toy. For a long while he remained motionless, save for his eyes, which followed all movements of the glittering thing.

The owner paid no attention to the spectator but continued his joyous imitations of phases of the career of a fire engine. His gleeful baby laugh rang against the calm fronts of the houses. After a little, the wandering baby began quietly to sidle nearer. His bit of rope, now forgotten, dropped at his feet. He removed his eyes from the toy and glanced expectantly at the other child.

"Say," he breathed, softly.

The owner of the toy was running down the walk at top speed. His tongue was clanging like a bell and his legs were galloping. An iron post on the corner was all ablaze. He did not look around at the coaxing call from the small, tattered figure on the curb.

The wandering baby approached still nearer and, presently, spoke again. "Say," he murmured, "le' me play wif it?"

The other child interrupted some shrill tootings. He bended his head and spoke disdainfully over his shoulder.

"No," he said.

The wanderer retreated to the curb. He failed to notice the bit of rope, once treasured. His eyes followed as before the winding course of the engine, and his tender mouth twitched.

"Say," he ventured at last, "is dat yours?"

"Yes," said the other, tilting his round chin. He drew his property suddenly behind him as if it were menaced. "Yes," he repeated, "it's mine."

"Well, le' me play wif it?" said the wandering baby, with a trembling note of desire in his voice.

"No," cried the pretty child with determined lips. "It's mine! My ma-ma buyed it."

"Well, tan't I play wif it?" His voice was a sob. He stretched forth little, covetous hands.

"No," the pretty child continued to repeat. "No, it's mine."

"Well, I want to play wif it," wailed the other. A sudden, fierce frown mantled his baby face. He clenched his thin hands and advanced with a formidable gesture. He looked some wee battler in a war.

"It's mine! It's mine," cried the pretty child, his voice in the treble of outraged rights.

"I want it," roared the wanderer.

"It's mine! It's mine!"

"I want it!"

"It's mine!"

The pretty child retreated to the fence, and there paused at bay. He protected his property with outstretched arms. The small vandal made a charge. There was a short scuffle at the fence. Each grasped the string to the toy and tugged. Their faces were wrinkled with baby rage, the verge of tears.

Finally, the child in tatters gave a supreme tug and wrenched the string from the other's hands. He set off rapidly down the street, bearing the toy in his arms. He was weeping with the air of a wronged one who has at last succeeded in achieving his rights. The other baby was squalling lustily. He seemed quite helpless. He wrung his chubby hands and railed.

After the small barbarian had got some distance away, he paused and regarded his booty. His little form curved with pride. A soft, gleeful smile loomed through the storm of tears. With great care, he prepared the toy for traveling. He stopped a moment on a corner and gazed at the pretty child whose small figure was quivering with sobs. As the latter began to show signs of beginning pursuit, the little vandal turned and vanished down a dark side street as into a swallowing cavern.

Appendix B: The Slum and Its Reformers

1. From Jacob A. Riis, *How the Other Half Lives* (1890)

[Riis (1849-1915) was a police reporter for the *New York Tribune*. His influential 1890 book *How the Other Half Lives: Studies Among the Tenements of New York* (New York: Charles Scribner's Sons, 1890) was a detailed anatomy of the Lower East Side slum and its inhabitants. President Theodore Roosevelt famously described Riis as "the most useful citizen of New York" and tried, unsuccessfully, to persuade him to take public office. Crane heard Riis lecture in 1892. The following selections are from Chapter 18, "The Reign of Rum," and Chapter 19, "The Harvest of Tares."]

Where God builds a church the devil builds next door—a saloon, is an old saying that has lost its point in New York. Either the Devil was on the ground first, or he has been doing a good deal more in the way of building. I tried once to find out how the account stood, and counted to 111 Protestant churches, chapels, and places of worship of every kind below Fourteenth Street, 4,065 saloons. The worst half of the tenement population lives down there, and it has to this day the worst half of the saloons. Uptown the account stands a little better, but there are easily ten saloons to every church to-day. I am afraid, too, that the congregations are larger by a good deal; certainly the attendance is steadier and the contributions more liberal the week round, Sunday included. Turn and twist it as we may, over against every bulwark for decency and morality which society erects, the saloon projects its colossal shadow, omen of evil wherever it falls into the lives of the poor.

Nowhere is its mark so broad or so black. To their misery it sticketh closer than a brother, persuading them that within its doors only is refuge, relief. It has the best of the argument, too, for it is true, worse pity, that in many a tenement-house block the saloon is the one bright and cheery and humanly decent spot to be found. It is a sorry admission to make, that to bring the rest of the neighborhood up to the level of the saloon would be one way of squelching it; but it is so. Wherever the tenements thicken, it multiplies. Upon the direst poverty of their crowds it grows fat and prosperous, levying upon it a tax heavier than all the rest of its grievous burdens combined. It is not yet two years since the Excise Board made the rule that no three corners of any street-crossing, not already so occupied, should thenceforward be licensed for rum-selling. And the tardy prohibition was intended for the tenement districts. Nowhere else is there need of it. One may walk many miles through the homes of the poor searching vainly for an open reading-room, a cheerful coffee-house, a decent club that is not a cloak for the traffic in rum. The dramshop yawns at every step, the poor man's club, his forum and his haven of rest when weary and disgusted with the crowding, the quarrelling, and the wretchedness at home. With the poison dealt out there he takes his politics, in quality not far apart. As the source, so the stream. The rumshop turns the political crank in New York. The natural yield is rum politics. Of what that means, successive Boards of Aldermen, composed in a measure, if not of a majority, of dive-keepers, have given New York a taste. The disgrace of the infamous "Boodle Board"[1] will be remembered until some corruption even fouler crops out and throws it into the shade.

What relation the saloon bears to the crowds, let me illustrate by a comparison. Below Fourteenth Street were, when the Health Department took its first accurate census of the tenements a year and a half ago, 13,220 of the 32,390 buildings classed as such in the whole city. Of the eleven hundred thousand tenants, not quite half a million, embracing a host of more than sixty-three thousand children under five years of age, lived below that line. Below it, also, were 234 of the cheap lodging-houses accounted for by the police last year, with a total of four millions and a half of lodgers for the twelvemonth, 59 of the city's 110 pawnshops, and 4,065 of its 7,884 saloons. The four most densely peopled precincts, the Fourth, Sixth, Tenth, and Eleventh, supported together in round numbers twelve hundred saloons, and their returns showed twenty-seven per cent. of the whole number of arrests for the year. The Eleventh Precinct, that has the greatest and the poorest crowds of all—it is the Tenth Ward—and harbored one-third of the army of homeless lodgers and fourteen per cent of all the prisoners of the year, kept 485 saloons going in 1889. It is not on record that one of them all failed for want of support. A number of them, on the contrary, had brought their owners wealth and prominence. From their bars these eminent citizens stepped proudly into the councils of the city and the State. The very floor of one of the bar-rooms, in a neighborhood that

---

[1] The corrupt Board of Aldermen under the effective control of William Marcy Tweed (1823-78) and guilty of defrauding the city of some $30 million.

lately resounded with the cry for bread of starving workmen, is paved with silver dollars!

East Side poverty is not alone in thus rewarding the tyrants that sweeten its cup of bitterness with their treacherous poison. The Fourth Ward points with pride to the honorable record of the conductors of its "Tub of Blood," and a dozen bar-rooms with less startling titles; the West Side to the wealth and "social" standing of the owners of such resorts as the "Witches' Broth" and the "Plug Hat" in the region of Hell's Kitchen three-cent whiskey, names ominous of the concoctions brewed there and of their fatally generous measure. Another ward, that boasts some of the best residences and the bluest blood on Manhattan Island, honors with political leadership in the ruling party the proprietor of one of the most disreputable black-and-tan dives and dancing-hells to be found anywhere. Criminals and policemen alike do him homage. The list might be strung out to make texts for sermons with a stronger home flavor than many that are preached in our pulpits on Sunday. But I have not set out to write the political history of New York. Besides, the list would not be complete. Secret dives are skulking in the slums and out of them, that are not labelled respectable by a Board of Excise and support no "family entrance." Their business, like that of the stale-beer dives, is done through a side-door the week through. No one knows the number of unlicensed saloons in the city. Those who have made the matter a study estimate it at a thousand, more or less. The police make occasional schedules of a few and report them to headquarters. Perhaps there is a farce in the police court, and there the matter ends. Rum and "influence" are synonymous terms. The interests of the one rarely suffer for the want of attention from the other.

With the exception of these free lances that treat the law openly with contempt, the saloons all hang out a sign announcing in fat type that no beer or liquor is sold to children. In the down-town "morgues" that make the lowest degradation of tramp-humanity pan out a paying interest, as in the "reputable resorts" uptown where Inspector Byrnes's[1] men spot their worthier quarry elbowing citizens whom the idea of associating with a burglar would give a shock they would not get over for a week, this sign is seen conspicuously displayed. Though apparently it means submission to a beneficent law, in reality the sign is a heartless, cruel joke. I doubt if one child in a thousand, who brings his growler[2]

---

[1] Byrnes was Chief Inspector of Police in New York City.
[2] A growler was a can used for carrying beer.

to be filled at the average New York bar, is sent away empty-handed, if able to pay for what he wants. I once followed a little boy, who shivered in bare feet on a cold November night so that he seemed in danger of smashing his pitcher on the icy pavement, into a Mulberry Street saloon where just such a sign hung on the wall, and forbade the barkeeper to serve the boy. The man was as astonished at my interference as if I had told him to shut up his shop and go home, which in fact I might have done with as good a right, for it was after 1 A.M., the legal closing hour. He was mighty indignant too, and told me roughly to go away and mind my business, while he filled the pitcher. The law prohibiting the selling of beer to minors is about as much respected in the tenement-house districts as the ordinance against swearing. Newspaper readers will recall the story, told little more than a year ago, of a boy who after carrying beer a whole day for a shopful of men over on the East Side, where his father worked, crept into the cellar to sleep off the effects of his own share in the rioting. It was Saturday evening. Sunday his parents sought him high and low; but it was not until Monday morning, when the shop was opened, that he was found, killed and half-eaten by the rats that overran the place.

All the evil the saloon does in breeding poverty and in corrupting politics; all the suffering it brings into the lives of its thousands of innocent victims, the wives and children of drunkards it sends forth to curse the community; its fostering of crime and its shielding of criminals— it is all as nothing to this, its worst offence. In its affinity for the thief there is at least this compensation that, as it makes, it also unmakes him. It starts him on his career only to trip him up and betray him into the hands of the law, when the rum he exchanged for his honesty has stolen his brains as well. For the corruption of the child there is no restitution. None is possible. It saps the very vitals of society; undermines its strongest defences, and delivers them over to the enemy. Fostered and filled by the saloon, the "growler" looms up in the New York street boy's life, baffling the most persistent efforts to reclaim him. There is no escape from it; no hope for the boy, once its blighting grip is upon him. Thenceforward the logic of the slums, that the world which gave him poverty and ignorance for his portion "owes him a living," is his creed, and the career of the "tough" lies open before him, a beaten track to be blindly followed to a bad end in the wake of the growler.

★ ★ ★ ★ ★

Along the water-fronts, in the holes of the dock-rats, and on the avenues, the young tough finds plenty of kindred spirits. Every corner has its gang, not always on the best of terms with the rivals in the next block, but all with a common programme: defiance of law and order, and with a common ambition: to get "pinched," *i.e.*, arrested, so as to pose as heroes before their fellows. A successful raid on the grocer's till is a good mark, "doing up" a policeman cause for promotion. The gang is an institution in New York. The police deny its existence while nursing the bruises received in nightly battles with it that tax their utmost resources. The newspapers chronicle its doings daily, with a sensational minuteness of detail that does its share toward keeping up its evil traditions and inflaming the ambition of its members to be as bad as the worst. The gang is the ripe fruit of tenement-house growth. It was born there, endowed with a heritage of instinctive hostility to restraint by a generation that sacrificed home to freedom, or, left its country for its country's good. The tenement received and nursed the seed. The intensity of the American temper stood sponsor to the murderer in what would have been the common "bruiser" of a more phlegmatic clime. New York's tough represents the essence of reaction against the old and the new oppression, nursed in the rank soil of its slums. Its gangs are made up of the American-born sons of English, Irish, and German parents. They reflect exactly the conditions of the tenements from which they sprang. Murder is as congenial to Cherry Street or to Battle Row, as quiet and order to Murray Hill. The "assimilation" of Europe's oppressed hordes, upon which our Fourth of July orators are fond of dwelling, is perfect. The product is our own. […]

From all this it might be inferred that the New York tough is a very fierce individual, of indomitable courage and naturally as blood-thirsty as a tiger. On the contrary he is an arrant coward. His instincts of ferocity are those of the wolf rather than the tiger. It is only when he hunts with the pack that he is dangerous. Then his inordinate vanity makes him forget all fear or caution in the desire to distinguish himself before his fellows, a result of his swallowing all the flash literature and penny-dreadfuls he can beg, borrow, or steal—and there is never any lack of them—and of the strongly dramatic element in his nature that is nursed by such a diet into rank and morbid growth. He is a queer bundle of contradictions at all times. Drunk and foul-mouthed, ready to cut the throat of a defenseless stranger at the toss of a cent, fresh from beating his decent mother black and blue to get money for rum, he will resent as an intolerable insult the imputation that he is "no gentleman." Fighting his battles with the coward's weapons, the brass-knuckles and the deadly sand-bag, or with brick-bats from the housetops, he is still in all seriousness a lover of fair play, and as likely as not, when his gang has downed a policeman in a battle that has cost a dozen broken heads, to be found next saving a drowning child or woman at the peril of his own life. It depends on the angle at which he is seen, whether he is a cowardly ruffian, or a possible hero with different training and under different social conditions. Ready wit he has at all times, and there is less meanness in his make-up than in that of the bully of the London slums; but an intense love of show and applause, that carries him to any length of bravado, which his twin-brother across the sea entirely lacks. I have a very vivid recollection of seeing one of his tribe, a robber and murderer before he was nineteen, go to the gallows unmoved, all fear of the rope overcome, as it seemed, by the secret, exultant pride of being the centre of a first-class show, shortly to be followed by that acme of tenement-life bliss, a big funeral. He had his reward. His name is to this day a talisman among West Side ruffians, and is proudly borne by the gang of which, up till the night when he "knocked out his man," he was an obscure though aspiring member.

2. From Thomas De Witt Talmage, *Night Scenes of City Life* (1892)

[Reverend Talmage (1823-1902) was minister to the Central Presbyterian Church in Brooklyn, but his reputation as a fiery preacher and lecturer stretched far beyond this parish. His sermons were published in thousands of newspapers. The following extracts are from Chapter V, "Under the Police Lantern," of his *Night Scenes of City Life* (Chicago: Donohue and Henneberry, 1892).]

I unroll the scroll of new revelations. With city missionary, and the police of New York and Brooklyn, I have seen some things that I have not yet stated in this series of discourses on the night side of city life. The night of which I speak now is darker than any other. No glittering chandelier, no blazing mirror adorns it. It is the long, deep exhaustive night of city pauperism. "We won't want a carriage to-night," said the detectives. "A carriage would hinder us in our work; a carriage going through the streets where we are going would only bring out the people to see what was the matter." So on foot we went up the dark lanes of poverty. Everything revolting to eye, and ear, and nostril. Population unwashed, uncombed, rooms unventilated. Three midnights overlapping each other—midnight of the natural world, midnight of crime, midnight of pauperism. Stairs oozing with filth. The inmates, nine-tenths of the journey to their final doom, traveled. They started in some unhappy home of the city or of the country. They plunged into the shambles of death within ten minutes' walk of the Fifth Avenue Hotel, New York, and then came on gradually down until they have arrived at the Fourth Ward. When they move out of the Fourth Ward they will move into Bellevue Hospital; when they move out of Bellevue Hospital they will move to Blackwell's Island; when they move from Blackwell's Island they will move to the Potter's Field; when they move from the Potter's Field they will move into Hell.[1] Bellevue Hospital and Blackwell's Island take care of 18,000 patients in one year. As we passed on, the rain pattering on the street and dripping around the doorways made the night more dismal. I said, "Now let the police go ahead," and they flashed their light, and there were fourteen persons trying to sleep, or sleeping, in one room. Some on a bundle of straw; more with nothing under them and nothing over them. "Oh!" you say, "this is exceptional." It is not. Thousands lodge in that way. One hundred and seventy thousand families living in tenement houses, in more or less inconvenience, more or less squalor. Half a million people in New York City—five hundred thousand people living in tenement-houses; multitudes of these people dying by inches. Of the twenty-four thousand that die yearly in New York fourteen thousand die in tenement-houses. No lungs that God ever made could for a long while stand the atmosphere we breathed for a little while. In the Fourth Ward, 17,000 people within the space of thirty acres. You say, "Why not clear them out? Why not, as at Liverpool, where 20,000 of these people were cleared out of the city, and the city saved from a moral pestilence, and the people themselves from being victimized?" There will be no reformation for these cities until the tenement-house system is entirely broken up. The city authorities will have to buy farms, and will have to put these people on those farms, and compel them to work. By the strong arm of the law, by the police lantern conjoined with Christian charity, these places must be exposed and must be uprooted. Those places in London which have become historical for crowded populations—St. Giles, Whitechapel, Hollborn, the Strand—have their

---

[1] Bellevue Hospital, located on First Avenue at 27th street, is the oldest public hospital in the United States; on Blackwell's Island see note to page 27; Potter's Field, on Hart Island in Long Island Sound, was the mass burial ground of New Yorkers unable to afford private interment.

match at last in the Sixth Ward, Eleventh Ward, Fourteenth Ward, Seventeenth Ward of New York. No purification for our cities until each family shall have something of the privacy and seclusion of a home circle. As long as they herd like beasts, they will be beasts.

What is that heavy thud on the wet pavement? Why, that is a drunkard who has fallen, his head striking against the street—striking very hard. The police try to lift him up. Ring the bell for the city ambulance. No. Only an outcast, only a tatterdemalion[1]—a heap of sores and rags. But look again. Perhaps he has some marks of manhood on his face; perhaps he may have been made in the image of God; perhaps he has a soul which will live after the dripping heavens of this dismal night have been rolled together as a scroll; perhaps he may have been died for, by a king; perhaps he may yet be a conqueror charioted in the splendors of heavenly welcome. But we must pass on. We cross the street, and, the rain beating in his face, lies a man entirely unconscious. I wonder where he comes from. I wonder if any one is waiting for him. I wonder if he was ever rocked in a Christian cradle. I wonder if that gashed and bloated forehead was ever kissed by a fond mother's lips. I wonder if he is stranded for eternity. But we cannot stop. We passed on down, the air loaded with blasphemies and obscenities, until I heard something that astounded me more than all. I said, "What is that?" It was a loud, enthusiastic Christian song, rolling out on the stormy air. I went up to the window and looked in. There was a room filled with all sorts of people, some standing, some kneeling, some sitting, some singing, some praying, some shaking hands as if to give encouragement, some wringing their hands as though over a wasted life. What was this? Oh! it was Jerry McAuley's glorious Christian mission.[2] There he stood, himself snatched from death, snatching others from death. That scene paid for all the nausea and fatigue of the midnight exploration. Our tears fell with the rain-tears of sympathy for a good man's work; tears of gratitude to God that one lifeboat had been launched on that wild sea of sin and death; tears of hope that there might be lifeboats enough to take off all the wrecked, and, that, after a while, the Church of God, rousing from its fastidiousness, might lay hold with both hands of this work, which must be done if our cities are not to go down in darkness and fire and blood. [...]

---

[1] A poor, ragged person.
[2] Irish-born McAuley (1839–84) opened his first mission in Water Street, New York City, in 1871.

Hear it, you ministers of religion, and utter words of sympathy for the suffering, and thunders of indignation against the cause of all this wretchedness. Hear it, mayoralties and judicial bench, and constabularies. Unless we wake up, the Lord will scourge us as the yellow fever never scourged New Orleans, as the plague never smote London, as the earthquake never shook Carraccas, as the fire never overwhelmed Sodom. I wish I could throw a bomb-shell of arousal into every city hall, meeting-house and cathedral on the continent. The factories at Fall River and at Lowell sometimes stop for lack of demand, and for lack of workmen, but this million-roomed factory of sin and death never stops, never slackens a band, never arrests a spindle. The great wheel of that factory keeps on turning, not by such floods as those of the Merrimac or the Connecticut, but crimson floods rushing forth from the groggeries, and the wine-cellars, and the drinking saloons of the land, and the faster the floods rush the faster the wheel turns; and the band of that wheel is woven from broken heart-strings, and every time the wheel turns, from the mouth of the mill come forth blasted estates, squalor, vagrancy, crime, sin, woe—individual woe, municipal woe, national woe—and the creaking and the rumbling of the wheels are the shrieks and the groans of men and women lost for two worlds, and the cry is, "Bring on more fortunes, more homes, more States, more cities, to make up the awful grist of this stupendous mill." "Oh," you say, "the wretchedness and the sin of the city will go out from lack of material after awhile." No, it will not. The police lantern flashes in another direction. Here come 15,000 shoeless, hatless, homeless children of the street, in this cluster of cities. They are the reserve corps of this great army of wretchedness and crime that are dropping down into the Morgue, the East river, the Potter's Field, the prison. A philanthropist has estimated that if these children were placed in a great procession, double-file, three feet apart, they would make a procession eleven miles long. Oh! what a pale, coughing, hunger-bitten, sin-cursed, ophthalmic throng—the tigers, the adders, the scorpions ready to bite and sting society, which they take to be their natural enemy. Howard Mission has saved many. Children's Aid Society[1] has saved many. Industrial Schools have saved many. One of these societies transported 30,000 children from the streets of our cities, to farms at the West, by a stratagem of charity, turning them from vagrancy into useful citizenship, and out of 21,000 children thus transported from the cities to farms only twelve turned out badly. But still the reserve corps of sin and wretchedness marches on. [...]

---

[1]   The Children's Aid Society was founded by Charles Loring Brace in 1853 (see Appendix B3).

I am here this morning to tell you that there are deathful and explosive influences under all our cities, ready to destroy us with a great moral convulsion. Some men say: "I don't see anything of this, and I am not interested in it." You ought to be. You remind me of a man who has been shipwrecked with a thousand others. He happens to get up on the shore, and the others are all down in the surf. He goes up in a fisherman's cabin, and sits down to warm himself. The fisherman says: "Oh! this won't do. Come out and help me to get these others out of the surf." "Oh, no!" says the man; "it's my business now to warm myself." "But," says the fisherman, "these men are dying; are you not going to give them help?" "Oh, no! I've got ashore myself, and I must warm myself!" That is what people are doing in the church to-day. A great multitude are out in the surf of sin and death, going down forever; but men sit by the fire of the church, warming their Christian graces, warming their faith, warming their hope for heaven, and I say, "Come out, and work to-day for Christ." "Oh, no," they say; "my sublime duty is to warm myself!" Such men as that will not come within ten thousand miles of heaven! Help foreign missions. Those of my own blood are toiling in foreign lands with Christ's Word. Send a million dollars for the salvation of the heathen—that is right—but look after the heathen also around the mouths of the Hudson and East rivers. Send missionaries if you will to Borioboola-gha, but send missionaries also through Houston street, Mercer street, Greene street, Navy street, Fulton street, and all around about Brooklyn Atlantic Docks. If you will, send quilted coverlets to Central Africa to keep the natives warm in summer-time, and send ice-cream freezers to Greenland, but do have a little common sense and practical charity, and help these cities here that want hats, want clothes, want shoes, want fire, want medicines, want instruction, want the Gospel, want Christ.

3. From Charles Loring Brace, *The Dangerous Classes of New York* (1872)

[Brace (1826-90) was a missionary in New York City and founder of the Children's Aid Society in 1853. The following extract is taken from Chapter X, "Street Girls: Their Sufferings and Crimes," of his *The Dangerous Classes of New York; and Twenty Years' Work Among Them* (New York: Wynkoop and Hellenbeck, 1872).]

Then the strange and mysterious subject of sexual vice comes in. It has often seemed to me one of the most dark arrangements of this singular world that a female child of the poor should be permitted to start on its immortal career with almost every influence about it degrading, its inherited tendencies overwhelming toward indulgence of passion, its examples all of crime or lust, its lower nature awake long before its higher, and then that it should be allowed to soil and degrade its soul before the maturity of reason, and beyond all human possibility of cleansing!

For there is no reality in the sentimental assertion that the sexual sins of the lad are as degrading as those of the girl. The instinct of the female is more toward the preservation of purity, and therefore her fall is deeper—an instinct grounded in the desire of preserving a stock, or even the necessity of perpetuating our race.

Still, were the indulgences of the two sexes of a similar character—as in savage races—were they both following passion alone, the moral effect would not perhaps be so different in the two cases. But the sin of the girl soon becomes what the Bible calls "a sin against one's own body," the most debasing of all sins. She soon learns to offer for sale that which is in its nature beyond all price, and to feign the most sacred affections, and barter with the most delicate instincts. She no longer merely follows blindly and excessively an instinct; she perverts a passion and sells herself. The only parallel case with the male sex would be that in some Eastern communities which are rotting and falling to pieces from their debasing and unnatural crimes. When we hear of such disgusting offenses under any form of civilization, whether it be under the Rome of the Empire, or the Turkey of today, we know that disaster, ruin, and death, are near the State and the people.

This crime, with the girl, seems to sap and rot the whole nature. She loses self-respect, without which every human being soon sinks to the lowest depths; she loses the habit of industry, and cannot be taught to work. Having won her food at the table of Nature by unnatural means, Nature seems to cast her out, and henceforth she cannot labor. Living in a state of unnatural excitement, often worked up to a high pitch of nervous tension by stimulants, becoming weak in body and mind, her character loses fixedness of purpose and tenacity and true energy. The diabolical women who support and plunder her, the vile society she keeps, the literature she reads, the business she has chosen or fallen into, serve continually more and more to degrade and defile her. If, in a moment of remorse, she flee away and take honest work, her weakness and bad habits follow her; lazy; she craves the stimulus and hollow gayety of the wild life she has led; her ill name dogs her; all the wicked have an instinct of her former evil courses; the world and herself are against reform, and, unless she chance to have a higher moral nature or stronger will than most of her class, or unless Religion should touch even her polluted soul, she soon falls back, and gives one more sad illustration of the immense difficulty of a fallen woman rising again.

[The great majority of prostitutes, it must be remembered, have had no romantic or sensational history, though they always affect this.]They usually relate, and perhaps even imagine, that they have been seduced from the paths of virtue suddenly and by the wiles of some heartless seducer. Often they describe themselves as belonging to some virtuous, respectable, and even wealthy family. Their real history, however, is much more commonplace and matter-of-fact. They have been poor women's daughters, and did not want to work as their mothers did; or they have grown up in a tenement-room, crowded with boys and men, and lost purity before they knew what it was; or they have liked gay company, and have had no good influences around them, and sought pleasure in criminal indulgences; or they have been street-children, poor, neglected, and ignorant, and thus naturally and inevitably have become depraved women. Their sad life and debased character are the natural outgrowth of poverty, ignorance, and laziness. The number among them who have "seen better days," or have fallen from heights of virtue, is incredibly small. They show what fruits neglect in childhood, and want of education and of the habit of labor, and the absence of pure examples, will inevitably bear. Yet in their low estate they always show some of the divine qualities of their sex.[The physicians in the Blackwell's Island Hospital[1] say that there are no nurses so tender and devoted to the sick and dying as these girls.]And the honesty of their dealings with the washerwomen and shopkeepers, who trust them while in their vile houses, has often been noted. The words of sympathy and religion always touch their hearts, though the effect passes like the April cloud. On a broad scale, probably no remedy that man could apply would ever cure this fatal disease of society. It may, however, be diminished in its ravages, and prevented in a large measure. The check to its devastations in a laboring or poor class will be the facility of marriage, the opening of new channels of female work, but, above all, the influences of education and Religion.

---

[1] See note page 27.

Appendix C: Slum Fiction: From Edgar Fawcett, The Evil That Men Do *(New York: Belford, 1889)*

[Fetching up in New York City, pretty, small-town girl Cora Strang finds low-grade work in the garment industry. Her youthfulness and striking good looks attract compliments and with them offers of money. The narrative details, approvingly, Cora's resistance to temptation then goes on to describe the "hell-broth" of the Bowery.]

If it had been so much plain alms, well and good. There had been the scent of a bribe and lure about it in this case, and therefore avoidance was discretion. She would put herself in no man's power; freedom was about all that she had to call her very own, and that she meant to keep. She had seen such sights of woe where girls went wrong. Besides, there was always that past of hers, at home in the country, to influence her, to remind her, to smile at her from afar, as the wild, sweet light of a dead sunset smiles over distances of deserted land.

The Bowery, down in this crowded part of it, clamored to-day with hobgoblin noises. Ragged boys were yelling "extra," in voices of unusual keenness, for that morning, at the Tombs near by, a quaking little Italian wife-murderer had been legally choked to death after four years' imprisonment and three elaborate trials. The broad street itself was crammed with vehicles, whose various wheels jarred upon its cobble-stones with every species of dissonance, and across these, in a kind of vocal sword-thrust, darted the cry of the orange-and-banana vendors, with their laden carts trundled along the curb.

In the lower Bowery life seethes as though it were some sort of bubbling broth in a cauldron—hell-broth, perhaps. Here is no hint of the ease born from wealth as bud from bough. It is mostly struggle and fret, with spurts of false, hectic joy sometimes, but oftener of joy that is amazingly genuine. There are many grim faces, but still there are many in which contentment has found an abiding haunt. You see want everywhere; in the cheap goods that swing for sale from the awnings of shops; in the uncouth shoes that are festooned before the windows of their purveyors like strings of sausages, each telling you at a glance of its pegged sole and insecure stitchings; in the blistered and veiny cigars that tobacconists expose behind their gaudy-painted wooden statues, or in the vulgar, pinchbeck jewelry, flaring crudely from at least five windows on every block. (Chapter 1)

* ★ ★ ★ ★ ★

[The squalor of the Lower East Side is further described through the figure of Cora's friend, Em Cratchett:]

Em Cratchett was a sewing-girl who supported a bed-ridden mother, an idiot brother seven years old, and two sisters, aged about nine and eleven. This family had once occupied two rooms in the Prince Street tenement-house, and there Cora had got to know Em even better than she knew Effie and Ann Flynn. Em had been forced to find cheaper quarters, and a tenement-house close to Grand Street had supplied them. It was a den of filth, but its two yet smaller rooms were a dollar and a half lower per month, and to Em that meant a great sum. She had more than once told Cora that she believed that if it wasn't for the strong tea, starvation would have killed her long ago. She took it as black as ink, and no doubt it buoyed her up among the fearful sights and smells on every side. Not a cent, with Em, but counted; and when they raised the electric light within a few yards of her windows it brought her one more chance to save. For a monstrous iron structure had been built, of late, just over the way, and its bulk had darkened the sunshine, so that morning seemed like afternoon and three o'clock in the day was like dusk. But when night came the electric light flooded Em's front room with its keen, pale splendor, as though it had been the marvellous moonlight of another planet. One evening a sudden thought seized the girl, and she tried those acute white rays to sew by. Always afterward she did her work at night; and took what rest she could get between morning and the hours that followed. Soon others in the house imitated her—such as were not too slothful and drunken among womankind. Those cold and colorless beams poured in upon bent shapes and wan faces, night after night. The late feasts of luxury and dissipation in other parts of the town were copied here with tints of frightful parody and irony. These were revellers with cups of gall for their wine, and spectres of want to serve as footmen. Sin rioted in the reeking house, whose very stairs had rotten creaks when you trod them, as though fatigued by the steps of sots and trulls. To enter some of the rooms was to smell infection and to face beastliness. Fever lived in the sinks and closets along the halls, where festered refuse more rancid and stenchful than stale swill, and so vile that to name it would be to deal with words which are the dung of lexicons. Those halls had nooks of gloom where miasma might have fled in fright before the human grossness that spawned there. Little children dipped their chastity in poison between the scurfy-grained wainscots of every corridor, and twisted their soft lips into the shaping of oaths that would scare brothels. Now and then, in the lull of midnight, when the sewing-machines clattered from rooms like Em's and her toilful sisters, high yells would ring out as the beaten wife cowered and shivered, murder had been done. There was a room with a ghost in it of a hanged desperado, which had so lowered its rent by its uncanny pranks that an Italian couple with six little ones had got it cheap after quitting the steamer. Malaria forever kept busy her minions of disease, and the just historian of this noxious house must have collected his annals ill if he forgot to tell how often pine-wood coffins of the Potter's Field[1] undertaker had been hustled over its noisome floors. (Chapter 8)

★　★　★　★　★

[Cora falls in love with Casper Drummond, son of a wealthy New York entrepreneur. He gets her work and she secretly moves into his town house. Casper's parents, however, have arranged for his marriage to a rich young woman, and he is forced to break off with Cora. She is homeless and begins to drink heavily. The narrative accounts for her fall thus:]

She had no philosophy, no aidful optimism born of culture, no courage of the sort that is nurtured by an educated view of just how much self-blame might be one's rightful desert. She had, and still possessed, a fair share of religious awe and reverence; but this endowment, in so far as it served her at all, served her ill, since it pierced her with a recognition of her own repulsive sin, and deepened her forlorn realization that the coming scourge and contumely of society would be wreaked only through the just consequences of her merited wrong-doing. When a woman has lost her purity before the eyes of the world she is like some delicate piece of porcelain from which the limed charm of fruit or flower has been rudely scratched. It needs the most careful and skilled craft to re-enamel that injured surface, and for poor Cora, there was no such deft-fingered artisanship. She had tried very hard to be good; and she had failed hopelessly. This became the incessant haunting formula of her reflections, and week after week many a bitter evidence of how

---

[1]   See note page 164.

life teemed with sorrow and guilt not unlike her own turned the dreary hospital into a school of despair.

True, it was an edifice consecrated to pity; she perceived that most clearly, and often blessed it for the succor it had conferred upon her. But while it taught her that humanity is not wholly callous to the woes of its fellow-creatures, a subtler lesson was learned from it of the pitfalls into which those fellow-creatures are forever being plunged by the savage forces of birth, heredity and poverty. Hers was doubtless not the trained mind to perceive it, but she had striven to strike a pact of amity with the world, and the world had spit in her face and caught her by the throat as a return for the overture. A sentimental scream at "pessimism" is forever being raised against any cumulative view of instances like these; but it is none the less true that life shouts them to us from the house-tops while we stuff our ears with the cotton of individual dollar-getting, and turn even the divine selfishness of family love into an egotistic indifference that either soothes conscience-qualms by lazy alms-giving or quite murders philanthropy by a dull-blooded sloth [...]

[Most human souls are lax in their receptivity to sin proportionately as they have once been fierce in their resistance of it.] Cora did not satisfy herself with half-measures. The ruin was complete. Every moral beam and rafter trembled, every clamp and stanchion gave way [...] Cora changed her residence. For a time she dwelt in luxury; her delicate and graceful figure trailed silks and glittered with gems. A certain kind of adoration grovelled before her. The next summer went by for her in a whirl of spurious pomp and splendor. [She might have held her own through many seasons with a malignant magnificence, but for one cause—conscience.] That cried to her in every brilliant she strung about her throat, every crimson or purple in which she clad her shape. Her outraged moral sense demanded some sort of narcotic; love had no part in her new mode of life, or, if its influence entered there, the effect was one of reminded massacre and onslaught. She had murdered sentiment, but she could not lay its haunting ghost. Wine brought her peace, and the hands that paid her the wage of self-abasement lifted to her lips the cup that deadened remorse. For months her career became one of mad rashness. She felt herself harden, ossify. Her beauty lasted, though it became dulled and coarsened, gaining perhaps in an exuberance prophetic of decay, like that of a rose forced by its chemic heat from bud to bloom, and baring its fragrant heart at the price of langorous petals. Pleasure thrummed its viol in her ears, and vice dragged her by the waist into its rompish dance. The town blushed voluptuously before her sight; it had no more hints of want or toil in the hectic joys its days and nights proffered. Experience had flung aside its old austerities like the worn garments of a beggar suddenly dowered with millions. Time smothered his scythe in flowers, though the blade gleamed through their heavy tangles. Her clock ticked music, but there were hoarse notes in its cadence now and then, as harsh as when a grain of sand grits on the teeth in food cooked by the skill of deftest kitchens. Horrible moments of fatigue and self-disgust would be banished with draughts of stimulant that made existence abnormally jocund. Hope and courage were forced unnaturally from those lairs which they never quit, so summoned, except at the cost of fatal future depression. She drew great drafts on her nervous energy, regardless of that bankruptcy which awaits all such physical folly. There were times when she felt like shrinking from the very ardors that she aroused, as though they had been leprous and pestilent. Again she would be spurred by a fierce exultation in her own worst errors, and seem to taunt the very greed of fate, that it should have denied her so much, and yet left her these permitted funds and fonts of indulgence. There was then a bacchanal revolt[1] in her words and mien that carried with it a terrible and poignant charm. You might almost have fancied that she exhaled some odor at once delicious and deadly, like a blossom whose gaudy grace is akin to baleful creatures beamed on by the same tropic sun. "She'd be glorious if she were educated," a certain man of better class than she often met, once said of her. "She has beauty that's positively harrowing; her hair and her dimples and her coloring and those gold lights that swim in her brown eyes make her seem like a sorceress that has glided alive from the mists of song and story. But the moment she opens her lips the spell's broken. She has no more grammar than a lawyer's brief, and I don't believe she knows what's the capital of New York. Besides, she going at a killing gallop. In a year, at this rate, she'll be on the common streets."

[Drunk and destitute, Cora runs into Owen Slattery who, having once proposed marriage to her, is now a destitute alcoholic. Dismayed by her condition and the destruction of her beauty, he cuts her throat before killing himself.] (Chapters 27 and 28)

---

[1] Drunken revelry, an orgy.

Appendix D: Crane on Realism and Maggie

1. "Howells Discussed at Avon-by-the-Sea" (August 1891)

[Crane reported this lecture by Hamlin Garland for the *New York Tribune*, 18 August 1891. See Appendix F1]

At the Seaside Assembly the morning lecture was delivered by Professor Hamlin Garland, of Boston, on W.D. Howells, the novelist. He said: "No man stands for a more vital principle than does Mr. Howells. He stands for modern-spirit, sympathy and truth. He believes in the progress of ideals, the relative in art. His definition of idealism cannot be improved upon, 'the truthful treatment of material'. He does not insist upon any special material, but only that the novelist be true to himself and to things as he sees them. It is absurd to call him photographic. The photograph is false in perspective, in light and shade, in focus. When a photograph can depict atmosphere and sound, the comparison will have some meaning, and then it will not be used as a reproach. Mr Howells' work has deepened in insight and widened in sympathy from the first. His canvas has grown large, and has thickened with figures. Between 'Their Wedding Journey' and 'A Hazard of New Fortunes' there is an immense distance. 'A Modern Instance' is the greatest, most rigidly artistic novel ever written by an American, and ranks with the great novels of the world.[1] 'A Hazard of New Fortunes' is the greatest, sanest, truest study of a city in fiction. The test of the value of Mr Howells' work will come fifty years from now, when his sheafs of novels will form the most accurate, sympathetic and artistic study of American society yet made by an American. Howells is a many-sided man, a humorist of astonishing delicacy and imagination, and he has written of late some powerful poems in a full, free style. He is by all odds the most American and vital of our literary men to-day. He stands for all that is progressive and humanitarian in our fiction, and his following increases each day. His success is very great, and it will last."

---

[1] Howells's first novel, *Their Wedding Journey*, was published in 1872. *A Modern Instance* appeared in 1882, and *A Hazard of New Fortunes* in 1890.

2. From a Letter to Lily Brandon Munroe (April 1893)[1]

Hamlin Garland was the first to over-whelm me with all manner of extraordinary language. The book has made me a powerful friend in W.D. Howells. B.O. Flower of the *Arena*[2] has practically offered me the benefits of his publishing company for all that I may in future write. Albert Shaw of the "Review of Reviews" wrote me congratulations this morning and to-morrow I dine with the editor of the "Forum."

So I think I can say that if I "watch out" I'm almost a success. And "such a boy, too," they say.

I do not think, however, that I will get enough applause to turn my head. I don't see why I should. I merely did what I could, in a simple way, and recognition from such men as Howells, Garland, Flower and Shaw, has shown me that I was not altogether reprehensible. [...]

They tell me I did a horrible thing, but, they say, "it's great."

"And its style," said Garland to Howells, "Egad, it has no style! Absolutely transparent! Wonderful—wonderful." [...]

3. Letter to Ripley Hitchcock (February 1896)

[Hitchcock was an editor at D. Appleton and Company, publisher of Crane's *The Red Badge of Courage*. The success of that novel led to Appleton's offering to issue a revised version of *Maggie*.]

I am working at *Maggie*. She will be down to you in a few days. I have dispensed with a goodly number of damns. I have no more copies of the book or I would have sent you one.

I want to approach Appleton & Co on a delicate matter. I don't care much about money up here save when I have special need of it and just at this time there is a beautiful riding-mare for sale for a hundred dollars. The price will go up each week, almost, until spring and I am crazy to get her now. I don't want to strain your traditions but if I am worth $100. in your office, I would rather have it now.

---

[1] Letters in this appendix are reproduced from *The Correspondence of Stephen Crane*, ed. Stanley Wertheim and Paul Sorrentino (New York: Columbia UP, 1988). Reprinted with permission of the publisher.

[2] Benjamin Orange Flower (1858-1918), editor of *The Arena*.

4. Letter to Ripley Hitchcock (10 February 1896)

I am delighted with your prompt sympathy in regard to the saddle horse. It is a luxury to feel that some of my pleasures are due to my little pen. I will send you *Maggie* by detail. I have carefully plugged at the words which hurt. Seems to me the book wears quite a new aspect from very slight omissions. Did you know that the book is very short? Only about 20000 words?

5. Letter to Ripley Hitchcock (2 April 1896)

I am engaged on the preface.[1] Don't let anyone put chapter headings on the book. The proofs make me ill. Let somebody go over them—if you think best—and watch for bad grammatical form & bad spelling. I am too jaded with Maggie to be able to see it.

---

[1] The preface is lost, if indeed it was ever completed.

Appendix E: The New Journalism

1. From William Dean Howells, "The Man of Letters as a Man of Business," *Literature and Life* (New York: Harper, 1902)

[Howells wrote this essay in 1893.]

I think that every man ought to work for his living, without exception, and that when he has once avouched his willingness to work, society should provide him with work and warrant him a living. I do not think any man ought to live by an art. A man's art should be his privilege, when he has proven his fitness to exercise it, and has otherwise earned his daily bread; and its results should be free to all. There is an instinctive sense of this, even in the midst of the grotesque confusion of our economic being; people feel that there is something profane, something impious, in taking money for a picture, or a poem, or a statue. Most of all, the artist himself feels this. He puts on a bold front with the world, to be sure, and brazens it out as Business; but he knows very well that there is something false and vulgar in it; and that the work which cannot be truly priced in money cannot be truly paid in money. He can, of course, say that the priest takes money for reading the marriage service, for christening the new-born babe, and for saying the last office for the dead; that the physician sells healing; that justice itself is paid for; and that he is merely a party to the thing that is and must be. He can say that, as the thing is, unless he sells his art he cannot live, that society will leave him to starve if he does not hit its fancy in a picture, or a poem, or a statue; and all this is bitterly true. He is, and he must be, only too glad if there is a market for his wares. Without a market for his wares he must perish, or turn to making something that will sell better than pictures, or poems, or statues. All the same, the sin and the shame remain, and the averted eye sees them still, with its inward vision. Many will make believe otherwise, but I would rather not make believe otherwise; and in trying to write of Literature as Business I am tempted to begin by saying that Business is the opprobrium of Literature. (Section I)

★ ★ ★ ★ ★

Literature is at once the most intimate and the most articulate of the arts. It cannot impart its effect through the senses or the nerves as the other arts can; it is beautiful only through the intelligence; it is the mind speaking to the mind; until it has been put into absolute terms, of an invariable significance, it does not exist at all. It cannot awaken this emotion in one, and that in another; if it fails to express precisely the meaning of the author, if it does not say *him*, it says nothing, and is nothing. So that when a poet has put his heart, much or little, into a poem, and sold it to a magazine, the scandal is greater than when a painter has sold a picture to a patron, or a sculptor has modelled a statue to order. These are artists less articulate and less intimate than the poet; they are more exterior to their work; they are less personally in it; they part with less of themselves in the dicker. It does not change the nature of the case to say that Tennyson and Longfellow and Emerson[1] sold the poems in which they couched the most mystical messages their genius was charged to bear mankind. They submitted to the conditions which none can escape; but that does not justify the conditions, which are none the less the conditions of hucksters because they are imposed upon poets. If it will serve to make my meaning a little clearer we will suppose that a poet has been crossed in love, or has suffered some real sorrow, like the loss of a wife or child. He pours out his broken heart in verse that shall bring tears of sacred sympathy from his readers, and an editor pays him a hundred dollars for the right of bringing his verse to their notice. It is perfectly true that the poem was not written for these dollars, but it is perfectly true that it was sold for them. The poet must use his emotions to pay his provision bills; he has no other means; society does not propose to pay his bills for him. Yet, and at the end of the ends, the unsophisticated witness finds the transaction ridiculous, finds it repulsive, finds it shabby. Somehow he knows that if our huck-stering civilization did not at every moment violate the eternal fitness of things, the poet's song would have been given to the world, and the poet would have been cared for by the whole human brotherhood, as any man should be who does the duty that every man owes it.

The instinctive sense of the dishonor which money-purchase does to art is so strong that sometimes a man of letters who can pay his way otherwise refuses pay for his work, as Lord Byron[2] did, for a while, from a noble pride, and as Count Tolstoy[3] has tried to do, from a noble

---

[1] Alfred Lord Tennyson (1809–92), English poet; Henry Wadsworth Longfellow (1807–82), American poet; Ralph Waldo Emerson (1803–82), American essayist, philosopher, and poet.

[2] George Gordon Byron (1788–1824), English poet.

[3] Leo Tolstoy (1828–1910), Russian novelist.

conscience. But Byron's publisher profited by a generosity which did not reach his readers; and the Countess Tolstoy collects the copyright which her husband foregoes; so that these two eminent instances of protest against business in literature may be said not to have shaken its money basis. I know of no others; but there may be many that I am culpably ignorant of. Still, I doubt if there are enough to affect the fact that Literature is Business as well as Art, and almost as soon. At present business is the only human solidarity; we are all bound together with that chain, whatever interests and tastes and principles separate us, and I feel quite sure that in writing of the Man of Letters as a Man of Business, I shall attract far more readers than I should in writing of him as an Artist. Besides, as an artist he has been done a great deal already; and a commercial state like ours has really more concern in him as a business man. Perhaps it may sometimes be different; I do not believe it will till the conditions are different, and that is a long way off. [...] (Section II)

★   ★   ★   ★   ★

Under the regime of the great literary periodicals the prosperity of literary men would be much greater than it actually is, if the magazines were altogether literary. But they are not, and this is one reason why literature is still the hungriest of the professions. Two-thirds of the magazines are made up of material which, however excellent, is without literary quality. Very probably this is because even the highest class of readers, who are the magazine readers, have small love of pure literature, which seems to have been growing less and less in all classes. I say seems, because there are really no means of ascertaining the fact, and it may be that the editors are mistaken in making their periodicals two-thirds popular science, politics, economics, and the timely topics which I will call contemporanies; I have sometimes thought they were. But however that may be, their efforts in this direction have narrowed the field of literary industry, and darkened the hope of literary prosperity kindled by the unexampled prosperity of their periodicals. They pay very well indeed for literature; they pay from five or six dollars a thousand words for the work of the unknown writer, to a hundred and fifty dollars a thousand words for that of the most famous, or the most popular, if there is a difference between fame and popularity; but they do not, altogether, want enough literature to justify the best business talent in devoting itself to belles-lettres, to fiction, or poetry, or humorous sketches of travel, or light essays; business talent can do far better in drygoods, groceries, drugs, stocks, real estate, railroads, and the like. I do not think there is any danger of a ruinous competition from it in the field which, though narrow, seems so rich to us poor fellows, whose business talent is small, at the best. […]

The man of letters must make up his mind that in the United States the fate of a book is in the hands of the women. It is the women with us who have the most leisure, and they read the most books. They are far better educated, for the most part, than our men, and their tastes, if not their minds, are more cultivated. Our men read the newspapers, but our women read the books; the more refined among them read the magazines. If they do not always know what is good, they do know what pleases them, and it is useless to quarrel with their decisions, for there is no appeal from them. To go from them to the men would be going from a higher to a lower court, which would be honestly surprised and bewildered, if the thing were possible. As I say, the author of light literature, and often the author of solid literature, must resign himself to obscurity unless the ladies choose to recognize him. Yet it would be impossible to forecast their favor for this kind or that. Who could prophesy it for another, who guess it for himself? We must strive blindly for it, and hope somehow that our best will also be our prettiest; but we must remember at the same time that it is not the ladies' man who is the favorite of the ladies.

There are of course a few, a very few, of our greatest authors, who have striven forward to the first place in our Valhalla[1] without the help of the largest reading-class among us; but I should say that these were chiefly the humorists, for whom women are said nowhere to have any warm liking, and who have generally with us come up through the newspapers, and have never lost the favor of the newspaper readers. They have become literary men, as it were, without the newspapers' readers knowing it; but those who have approached literature from another direction, have won fame in it chiefly by grace of the women, who first read them, and then made their husbands and fathers read them. Perhaps, then, and as a matter of business, it would be well for a serious author, when he finds that he is not pleasing the women, and probably never will please them, to turn humorous author, and aim at the countenance of the men. Except as a humorist he certainly never will get it, for your American, when he is not making money, or trying to do it, is making a joke, or trying to do it. (Section VI)

---

[1] In Scandanavian mythology the palace in which heroes slain in battle feasted for eternity.

★ ★ ★ ★ ★

I hope that I have not been hinting that the author who approaches literature through journalism is not as fine and high a literary man as the author who comes directly to it, or through some other avenue; I have not the least notion of condemning myself by any such judgment. But I think it is pretty certain that fewer and fewer authors are turning from journalism to literature, though the entente cordiale between the two professions seems as great as ever. I fancy, though I may be as mistaken in this as I am in a good many other things, that most journalists would have been literary men if they could, at the beginning, and that the kindness they almost always show to young authors is an effect of the self-pity they feel for their own thwarted wish to be authors. When an author is once warm in the saddle, and is riding his winged horse to glory, the case is different: they have then often no sentiment about him; he is no longer the image of their own young aspiration, and they would willingly see Pegasus buck under him, or have him otherwise brought to grief and shame. They are apt to gird at him for his unhallowed gains, and they would be quite right in this if they proposed any way for him to live without them; as I have allowed at the outset, the gains *are* unhallowed. Apparently it is unseemly for an author or two to be making half as much by their pens as popular ministers often receive in salary; the public is used to the pecuniary prosperity of some of the clergy, and at least sees nothing droll in it; but the paragrapher can always get a smile out of his readers at the gross disparity between the ten thousand dollars Jones gets for his novel, and the five pounds Milton got for his epic.[1] I have always thought Milton was paid too little, but I will own that he ought not to have been paid at all, if it comes to that. Again, I say that no man ought to live by any art; it is a shame to the art if not to the artist; but as yet there is no means of the artist's living otherwise, and continuing an artist.

The literary man has certainly no complaint to make of the newspaper man, generally speaking. I have often thought with amazement of the kindness shown by the press to our whole unworthy craft, and of the help so lavishly and freely given to rising and even risen authors. To put it coarsely, brutally, I do not suppose that any other business receives so much gratuitous advertising, except the theatre. It is enormous, the space given in the newspapers to literary notes, literary

---

[1] John Milton (1608-74), *Paradise Lost* (1667).

announcements, reviews, interviews, personal paragraphs, biographies, and all the rest, not to mention the vigorous and incisive attacks made from time to time upon different authors for their opinions of romanticism, realism, capitalism, socialism, Catholicism, and Sandemanianism.[1] I have sometimes doubted whether the public cared for so much of it all as the editors gave them, but I have always said this under my breath, and I have thankfully taken my share of the common bounty. A curious fact, however, is that this vast newspaper publicity seems to have very little to do with an author's popularity, though ever so much with his notoriety. Those strange subterranean fellows who never come to the surface in the newspapers, except for a contemptuous paragraph at long intervals, outsell the famousest of the celebrities, and secretly have their horses and yachts and country seats, while immodest merit is left to get about on foot and look up summer board at the cheaper hotels. That is probably right, or it would not happen; it seems to be in the general scheme, like millionairism and pauperism; but it becomes a question, then, whether the newspapers, with all their friendship for literature, and their actual generosity to literary men, can really help one much to fortune, however much they help one to fame. Such a question is almost too dreadful, and though I have asked it, I will not attempt to answer it. I would much rather consider the question whether if the newspapers can make an author they can also unmake him, and I feel pretty safe in saying that I do not think they can. The Afreet once out of the bottle can never be coaxed back or cudgelled back; and the author whom the newspapers have made cannot be unmade by the newspapers. They consign him to oblivion with a rumor that fills the land, and they keep visiting him there with an uproar which attracts more and more notice to him. An author who has long enjoyed their favor, suddenly and rather mysteriously loses it, through his opinions on certain matters of literary taste, say. For the space of five or six years he is denounced with a unanimity and an incisive vigor that ought to convince him there is something wrong. If he thinks it is his censors, he clings to his opinions with an abiding constance, while ridicule, obloquy, caricature, burlesque, critical refutation and personal detraction follow unsparingly upon every expression, for instance, of his belief that romantic fiction is the highest form of fiction, and that the base, sordid, photographic, commonplace school of Tolstoy, Tourguenief,

---

[1] A movement led by Scots clergyman Robert Sandeman (1718-71) which held that Christ's kingdom was entirely spiritual and so beyond both state and church control.

Zola, Hardy, and James, are unworthy a moment's comparison with the school of Rider Haggard.[1] All this ought certainly to unmake the author in question, and strew his *disjecta membra* wide over the realm of oblivion. But this is not really the effect. Slowly but surely the clamor dies away, and the author, without relinquishing one of his wicked opinions, or in anywise showing himself repentant, remains apparently whole; and he even returns in a measure to the old kindness: not indeed to the earlier day of perfectly smooth things, but certainly to as much of it as he merits.

I would not have the young author, from this imaginary case, believe that it is well either to court or to defy the good opinion of the press. In fact, it will not only be better taste, but it will be better business for him to keep it altogether out of his mind. There is only one whom he can safely try to please, and that is himself. If he does this he will very probably please other people; but if he does not please himself he may be sure that he will not please them; the book which he has not enjoyed writing, no one will enjoy reading. Still, I would not have him attach too little consequence to the influence of the press. I should say, let him take the celebrity it gives him gratefully but not too seriously; let him reflect that he is often the necessity rather than the ideal of the paragrapher, and that the notoriety the journalists bestow upon him is not the measure of their acquaintance with his work, far less his meaning. They are good fellows, those poor, hard-pushed fellows of the press, but the very conditions of their censure, friendly or unfriendly, forbid it thoroughness, and it must often have more zeal than knowledge in it. (Section IX)

2. From David G. Croly, interview published in *Views and Interviews on Journalism*, ed. Charles F. Wingate (New York: F.B. Patterson, 1875)

The London *Spectator* some time since referred to the curious fact, which it may be well to note, that the modern novel and the newspaper are beginning to assimilate, and are becoming very much alike. The popular novel of two hundred years ago dealt with the ideal world, with

---

[1] Leo Tolstoy (1828-1910), Russian novelist; Ivan Turgenev (1818-83), Russian novelist and story writer; Émile Zola (1840-1902), French novelist; Thomas Hardy (1840-1928), English novelist and poet; Henry James (1843-1916), American-born novelist, critic, and short story writer; Sir (Henry) Rider Haggard (1856-1925), English popular novelist and author of *King Solomon's Mines* (1885).

fairies, ghosts, etc. Mrs. Radcliffe's and Monk Lewis' romances were among that list.[1] The popular novels, in their characters and plots, were remote from human interests. But the progress of fiction-writing has brought the novelist down to the affairs of everyday life. The popular novels of the day, like the contemporary plays, are intensely realistic. Anthony Trollope[2] deals with the love affairs and business interests which might occur to any respectable New York or London family. Had Trollope lived in the time of Mrs. Radcliffe he would have composed romances in the mysteries of Udolpho vein. Dickens and Thackeray[3] drew their characters from everyday life. On the other hand, the newspaper in times past thought it beneath its dignity to discuss anything of a domestic or social character. The topics treated were abstract, and remote from men's daily lives. But now journalism is taking greater hold of social questions. It is this feature which gives so much interest to our story papers and magazines. If people could find in their newspapers the same mental pabulum that they look for in their magazines, they would not read the magazines or novels so much as they do, for truth is really stranger than fiction. But, unfortunately, the newspaper has heretofore been compelled to deal with topics furnished by the police station and the divorce court. [...]

The larger a city grows the less value is its purely local news. When New York had a hundred thousand inhabitants, every one was interested in every target company that passed through the streets. Every fire, concert, ball and dog fight had its local value. But when New York becomes a real metropolis, the person who lives in the First Ward will take very little interest in what occurs in the Twelfth, except it be of human interest. An inhabitant of the Ninth Ward has scarcely more concern in a murder in Mackerelville than in one in Kansas. The tendency in very large cities is to give the go-by to purely local news, and to direct their attention to the general news of the world [...] When I lived in Orange, I was interested in church affairs, concerts and lectures, because in a small place you know everybody. In New York I do not know my next-door neighbour.

---

[1]   Ann Radcliffe (1764-1832), English novelist and author of *The Mysteries of Udolpho* (1794); Matthew Gregory Lewis (1775-1818), English novelist and playwright, author of the Gothic novel *The Monk* (1796).

[2]   English novelist, 1815-82.

[3]   Charles Dickens (1812-70) and William Makepeace Thackeray (1811-63), English novelists.

3. From Lincoln Steffens, *Autobiography* (New York: Harcourt Brace, 1931)

[As city editor of the *New York Commercial Advertiser* during the 1890s, Steffens adopted a policy of recruiting talented graduates from the Ivy League colleges.]

My inspiration was a love of New York, just as it was, and my ambition was to have it reported so that New Yorkers might see, not merely read of it, as it was: rich and poor, wicked and good, ugly but beautiful, growing, great. [...]

My reporters liked our attitude. They were picked men and women, picked for their unusual, literary pose. I hated the professional newspaper man; I had seen him going down, down, down, and I dreaded his fate. I remember once how one of them came to me for a job at the beginning of our enterprise when I needed reporters. I reconizged the type; I smelled it on his alcoholic breath, read it on his cynical lips. To stall him, I asked him what experience he had had.

"Experience!" he echoed. "I have been Washington correspondent of the *Herald*, city editor of the *Tribune*, London man for the *Times*. I"— he waved his arm contemptuously out over our long, big city room and concluded—"I have been the editor of this shebang."

"Then there is no place here for you now," I cried at him, my hands up in horror. [...]

I wanted fresh, young, enthusiastic writers who would see and make others see the life of the city. This meant individual styles, and old newspaper men wrote in the style of their paper.

[...]

In the main [...] the *Commercial* reporters were sought out of the graduating classes of the universities, Harvard, Yale, Princeton, and Columbia, where we let it be known that writers were wanted—not newspaper men, but writers.

My verbal advertisement and my announced rules drew the right kind of young men. I would take fellows, I said, whose professor of English believed they were going to be able to write and who themselves wanted to be writers, provided, however, that they did not intend to be journalists. "We" had use for any one who, openly or secretly, hoped to be a poet, a novelist, or an essayist [...] When a reporter no longer saw red at a fire, when he was so used to police news that a murder was not a human tragedy but only a crime, he could not write police news for us. We preferred the fresh staring eyes to the informed mind and the blunted pencil. To express if not to enforce this, I used to warn my staff that whenever a reporter became a good all-round newspaper man he would be fired. [...]

From Yale came Larkin G. Mead, a nephew of William Dean Howells, who couldn't spell, punctuate, or keep to the rules of primary grammar, but had a sensitive eye, red hair and freckles, and drove words like nails. [...]

We talked of such things on our paper. We dared to use such words as "literature," "art," "journalism," not only in the city room itself, but at a fire or in the barrooms where the Press drank. The old hacks hated it and ridiculed us [...]. Cynicism was a pose in the journalism of those days, and my staff did not take it. They meant to be writers, and they did not pretend to be working only for money. (Chapter XVII)

Appendix F: Reviews

1. Hamlin Garland, *Arena* (June 1893)

[Garland (1860-1940) was a short story writer and novelist. He propounded a theory of realistic fiction called "veritism," which may have influenced Crane's writing. Crane heard him lecture on William Dean Howells in August 1891 (see Appendix D1, and Garland would later try to secure a publisher for *Maggie*.]

This [*Maggie*] is of more interest to me, both because it is the work of a young man, and also because it is a work of astonishingly good style. It deals with poverty and vice and crime also, but it does so, not out of curiosity, not out of salaciousness, but because of a distinct art impulse, the desire to utter in truthful phrase a certain rebellious cry. It is the voice of the slums. It is not written by a dilettante; it is written by one who has lived the life. The young author, Stephen Crane, is a native of the city, and has grown up in the very scenes he describes. His book is the most truthful and unhackneyed study of the slums I have yet read, fragment though it is. It is pictorial, graphic, terrible in its directness. It has no conventional phrases. It gives the dialect of the slums as I have never before seen it written—crisp, direct, terse. It is another locality finding voice.

It is important because it voices the blind rebellion of Rum Alley and Devil's Row. It creates the atmosphere of the jungles, where vice festers and crime passes gloomily by, where outlawed human nature rebels against God and man.

The story fails of rounded completeness. It is only a fragment. It is typical only of the worst elements of the alley. The author should delineate the families living on the next street, who live lives of heroic purity and hopeless hardship.

The dictum is amazingly simple and fine for so young a writer. Some of the works illuminate like flashes of light. Mr. Crane is only twenty-one years of age, and yet he has met and grappled with the actualities of the street in almost unequalled grace and strength. With such a *technique* already at command, with life mainly *before him*, Stephen Crane is to be henceforth reckoned with. 'Maggie' should be put beside 'Van Bibber'[1] to see the extremes of New York as stated by two young men. Mr. Crane

---

[1]   *Van Bibber and Others* (1892) by Richard Harding Davis.

need not fear comparisons so far as *technique* goes, and Mr. Davis will need to step forward right briskly or he may be overtaken by a man who impresses the reader with a sense of almost unlimited resource.

2. From William Dean Howells, "New York Low Life in Fiction," *New York World* (26 July 1896)

[Howells (1837-1920) was a novelist and critic who served as editor of the *Atlantic Monthly* and, later, *Harper's Monthly*. He made frequent references to Crane's work as part of a more general analysis of literary realism.]

The fiction meant to be read, as distinguishable from the fiction meant to be represented, has been much later in dealing with the same material, and it is only just beginning to deal with it in the spirit of the great modern masters. I cannot find that such clever and amusing writers as Mr. Townsend, or Mr. Ralph, or Mr. Ford[1] has had it on their consciences to report in the regions of the imagination the very effect of the life which they all seem at times to have seen so clearly. There is apparently nothing but the will that is wanting in either of them, but perhaps the want of the will is the want of an essential factor, though I should like very much to have them try for a constant reality in their studies; and I am far from wishing to count them out in an estimate of what has been done in that direction. It is only just to Mr. Stephen Crane, however, to say that he was first in the field where they made themselves known earlier. His story of *Maggie, a Girl of the Streets*, which has been recently published by the Appletons, was in the hands of a few in an edition which the author could not even give away three years ago; and I think it is two years, now, since I saw *George's Mother*, which Edward Arnold has brought out, in the manuscript.

Their present publication is imaginably due to the success of *The Red Badge of Courage*, but I do not think that they will owe their critical acceptance to the obstreperous favor which that has won. As a piece of art they are altogether superior to it, and as representations of life their greater fidelity cannot be questioned. [...]

---

[1]   Edward W. Townsend (1855-1942) American, author of *Chimmie Faden* (1895); Julian Ralph (1853 1903) American, journalist and short story writer; Paul Leicester Ford (1865-1902) American, novelist and historian.

There is a curious unity in the spirit of the arts; and I think that what strikes me most in the story of *Maggie* is that quality of fatal necessity which dominates Greek tragedy. From the conditions it all had to be, and there were the conditions. I felt this in Mr. Hardy's *Jude*,[1] where the principle seems to become conscious in the writer; but there is apparently no consciousness of any such motive in the author of *Maggie*. Another effect is that of an ideal of artistic beauty which is as present in the working out of this poor girl's squalid romance as in any classic fable. This will be foolishness, I know, to the foolish people who cannot discriminate between the material and the treatment in art, and who think that beauty is inseparable from daintiness and prettiness, but I do not speak to them. I appeal rather to such as feel themselves akin with every kind of human creature, and find neither high nor low when it is a question of inevitable suffering, or of a soul struggling vainly with an inexorable fate.

My rhetoric scarcely suggests the simple terms the author uses to produce the effect which I am trying to report again. They are simple, but always most graphic, especially when it comes to the personalities of the story. [...]

[I]t is notable how in all respects the author keeps himself well in hand. He is quite honest with his reader. He never shows his characters or his situations in any sort of sentimental glamour; if you will be moved by the sadness of common fates you will feel his intention, but he does not flatter his portraits of people or conditions to take your fancy. [...]

3. William Dean Howells, *Academy* (18 August 1900)

[Howells addressed this letter to Mrs. Stephen Crane (Cora Taylor) on 19 July 1900; Crane had died on 5 June.]

Hamlin Garland first told me of *Maggie*, which your husband then sent me. I was slow in getting at it, and he wrote me a heartbreaking note to the effect that he saw I did not care for his book. On this I read it, and found that I did care for it immensely. I asked him to come and see me, and he came to tea and stayed far into the evening, talking about his work, and the stress there was on him to put in the profanities which I thought would shock the public from him, and about the semi-savage poor, whose types he had studied in that book. He spoke wisely and kindly about them, and especially about the Tough, who was tough

---

[1] Thomas Hardy, *Jude the Obscure* (1895).

because, as he said, he felt that 'everything was on him.' He came several times afterwards, but not at all oftener than I wished, or half so often, and I knew he was holding off from modesty. He never came without leaving behind him some light on the poor, sad life he knew so well in New York, so that I saw it more truly than ever before. He had thought wisely and maturely about it, but he had no plan for it, perhaps not even any hope without a plan. He was the great artist which he was because he was in no wise a sentimentalist. Of course I was struck almost as much by his presence as by his mind, and admired his strange, melancholy beauty, in which there was already the forecast of his early death. His voice charmed me, and the sensitive lips from which it came, with their intelligent and ironical smile, and his mystical, clouded eyes. Inevitably there was the barrier between his youth and my age that the years make, and I could not reach him where he lived as a young man might. I cannot boast that I understood him fully; a man of power, before he comes to its full expression, is hard to understand. It is doubtful if he is quite in the secret himself, but I was always aware of his power, and nothing good that he did surprised me. He came to see me last just before he sailed for England the last time, and then he showed the restlessness of the malarial fever that was preying on him; he spoke of having got it in Cuba. But even then, with the sense that we were getting at each other less than ever, I felt his rare quality. I do not think America has produced a more distinctive and vital talent.

4. From Unsigned review, *Nashville Banner* (15 August 1896)

The details of this story are strongly presented, and with a peculiar power they hold the interest unfaltering to the end. But the fascination is a miserable and depressing one, and the average reader will regret his inability to lay the book aside until its dreary story is finished.

Maggie, a child of the slums, is cursed with the triple burden of a drunken and sullen father, a drunken virago for a mother, and a drunken bully for a brother. Drink, shiftlessness, ill-temper [...] make her childhood a terror, and her girlhood a tragedy which ends with her death. Yet in the midst of this environment the girl feebly struggles toward something better, and the pathetic proof of her higher sensibility is that when the innocence is gone and the man who has represented all that is good in life to her has proved himself as false and base as the rest, her feeling is still fine enough to wither under the shame of her sin, and she prefers death to further degradation. And the pathos of her tragedy is immeasurably increased by the description of poor Maggie's hero. [...]

We are told that Maggie is pretty. She is a flower that has 'blossomed in a mud-puddle,.... a most rare and wonderful product of a tenement district, a pretty girl.' And it is her beauty and her fatal aspirations that work her ruin, and that finally envelop the gloom of the story in the black hideousness of midnight, without one star to illume the darkness. And it is in this that the story is a failure, in spite of its strength. It is too hopeless, too full of misery, degradation and dirt. The reader flounders in a mire of pessimism, never once receiving from the author the offer of a helping hand or a word of encouragement, and the memory of the book is a nightmare, and the thought of it inexpressible [...], hopeless and depressing. And yet it is not an unmoral book, and in spite of the grime, the suffering, and the bitterness with which its pages are imbued, it is remarkably free from the disgusting impurities in which the pen of the ordinary realist is wont to revel. And, indeed, as a philanthropic work, the story is a strong sermon, urging the need of greater charity of sentiment, as well as of gold for the poverty-hardened people of the slums. But as a literary production, and as such it invites our attention, it is a magnificent piece of realism, which loses its artistic value because its shadows are too deep and its lights too faint and evasive, missing, indeed, the highest aim of literature, which is to give some small degree of pleasure, at least, to the world, and to prove itself not a clog, but an aspiration in the uplifting of humanity's heart.

A noticeable thing about the book is the resemblance of its methods to those of Victor Hugo,[1] a resemblance merely suggestive at first, but which becomes more pronounced on a second reading. Sentences like these: 'He menaced mankind at the intersection of the streets'; 'He himself occupied a downtrodden position which had a private, but distinct element of grandeur in its isolation'; 'The girl, Maggie, blossomed in a mud-puddle'; 'The disorder and dirt of her home of a sudden appeared before her and began to take a potential aspect'; 'Here was one whose knuckles could ring defiantly against the granite of law,' might have been taken verbatim from some volume of the great Frenchman. But this influence, which has resulted in a probably unconscious imitation, is no discredit to Mr. Crane, for he has absorbed and reproduced not only Hugo's habit of language, but much of the over-largeness of thought which seems to fill up his curt sentences and overflow them with

---

[1] French novelist, 1802-85.

a half-latent strength of meaning, which never ceases to increase—a power-ful form of writing to which is due much of Hugo's unrivaled greatness.

5. From H.D. Traill, *Fortnightly Review* (1 January 1897)

In a day when the spurious is everywhere supposed to be successfully disguised and sufficiently recommended to the public by merely being described as new, it need not surprise us to find our attention solicited by a New Realism, of which the two most obvious things to be said are that it is unreal with the falsity of the half truth, and as old as the habit of exaggeration. One of the latest professors of this doubtful form of art, is the very young American writer, Mr. Stephen Crane, who first attracted notice in this country by a novel entitled *The Red Badge of Courage*. Whether that work was or was not described by its admirers as an achievement in realism, I am not aware. As a matter of fact, and as the antecedents, and indeed the age, of the writer showed, it was not a record of actual observation. Mr. Crane had evidently been an indus-trious investigator and collator of the emotional experiences of Soldiers, and had evolved from them a picture of the mental state of a recruit going into action. It was artistically done and obtained a not undeserved success; but no method, of course, could be less realistic, in the sense on which the professors of the New Realism insist, than the process which resulted in this elaborate study of the emotions of the battlefield from the pen of a young man who has never himself smelt powder.

Since then, however, Mr. Crane has given us two small volumes, which are presumably realistic or nothing. If circumstances have prevented the author from writing about soldiers in action 'with his eye on the object,' there are no such obstacles to his studying the Bowery and 'Bowery boys' from the life; we may take it, therefore, that *Maggie* and *George's Mother* are the products of such study. According to Mr. Howell's effusive 'Appreciation,' which prefaces it, *Maggie* is a remark-able story having 'that quality of fatal necessity which dominates Greek tragedy.' Let us see then what this Sophoclean[1] work is.

The story of *Maggie* opens with a fight between the boys of Rum Alley and those of Devil's Row. Jimmie, the heroine's brother, is a boy of Rum Alley, aged nine, and when the curtain draws up he is the centre of a circle of urchins who are pelting him with stones. [Traill Paraphrases Chapter 1.]

---

[1]   Sophocles (c. 496-405 BC), Greek tragedist.

That is the first chapter much condensed. In the original there are eight pages of it. Is it art? If so, is the making of mud-pies an artistic occupation, and are the neglected brats who are to be found rolling in the gutters of every great city unconscious artists?

In the next chapter Jimmie pummels his little sister, and his mother quarrels with and rates her husband till she drives him to the public-house, remaining at home to get drunk herself. In the third chapter, Jimmie, who has stopped out to avoid an outbreak of her intoxicated fury, steals home again late at night, listens outside the door to a fight going on within between his father and mother, and at last creeps in with his little sister to find both parents prostrate on the floor in a drunken stupor and to huddle in a corner until daybreak, cowering with terror lest they should awaken. For when you are a 'realist's' little boy, you have to be very handy and adaptable and do exactly what that realist requires of you: so that, though you may have been defying and cursing your father at one moment, like the daring little imp you have been described as being, you may at the next moment, and for the purpose of another sort of painful picture, have to behave like a cowed and broken-spirited child of a totally different type.

These opening scenes take up about one-fifth of the short book, and those that follow are like unto them. There is a little less fighting, but a good deal more drinking. Jimmie becomes a truck driver, and fights constantly with other drivers, but the fights are not described at length. His father dies, probably of drink, and his mother takes to drinking harder than ever. Maggie is seduced and deserted by Pete, the youth who appeared on the scene during the opening fight and hits one of the infant fighters on the back of the head. Jimmie resents the proceedings of the Bowery Lovelace as a breach of good manners, and, going with a friend to the tavern where Pete acts as 'bar-tender,' the two set upon him and there ensues a fight, in the course of which the lips of the combatants 'curl back and stretch tightly over the gums in ghoul-like grins.' It lasts for four pages, and is brought to a close by the intervention of the police, and the escape of Jimmie 'with his face drenched in blood.' How this story continues, how Maggie falls lower and lower and finally dies, and how after her death her gin-sodden mother is passionately entreated to forgive her, and at last graciously consents to do so—all this may be read in Mr. Crane's pages, and shall not here be summarised from them. Is it necessary to do so? Or to give a *précis* of the companion volume, *George's Mother*, the story of a 'little old woman' actually of sober and industrious habits, and of her actually not vicious though weak son, of whose backslidings she dies? Need I give specimen extracts from it? I hope not—I think not. The extracts which have been already given are perfectly fair samples of Mr. Crane's work. Anyone who likes to take it from the writer of this article, that to read these two little books through would be to wade through some three hundred and thirty pages of substantially the same stuff as the above extracts, will do Mr. Crane no injustice. So I will pass from him to a Realist of considerably larger calibre.

For Mr. Arthur Morrison, author of *Tales of Mean Streets* and *A Child of the Jago*, undoubtedly carries heavier guns than Mr. Crane. To begin with, he can tell a story, where Mr. Crane can only string together a series of loosely cohering incidents. Many of his characters are vividly and vigorously drawn, while the American writer puts us off for the most part with sketches and shadowy outlines. Mr. Morrison's ruffians and their ruffianism are better discriminated, and though there is plenty of fighting and drinking and general brutality in his last and strongest work—one of the faction fights in which, indeed, is related at quite inordinate length—he understands that the description of these things alone will not suffice to make a satisfactory story even about blackguards, and he has outgrown that touching *naïveté* displayed in the younger realist's obvious belief in the perpetual freshness and charm of mere squalor. He perceives that merely to follow his characters, as Mr. Crane does his, from the drinking-bar to the low music-hall and thence home again, day after day, with interludes of brawling and 'bashing' and other like recreations, becomes, after a hundred pages or so, a little monotonous, and that the life of the criminal in his constant struggle with the law, and in perpetual danger from its officers, possesses at least the element of 'sport,' and presents features of variety and interest which that of the mere so and tavern-brawler cannot possibly offer. Above all, Mr. Morrison wields a certain command of pathos, a power in which Mr. Crane is not only deficient, but of which he does not even appear to know the meaning; and were it not for a certain strange and, in truth, paradoxical defect, of which more hereafter, in his method of employing it, he would at times be capable of moving his readers very powerfully indeed. In a word, the English writer differs from the American by all the difference which divides the trained craftsman from the crude amateur, and deserves to that extent more serious and detailed criticism.

Select Bibliography

Baum, Rosalie Murphy. "Alcoholism and Family Abuse in *Maggie* and *The Bluest Eye*." *Mosaic: A Journal for the Interdisciplinary Study of Literature* 19.3 (1986): 91–105.

Begiebing, Robert J. "Stephen Crane's *Maggie*: The Death of the Self." *American Imago* 34 (1977): 50–71.

Bergon, Frank. *Stephen Crane's Artistry*. New York: Columbia UP, 1975.

Bradbury, Malcolm. "Romance and Reality in Maggie." *Journal of American Studies* 3 (1969): 111–21.

Brennan, Joseph X. "Ironic and Symbolic Structure in Crane's *Maggie*." *Nineteenth-Century Fiction* 16 (1962): 303–15.

Bruccoli, Matthew J. "Maggie's Last Night." *Stephen Crane Newsletter* 2.1 (1967): 10.

Cady, Edwin H. "Stephen Crane: Maggie, a Girl of the Streets." *Landmarks of American Writing*. Ed. Hennig Cohen. New York: Basic Books, 1969. 172–81.

Davis, Linda H. *Badge of Courage: The Life of Stephen Crane*. Boston and New York: Houghton Mifflin, 1998.

Dooley, Patrick Kiaran. *The Pluralistic Philosophy of Stephen Crane*. Urbana: U of Illinois P, 1993.

———. *Stephen Crane: An Annotated Bibliography of Secondary Scholarship*. New York: G.K. Hall, 1992.

Dow, William. "Performative Passages: Davis's *Life in the Iron Mills*, Crane's *Maggie*, and Norris's *McTeague*." *Twisted from the Ordinary: Essays on American Literary Naturalism*. Ed. Mary E. Papke. Knoxville, TN: U of Tennessee P, 2003.

Fitelson, David. "*Maggie: A Girl of the Streets* Portrays a 'Survival of the Fittest' World." *Readings on Stephen Crane*. Ed. Bonnie Szumski. San Diego, CA: Greenhaven, 1998. 168–79.

Ford, Philip H. "Illusion and Reality in Crane's *Maggie*." *Arizona Quarterly* 25 (1969): 293–303.

Fox, Austen. "Crane Is Preoccupied with the Theme of Isolation." *Readings on Stephen Crane*. Ed. Bonnie Szumski. San Diego, CA: Greenhaven, 1998. 56–62.

Fried, Michael. *Realism, Writing, Disfiguration: On Thomas Eakins and Stephen Crane*. Chicago: U of Chicago P, 1987.

Fudge, Keith. "Sisterhood Born from Seduction: Susanna Rowson's Charlotte Temple, and Stephen Crane's Maggie Johnson." *Journal of American Culture* 19.1 (1996): 43-50.

Gandal, Keith. "Stephen Crane's 'Maggie' and the Modern Soul." *ELH* 60.3 (1993): 759-85.

——. *The Virtues of the Vicious: Jacob Riis, Stephen Crane, and the Spectacle of the Slum.* Oxford, England: Oxford UP, 1997.

Gibson, Donald. *The Fiction of Stephen Crane.* Carbondale and Edwardsville: Southern Illinois UP, 1968.

Golemba, Henry. "'Distant Dinners' in Crane's *Maggie*: Representing 'the Other Half.'" *Essays in Literature* 21.2 (1994): 235-50.

Graff, Aida Farrag. "Metaphor and Metonymy: The Two Worlds of Crane's *Maggie*." *English Studies in Canada* 8.4 (1982): 422-36.

Graham, Don B. "Dreiser's Maggie." *American Literary Realism* 7 (1974): 169-70.

Gullason, Thomas. "The Sources of Stephen Crane's *Maggie*." *Philological Quarterly* 38 (1959): 497-502.

——. "The Symbolic Unity of 'The Monster.'" *Modern Language Notes* 75 (1960): 663-68.

——. "Thematic Patterns in Stephen Crane's Early Novels." *Nineteenth-Century Fiction* 16 (1961): 59-67.

——. *Stephen Crane's Career: Perspectives and Evaluations.* New York: New York UP, 1972.

——. "The Prophetic City in Stephen Crane's 1893 *Maggie*." *Modern Fiction Studies* 24 (1978): 129-37.

——. "Tragedy and Melodrama in Stephen Crane's *Maggie*." *Maggie: A Girl of the Streets, An Authoritative Text.* Ed. Donald Pizer. New York: Norton, 1979. 245-53.

Halliburton, David. *The Color of the Sky: A Study of Stephen Crane.* Cambridge: Cambridge UP, 1989.

Hapke, Laura. "The Alternate Fallen Woman in *Maggie: A Girl of the Streets*." *Markham Review* 12 (1983): 41-43.

Holton, Milne. "The Sparrow's Fall and the Sparrow's Eye: Crane's *Maggie*." *Studia Neophilologica* 41 (1969): 115-29.

——. *Cylinder of Vision: The Fiction and Journalistic Writing of Stephen Crane.* Baton Rouge: Louisiana State UP, 1972.

Horwitz, Howard. "Maggie and the Sociological Paradigm." *American Literary History* 10.4 (1998): 606-38.

Hussman, Lawrence E., Jr. "The Fate of the Fallen Woman in *Maggie* and *Sister Carrie*." *The Image of the Prostitute in Modern Literature.* Ed. Pierre L. Horn and Mary Beth Pringle. New York: Ungar, 1984. 91-100.

Kahn, Sy. "Stephen Crane and the Giant Voice in the Night: An Explication of 'The Monster.'" *Essays in Modern American Literature*. Ed. Richard E. Langford. Deland: Stetson UP, 1963. 35-45.

Kaplan, Amy. *The Social Construction of American Realism*. Chicago and London: U of Chicago P, 1988.

Karlen, Arno. "The Craft of Stephen Crane." *Georgia Review* 28 (1974): 473-77.

———. "Stylistic Weakness in *Maggie*." *Readings on Stephen Crane*. Ed. Bonnie Szumski. San Diego, CA: Greenhaven, 1998. 180-84.

Katz, Joseph. "The Maggie Nobody Knows." *Modern Fiction Studies* 12 (1966): 200-12.

Katz, Joseph. Ed. *Stephen Crane in Transition: Centenary Essays*. DeKalb, IL: Northern Illinois UP, 1972.

Knapp, Daniel. "Son of Thunder: Stephen Crane and the Fourth Evangelist." *Nineteenth-Century Fiction* 24 (1969): 259-66.

Kramer, Maurice. "Crane's *Maggie: A Girl of the Streets*." *Explicator* 22 (1964): Item 49.

Krause, Sydney J. "The Surrealism of Crane's Naturalism in *Maggie*." *American Literary Realism* 16.2 (1983): 253-61.

La France, Marston. *A Reading of Stephen Crane*. Oxford: Clarendon Press, 1971.

———. "George's Mother and the Other Half of Maggie." *Stephen Crane in Transition*. Ed. Joseph Katz. De Kalb: Northern Illinois UP, 1972. 35-53.

Minks, Tamara S. "Maggie Johnson: An American in a Fallen Eden." *Recovering Literature: A Journal of Contextualist Criticism* 16 (1988): 23-35.

Monteiro, George. "Amy Leslie on Stephen Crane's Maggie." *Journal of Modern Literature* 9.1 (1981): 147-48.

Nagel, James. *Stephen Crane and Literary Impressionism*. University Park: Pennsylvania State UP, 1980.

Novotny, George T. "Crane's *Maggie, A Girl of the Streets*." *Explicator* 50.4 (1992): 225-28.

Parker, Hershel, and Brian Higgins. "Maggie's 'Last Night': Authorial Design and Editorial Patching." *Studies in the Novel* 10.1 (1978): 64-75.

Petry, Alice Hall. "Gin Lane in the Bowery: Crane's Maggie and William Hogarth." *American Literature: A Journal of Literary History, Criticism, and Bibliography* 56.3 (1984): 417-26.

Pizer, Donald. "Nineteenth-Century American Naturalism: An Essay in Definition." *Bucknell Review* 13 (1965): 1-18.

———. "Stephen Crane's Maggie and American Naturalism." *Criticism* 7 (1965): 168-75.

———. "Maggie and the Naturalistic Aesthetic of Length." *American Literary Realism* 28.1 (1995): 58–65.

Robertson, Michael. *Stephen Crane, Journalism, and the Making of Modern American Literature.* New York: Columbia UP, 1997.

Simoneaux, Katherine G. "Color Imagery in Crane's *Maggie: A Girl of the Streets.*" *CLA Journal* 18 (1974): 91–100.

Solomon, Eric. *Stephen Crane, from Parody to Realism.* Cambridge: Harvard UP, 1966.

Stallman, R.W. "Stephen Crane's Revision of *Maggie: A Girl of the Streets.*" *American Literature* 26 (1955): 528–36.

Stein, William Bysshe. "New Testament Inversions in Crane's *Maggie.*" *Modern Language Notes* 73 (1958): 268–72.

Stein, William Bysshe. "Crane's Use of Biblical Parables in *Maggie.*" *Readings on Stephen Crane.* Ed. Bonnie Szumski. San Diego, CA: Greenhaven, 1998. 185–90.

Sweeney, Gerard M. "The Syphilitic World of Stephen Crane's *Maggie.*" *American Literary Realism* 24.1 (1991): 79–85.

Trachtenberg, Alan. *The Incorporation of America: Culture and Society in the Gilded Age.* New York: Hill and Wang, 1982.

Waldron, Karen E. "No Separations in the City: The Public-Private Novel and Private-Public Authorship." *Separate Spheres No More: Gender Convergence in American Literature, 1830–1930.* Ed. Monika M. Elbert. Tuscaloosa, AL: U of Alabama P, 2000. 92–113.

Weatherford, Richard M. *Stephen Crane: The Critical Heritage.* London and New York: Routledge, 1977.

Westbrook, Max. "Stephen Crane's Social Ethic." *American Quarterly* 14 (1962): 587–96.